Lock Down Publications and Ca$h

Presents

THE BIRTH OF
A GANGSTER 3

A Novel by *Delmont Player*

First Edition May 2023

Printed in the United States of America

This is a work of fiction. Names, characters, places, and incidents either
are products of the author's imagination or are used fictitiously. Any
similarity to actual events or locales or persons, living or dead, is entirely
coincidental.

Lock Down Publications
P.O. Box 944
Stockbridge, GA 30281
www.lockdownpublications.com

Like our page on Facebook: Lock Down Publications
www.facebook.com/lockdownpublications.ldp

Book interior design by: Shawn Walker
Edited by: Nuel Uyi

Stay Connected with Us!

Text **LOCKDOWN** to 22828 to stay up-to-date with new releases, sneak peaks, contests and more…

Like our page on Facebook:
Lock Down Publications

Join Lock Down Publications/The New Era Reading Group

Visit our website:
www.lockdownpublications.com

Follow us on Instagram:
Lock Down Publications

Email Us: We want to hear from you!

Dedication

This book is dedicated to all the beautiful women and innocent children; the matriarch Evelyn Player, Alia Smith, Royal Quinn, Jody Leconrnu, Alexis, Korryn Gains, Ja'Nyi Wheaten, the Vicosa sisters, Taylor Hayes, Wendy Black, Leandrea Sampson, Ashley Lambert, Denita Barrett, Tiffany Wiggins, Danielle Parnell, Sophia W., Baby Mayorla Bennett, Sianni Williams, Jacquelyn Smith, Cheryl McCormack, Maliyah Turner. Baltimore City police officer Keona Holley, Monique Billinger, Linda Dennis and Hanna Choi—to name a few who have lost their lives to a different kind of pandemic, i.e. ignorance, reckless gun violence, domestic violence, etc.—which continues to plague the streets of Baltimore City. As "men" we have to do more to hold each other accountable for the destruction—whether intentional or not—of our own communities. The constant disregard for the lives of our women, children and human beings in general has got to stop. It's time to step up and step forward. If you're not willing to do that, then you need to step off! Because this is a call to all real men! Men who would gladly give their lives to protect the women and children in our communities, because that is what it may take. I don't care what these women may have done. How they may have been living, or what we may think of them. They are our women! Which means they deserve our love, respect and highest honor. But more importantly, they deserve our protection!

We're always crying foul when a cop kills one of us because we expect them to be better. We're always screaming. "Black Lives Matter" and talking about how Amerikkka and the justice system values white life. But, I never hear us complain about how much we slaughter each other in cities like Chicago, Philadelphia, St. Louis, New

Orleans and Baltimore—which has seen 300 plus homicides for eight years straight. We don't even lose any sleep when our women and children are senselessly gunned down. And I'm not saying nothing is really right about the street-life. But there used to be rules and codes of conduct. There used to be structure. Furthermore, there used to be consequences! Where are they now? Where are "We" now? When do we begin to hold each other accountable? Yeah, I know "WE" may have it together. Which may make "us" think that we are good. But, good for what? Good for who? We're good for nothing, unless we're helping to protect, build and better our women, children and respective communities. So, let's go to work, brothers. Because a man's work is never done. So, when you see our women out there being disrespected, our children abandoned, make it your business to give them some knowledge, wisdom, understanding and time. Some love leadership because, if you don't, they may just be the one who pays the price for our actions or lack thereof.

Don't tell me black lives matter when you are out there killing yourself and kind with guns, ignorance and all types of drugs. Think about that! We must offer our (women & children) communities love, education, commitment and patience because they are our reflection and our future. Mere knowledge accounts for nothing, unless it is carried into practice. Need I say more?

ACKNOWLEDGEMENTS

I would just like to acknowledge all the men and women who get up everyday and strive to make the world a better place for the entire human family.
Thank you.

Chapter One

Gangster Service

"No, that's too much! Oh my gawd! Baby, please. I don't know how that little girl handles all of this!" Diann cried out and tried to run as Jamaine went balls deep.

"Didn't I tell you to stop running?" Jamaine slapped Diann across the soft ass cheeks and watched them wiggle before grabbing her waist again.

"I can't help it," Diann confessed like she was out of breath. "It's too big," she added and bit down on a pillow. The truth was that the forty-nine-year-old was no different from any other good girl. She had been getting dicked down, gangster-style, and ended up finding out first-hand why good girls loved bad boys.

Jamaine smiled inside, gripped Diann's hips tighter and began getting up in the good ol' real estate agent's pussy nice and slow as pussy juice ran all down the back of Diann's thighs and began to clod up around the base of his dick and nuts. But Jamaine loved every minute of it. It was just something about older women that did it for him. The way they used their entire body to make love to a young nigga. The way they complained and acted as if they didn't love being bent up in all kinds of new positions, getting dicked down like a young girl. And the way they took care of a man and made him feel like a king. Jamaine flipped Diann around for another good thirty minutes, before pulling out and falling back on the loveseat. "Man, that old pussy fire!" he admitted with sweat running down his chest.

"Why did you take it out?" Diann ran her hand through her tousled hair and exhaled, "Please put it back in."

Jamaine could hear the passion in her voice and see the hunger in her eyes. "Nah, come suck this motherfucker." Jamaine leaned back, opened his legs and placed his arms across the back of the couch.

"Let me clean it first." Diann reached for the warm wet cloth they'd been using since the beginning of their sexapade.

"Nahh, clean it with your mouth," Jamaine demanded as his cum-soaked dick dangled like a baby arm between his legs.

Diann crawled between Jamaine's legs slowly as if dreading the task at hand. But deep down inside, she secretly loved when Jamaine treated her like a common slut. "I don't even be doing this for my husband," Diann confessed, taking Jamaine's slippery dick into her soft hands. "Lord, have mercy, this thing is big." Diann slowly stared at Jamaine's dick in amazement and stroked it. She couldn't understand them young girls. If her husband had a piece of prime beef between his legs like Jamaine, she'd worship it so much that he wouldn't have the time nor the energy for anyone else. "My husband would kill me if he knew the shit I let you do to me." Diann shook her head as though she couldn't believe it herself and began licking the cum off of Jamaine's nuts.

"He'd probably kill me too if he knew the way I taught you to suck my dick." Jamaine took a handful of Diann's hair into his fist and directed her lips to the tip of his dick. "Show me what I taught you."

Diann stared Jamaine in the eyes and slowly opened her mouth. Then, she teased the tip of his dick with her tongue and let her mouth carefully engulf him all the way down to the balls. Jamaine's eyes rolled into the back of his head and his head fell back as Diann toyed with the rim of his asshole. "Mmmhhh," Diann moaned and put a little pressure on Jamaine's asshole. She knew exactly what he liked and exactly what he needed. Diann gagged and pulled back a little. Then she proceeded to bob up and down on Jamaine's dick while using both of her hands to stroke his dick and finger his ass. "Mmmmmhhh."

Jamaine loved the way Diann deep-throated him. He wished young bitches would take notes. They could really learn something about keeping a man. Because it doesn't speak well for proper instruction as regards whoever was giving out the lessons that had them bitches faking like something was wrong with being a freak for your man. Such bitches needed to be retired or retained by an older bitch like Diann. "Damn, I wish I could take you home to show my girl how it's done," Jamaine exclaimed as Diann came up for some air and held his dick straight up before ducking low to start licking his balls and ass.

"Turn over!" Jamaine pushed Diann's face from between his legs. "You know what I want."

"Jamaine, please don't be rough. You know what happened the last time." Diann pleaded, rolling over on her stomach as memories of walking around funny for a week popped into her head. Diann felt so dirty as she secretly craved what Jamaine was about to give her. She pushed herself up to her knees and waited.

"I got you, baby." Jamaine slid up behind Diann and used her pussy to get the tip of his dick nice and wet, then he slowly began rubbing the thick head of his dick back and forth across her asshole.

"Jamaine, baby, hold up!" Diann begged, jumping forward as Jamaine began stretching her open. "Eat my pussy first. So it will loosen up."

Jamaine knew that he had to take good care of her. He stopped, got down behind Diann and started eating her pussy from behind. "You like that?" he asked in between licking and kissing her clitoris as he fingered her, but Diann only moaned. Jamaine knew that he was about his work, so he continued to slowly devour Diann's old pussy, nibbling on her clitoris and softly kissing her ass.

Jamaine reached over and took one of the ice cubes out of Diann's water glass, put it in his mouth and began blowing on her pussy.

"Ooooh baby!" Diann's toes curled when Jamaine's cool tongue made contact with her pussy. She'd never felt anything better. She loved the way Jamaine's cool lips felt on the edges of her warm pussy lips. She had chills all over. Diann zoned out and began to cum like crazy as Jamaine's hands and mouth went from her pussy to her thighs to her back, around to her nipples and up to her neck.

"Showtime, baby." Jamaine held Diann's ass cheeks wide open and took a good look at the asshole. She was definitely ready now. "Damn, baby, I wish I could take this ass every night." Jamaine straightened up and gently slapped her across the ass.

Diann's entire body was filled with lust. Every pore was on fire. She was wide open as she felt the head of Jamaine's dick forcing its way into her tight ass. "Easy baby, easy." Diann patted Jamaine's leg repeatedly. She knew that it was going to be a long ride before Jamaine finished kicking her back door in and probably nutting down her throat.

***

Dakaron

It only took about four days for me to get grabbed as a suspect in the shower incident because Monique's so-called sister dropped the correct spelling of my name to the administration and they found out that Monique was supposed to be on my enemy list. They fixed my motherfucking name after that though. There wasn't no more *Dokoron Truesdole* now. I wasn't mad though.

I would have gone down anyway because two weeks after the murder, my fingerprint as well as Bugeye's DNA was discovered on the murder weapon. The administration grabbed L.A. because they knew that whatever Bugeye and I were involved in, he was somehow connected too. Especially since we'd all gone down for the situation with Doogy and them. The funny part was that they really tried to play us against each other like niggas were amateurs or something. Like the fingerprints and DNA really meant something when everybody on the yard knew the knives changed hands three to four times a day.

The phone records had me on a call during the time of death. But the administration said they felt like I was involved somehow because they received a countless number of notes saying I did it. Yet, nobody was brave enough to come forward. That was one thing I was coming to love about prison. Though they were in abundance, rats were kept in check. I mean, I'm not saying they didn't tell and get niggas hemmed up when they could remain anonymous. But, when it was time to come out of the dark into the light, they mostly chose to stay in their respective holes. Because they knew that once they were exposed, there was nowhere to go, nowhere to hide. Because prison was too small.

After a few weeks of investigation, the administration still shipped me down to the Baltimore City Supermax. It was cool though because I was getting tired of Bugeye cursing me out—for leaving the knife in Monique's neck—every time he came out for recreation. Plus, it don't hurt being close to home while my name was ringing bells in the streets behind Monique's death. Niggas were saying that I wasn't nothing to be played with. On top of that, I now knew why Frank was so turned out on Ms. Sellmen's fine ass. Yeah, I was in the supermax hitting heads, gun-slinging or whatever niggas called it. And you can judge me all you want. I don't give a fuck. The women in the supermax were a different breed. They basically took the dick. I mean, they would call your mic and tell you straight up. "I'm trying to see something, nigga, or I'ma drop your level." They had a nigga living that Wild Wild West life. But the one thing I loved about it was the fact that they would stand there and let you knock their heads off until you nutted. No creep shit. You even had a few of them who were so nasty that they would press their faces against the glass and hold their mouths open while you busted all over the window like you were skeeting into their mouths. I was gone off that shit.

"What more can I say? / What more can I do? / You know this one's for you—" I freestyled over a Jay-Z instrumental playing on the 920-Q Thursday Throwback. *"It's never been a young nigga this G for so long / His name A-one, his integrity still strong—"* I continued to flow. "Let me big up my brothers / I have to big up my parents who made me G'd up enough to do it and blessed me with the DNA—"

I heard my neighbor banging on the wall. I pulled the headphones down. "Whoa!" I walked over to the vent that traveled through all the cells to make sure it was my neighbor. "That's you, Homicide?"

"Yeah," he replied.

"What's up, yo?" I inquired once I recognized his high-pitched voice because I wasn't trying to get caught up in a behind-the-door word game. The supermax was off the chain and also where foolish shit went on. Niggas used all kinds of war tactics to break your peace or make you lose your mind. Through piss or shit, you experience banging on your vent for days on end to keep you from getting any sleep, or yelling over top of you when you're trying to have a decent conversation, then there were the rats who would stay in their cells with the lights out, playing possum, trying to gather enough information to jump on your case or have your cell searched. Some of them even sold you out. Straight cowards; they called it, 'putting you under attack'. But the truth was, they were really infatuated with names, titles and representations; anyone of them who said different was lying. They either had a name, used to have a name, or knew that they would never have a name. That was why most of the dudes who they put 'under attack' were what I like to call, 'jailhouse celebrities'. Dudes with major names around the system. The sad part was that most of the gangsters with the names honestly didn't want them because after a while, the names became like a bad disease you could never get rid of.

"First of all, homie, stick to being a gangster, that rap shit not for you!" Homicide fired.

"Ahhh, nigga, stop hating. That was like six bars right off the dome. You don't want me to start writing."

"Yeah, I definitely don't want you to start putting that garbage on paper," Homicide laughed and it always amazed me how high-spirited he always was. Especially after he'd come down the supermax for putting in some extreme work for his blood-set; a set that was four-hundred strong. The same set that wrote him off and left him unable to even afford basic commissary items like soap and toothpaste.

"Yeah, okay, what's happening though?" I inquired, wondering why he'd interrupted my flow. "You bored over there, nigga!"

"Oh shit, my bad, big homie!" he fired like he had just remembered why he'd banged on the wall. "The police was calling your mic."

"What I tell you about that big homie shit?" I said, not ever wanting nobody to mistake me for a gang member.

"My bad, big dog," Homicide apologized. "But the folks were trying to get your attention real bad a minute ago."

"Thanks. I'll holler back later on." I tossed the headphones on the bed and went to the door to get the attention of the C.O. in the bubble. Every cell had a microphone fixture attached to help for media, courts, visits, and emergencies. I loved it because when the right female was working, I would get her on the mic and talk that shit. It was like being on the telephone.

"Yeah, what's up?" I asked the moment my mic cracked.

"You got a visit," said a female voice I thought I recognized.

"Who's this?" I inquired, stepping up to the toilet to get closer to the mic, not really wanting to Homicide to hear what I had to say. I mean, it wasn't that I was discussing something that I didn't have any business discussing. I just always liked to play my cards close to my chest. Especially since even some of the most thorough gangsters in the joint would do anything for a cute face and wicked body.

"Don't worry about it. Find out when you come out." She giggled girlishly. "And I know you heard me calling that mic too. You're in there sounding like a bad version of Jay-Z."

"Oh yeah?" I tried to catch the voice. I knew it wasn't Harper's pretty ass. She knew better than to play on my mic. "Who is this? Moreya?" I fired, referring to the bad ass stallion I had a thing for.

"This ain't no damn Moreya!" She snapped with an offensive attitude. "Just get ready for your visit."

"My bad!" I managed before the mic clicked off. *Damn*, I thought, stepping down off the toilet to brush my teeth and get ready as I realized exactly who I'd been talking to. It was Officer Martin. The fine ass, plain-Jane, older woman with the cute glasses and sexy brown eyes.

I fell in love with at least one female guard at every institution I'd ever touched. Over the jail it was Ms. Glover, in the 'Cut' it was Officer Turner and in the annex it was Shekey Sellmen. So, you know the supermax was no different. What was crazy though was the fact that I fell in love with Ms. Martin for all the reasons why everybody else hated her. She was picky about who she even conversed with. So, guys knew not to disrespect her verbally or sexually. She didn't wear make-up, didn't wear her uniform skin-tight, kept her hair in a basic ponytail, and she wasn't caught up in the prison 'food chain'. In other words, she wasn't being passed around, so her personal business wasn't all over the supermax. I love the way she conducted herself.

But I knew I'd fucked up by calling her by someone else's name and I could just picture her face as I walked past the bubble to go on my visit.

I got myself together and waited for my escort to show up. This would be my third visit. I was only allowed one visit a month because I'd just gone on level three and had 90 more days before I would be on level 4 and be able to buy tennis and stuff. The only thing that didn't change was the twenty-three-and-a-half-hour lockdown.

When I got inside the visit booth and saw Sweet Pea, all I could do was light up. She was always one of the first people to show up for me no matter the circumstances. Which was a lot more than I could say for a lot of other motherfuckers "What's up, Georges?" I slowly took Sweet Pea in from head to toe and shook my head. I never got tired of looking at her.

"What?" She blushed, biting the corner of her lip.

"You," I said, taking my shirt off real quick to show her what was underneath the hood.

"Boyyyy, mmhhhmmhhm! Mhhh!" It was her turn to shake her head.

"Yeah, I know." I smiled and put my shirt back on.

"You know what?" she began and paused to lock eyes with me knowingly. "I'm not fucking with you today. N-E-way, I saw the shit about Monique on the news."

"Yeah, I read it in the papers." I winked at her to confirm what she already knew. "Somebody did the game a favor."

"Good." Sweet Pea quickly changed the subject and began talking about Delmonte. I missed my baby like crazy. She was growing up so fast. Sweet Pea was telling me about how she don't like boys because their feet stink and they played too much. "That little girl a trip."

"That's my baby though," I declared.

"You should've seen all the shit she had in her book bag the first day of school. Toilet paper, food, washcloths. This little girl thought she was on *Survivor*."

Sweet Pea had me dying laughing. She went on to ask about my studies. Then, I brought her up to speed about China Doll and explained the whole inconsistent verdict and illegal sentence issues me and Frank were trying to get back in court on. Sweet Pea told me that Bugeye reached out to tell her that L.A. had been transferred out to the mountains in Hagerstown, Maryland.

"Damn, I know that nigga sick." I shook my head because I'd heard that it was fucked up out here.

"You heard from your girlfriend?" Sweet Pea inquired with a knowing grin.

"I told you in the letter that Lakeria and I ain't fucking around no more," I confessed, knowing very well that wasn't who Sweet Pea was referring to. "I'm too gangster for her country ass." That was a joke but the truth was, I missed Lakeria. I'd never dealt with a woman of her caliber before. A woman who wanted something more out of life.

"Nigga, you know who the fuck I'm talking about. Don't play with me!" Sweet Pea retorted, looking all sexy. "Ain't nobody thinking about that little off-brand, county bitch!"

"Oh, you talking about Chanae?" I teased.

"Yep, I'm talking about Chanae," Sweet Pea confirmed.

"What's up with her?" Sweet Pea asked.

"I don't know," I admitted. I hadn't heard anything from Chanae since she told me about who she was dealing with and asked me to buy her a birthday gift a few weeks before I ended up in the supermax.

"I still haven't heard nothing from her."

"Did you ever buy her that gift?"

"Imagine that! You think I would take care of another nigga's girl?" I fired seriously. "You know me better than that."

"I don't know, that's your girl," Sweet Pea teased.

"Yeah, okay. That's ol' boy girl."

"Who is she asking to buy her a gift though?" Sweet Pea raised her eyebrow, but I wasn't paying her simple ass no mind. She knew I was hip to Chanae's bullshit.

"Yeah, that's only because she thinks I'm sweet."

"You are," Sweet Pea said. "All a bitch gotta do is show you a little attention and you'll empty your little account. Chanae knows that just like I know it. That's why she never really goes too far."

"Yeah, well, it's a big difference between being there and simply being available," I explained. "Chanae is always available but she's not always there."

"That's why I told you that, any bitch who will try to deal with you while she's in a relationship ain't no good and can't be trusted. Because she has no respect for you, her nigga or herself. And if you accept that, then you just don't have any standards."

"For real, Sweet Pea, I'm not trying to hear that shit!" I mumbled, still hurt at the thought of Chanae falling for some clown and moving on.

"Can we talk about something else?"

I watched Sweet Pea as she absorbed my request and came to terms with my pain. "A'ight, I won't say nothing else about Chanae's phony ass." Sweet Pea rolled her eyes. "I'll just be here for you like I always have been. Not just available." Sweet Pea just had to make her point.

Chapter Two

Play the Game Gangster

By November 2005, the murder investigation surrounding Monique had been stalled and I was placed on the transfer list. I wasn't sure exactly where I would land, but I know that I was going somewhere up in Crackerville, Maryland because a big gang war had jumped off down the penitentiary annex and a whole lot of people had been stabbed, including a corrections officer. For some strange reason, I began reading the Bible a lot after one mysteriously slid underneath my cell door. I mean, shid, the laws of God appeared to be the only ones you just could not break without penalty. The game was in so much of a crisis that niggas in the city dropped a 'Stop Snitching' DVD to campaign against the countless number of guys eating the government's cheese for get-out-of-jail free cards. If that wasn't enough, the feds turned around and arrested my bitch, Lil' Kim for standing up for the G-Code and gave her one year when the niggas she'd tried to protect came up with an excuse not to protect her. Of course, she could've just pleaded the fifth instead of lying. But still, I felt like them dry-snitching ass niggas could've pleaded the fifth too and wrote her to tell her as much. If only they had been as thorough as her, everybody would've been okay.

In the little bit of time I'd been in the supermax, the game had changed and was going to shit. Niggas were even running around telling on women and correctional officers. It was like the non-players had more respect for the G-code than the niggas who were playing.

"Like I said, nigga, I don't care what niggas think about me. I'm about to go home! You the one got fifty years, bitch."

I was laid back on the rock, trying to block these two clowns out as they went back and forth out the door about nothing. But something about hearing people say that they didn't care what people thought about them always got my attention. Because all the motherfuckers I'd ever heard make that statement end up doing, saying or accepting anything to come up or get out of trouble. I shook my head and continued to listen for a moment. But the other buster isn't much different. I never understood how niggas could follow a guy who would not only say anything out of his mouth but would also put anything into it. A guy who already compromised his morals and principles. I didn't give a fuck if he slug the knife or not. Men don't follow no punk. It was times like these that I loved my parents even more. I mean, to be able to stand the way I did. To overcome the things I had. To walk the walk, I walked against all odds. I had to have strong parents.

***

"Damn, bro, you really did it," Detauwn stated as if he still couldn't believe that Antauwn had actually gotten married. "I thought Dakaron was going to fuck around and be the first one to get married."

"Shidd, I thought it would be you and ReRe or Keisha," Antauwn confessed.

"Yeah, I fucked that money up though," Detauwn admitted, knowing in his heart he'd let two good ones get away. Detauwn got silent for a moment. "Yeah, Samone's a good one."

"Yeah she cracked the code," Antauwn said. "That's my baby. I can't imagine myself with anybody else."

"Y'all just beef too much for me, but I respect y'all bond." Detauwn looked at Antauwn. "Just don't think marriage will change all your problems."

"Nigga, you're up next. You better tell that to yourself!" Antauwn said.

"Shidd," Detauwn retorted just as one of his daughters burst through the kitchen door.

"Daddy!" she exclaimed excitedly. "Come look at grandma!"

Detauwn and Antauwn followed Rupy into the living room to find their father in the middle of the floor, dancing with their mother. "Congratulations, son!" shouted Antauwn's mother as he rolled his wheelchair over to his wife and wrapped his arms around her. "You better take care of that girl, you hear me?"

"Yes, ma'am." Antauwn kissed Samone on her hips. "You know I got this, ma."

"Go grandma! Go grandma!" Mrs. Linda's grandchildren started chanting as she danced circles around her husband.

Detauwn slowly looked around the room and took everything in. The only thing missing was Dakaron. A tear rolled slowly down his cheek as he thought about his little brother. He wouldn't rest until shorty was home. Detauwn looked across the room and saw Sweet Pea dancing with Delmonte and knew that his little brother's presence was felt.

"Work that body, work that body. Make sure you don't hurt anybody!" Antauwn's aunt Joyce shouted, making him smile. He did it Truesdale style. Bad wife, big wedding, and a hand-picked guest list. There was only one more thing to do. Leave for his two-week honeymoon in Disney World. "I hope you're ready to have another baby?" Antauwn looked up at Samone.

"What?" Samone fired. "We're not having any more kids."

"Shiiid, I got at least two more daughters and a son in these nuts!" Antauwn said and Samone just shook her head laughing.

"I can't wait to spend the rest of my life with you, boy." Samone sat in Antauwn's lap.

"I can't wait to spend the rest of my night with you, baby," Antauwn joked, squeezing Samone's thick thighs. "Everybody wanna know how I keep your fine ass in the wheelchair. But ain't nothing wrong with that other leg and this tongue." Antauwn stuck his tongue out into Samone's ear, and she shivered and jumped out of his lap.

"Ewww, daddy!" Antauwn's youngest daughter twisted her face up as Samone ran across the room.

"Hey, Paulette! Tinika!" Antauwn called Samone's mother and cousin.

"Come here!" He rolled across the room as they too ran. "Now I see what Dak was talking about," Antauwn teased Tinika.

"Dakaron better keep wishing." Tinika paused, blushing because she knew that if Dakaron came home and took another swing at it, he'd definitely hit.

"Run, Tinika, run!" Samone warned as Antauwn closed in. She ran through the door and watched as Antauwn chased her cousin and mother. Next to giving birth to her daughter Jasmine, today was the happiest day of her life. The only thing that was missing was her brother Theo and Dakaron.

"Detauwn, don't help him!" Paulette exclaimed as Detauwn grabbed the back of Antauwn's wheelchair and pushed him towards them.

"Man, that's my little brother!" Detauwn said.

"That's cheating!" Tinika screamed, running behind Mr. Timmy and Mrs. Linda.

Samone just stood there laughing. It felt so good to be amongst family. The people who really loved her no matter what. Her daughter, her niece and nephews, her cousin, her brothers, her crazy father-in-law and mother-in-law, and her husband. Samone smiled just as Antauwn turned his attention to her and Detauwn pushed the wheelchair in her direction.

Chapter Three

It's Hell for a Gangster

I was transferred to the North Branch Correctional Institution in *Crackerville*—Cumberland, Maryland on December 13, 2005. The same day they executed Stanley 'Tookie' Williams. I remembered it was raining and everything. I also remembered thinking that if Tookie Williams didn't have a chance, then most of us were dead in the water. I mean, you were talking about a man who'd turned his entire life around and for what? To die because some racist governor wanted him to apologize for something that he'd maintained that he hadn't done? I had listened to the crooked radio host all morning before I left the supermax as he went on and on about why Tookie didn't deserve a second chance. He processed his anger against Snoop Dogg, Jamie Foxx and others for their support of the ex-gang member.

I wished I could call in so bad, especially about his stance on second chances and the value of life. I mean, this was the same crooked motherfucker who'd just been convicted of stealing the Baltimore City taxpayer's money. The same evil motherfucker who also said that he wouldn't mind seeing one of the 12 o'clock boys get hit by a car and die. I always found it ridiculous when a privileged mother fucker, who the system was designed to help at all costs, found it necessary and easy to judge people who they had nothing in common with. Yet, never offer any positive solution or resources to help address the problem. I respected 'Tookie' Williams though, because in the end, even in the face of death, he

23

refused to sell his soul to appease the ego of the coward who had the power. Even if it meant saving his own life.

On the ride through the city, before we hit the highway enroute to Cumberland, I stared out the transporter van's window and listened to music. I caught a song by an artiste named Lyfe Jennings and wondered if it would ever be that nice for me again. Nice to the point where I would find a woman to hold on to; a woman who'd stick around when the tough times got thick. A woman who I would put my faith and trust in.

When we arrived at North Branch Correctional Institution, I realized that it was just below the Mason-Dixon Line—the border between the US states of Maryland, Pennsylvania, Delaware and West Virginia that is thought of as the dividing line between the south of the US and the north. And everything I'd heard began to make sense. Especially since, in the past the Mason-Dixon line formed the northern border of the states when slaves were owned. I climbed out of the van and was ushered inside to a strip cell with large, red handprints painted on the back wall above a matching red box. "Lean forward and place your hands right on top of these hands." One of the three big, pot-bellied, rednecks pointed before spitting some chewing tobacco into a cup.

"Any sudden moves will be considered a sign of aggression," another one seconded with a shit-eating grin before his buddy went on to play 'Simone Says' with me.

"Left shoe over your right shoulder, right sock over your left shoulder. Turn around, lift your package. Lift your sack." He kept his eyes locked on me as I continued to comply. "Okay, face the wall again." He instructed. "Now lock your legs and slowly bend over at the waist–"

"What?" I looked back before he could finish and they immediately began to close in.

"He said, lock your legs and slowly bend at the waist, son."

I shook my head, exhaled in frustration and turned back around. Then I swallowed my pride and complied.

"Not so fast, boy! Do it again!" he demanded. "And this time, spread your buttocks and hold it. So that I can make sure there's nothing up there. I know how you guys are." He winked at his buddy.

After I popped, locked and dropped it like it was hot for them crackers, I turned around to see one of the other chumps giving his buddy a sneaky elbow and I wanted to punish one of them bitches. But, when I was ordered to gather my clothes, I just got my shit and decided to go on with my business.

Once I was fully dressed, I was given a bedroll and escorted to the building where I would be housed at by two hillbillies with racism oozing from their pores. I had never been a racist; never even truly felt like I knew what it was up until that moment, when those two cracks were walking me down the compound like cattle.

When I hit the housing unit and got on the tier, I spotted a few guys I knew. But it was Redburn's voice that made me light up. I tossed my stuff inside the cell, said a few words to my new cell-buddy and headed the dayroom to see what was what.

Redburn gave me the layout and happenings of the jail. Niggas were running around gossiping like girls, stealing like bitches and playing all types of dope-fiend games, ass-betting and shit because they knew that niggas weren't trying to see lock-up. But it really broke my heart to hear that so many men I'd once respected were walking around with their tails tucked between their legs and their heads down, letting the C.O.'s do and say anything to them without consequences.

Then, there were the snitches. Redburn explained that they were just out of control. "It's like they know that niggas are broken. Like they don't even care if niggas know that they're working with the police."

"That's serious," I admitted, shaking my head. "That's the first thing my cell-buddy told me too."

"Man, I don't even pay them dudes who knowingly deal with rats no mind. They can't tell me nothing." Redburn waved his hand as if dismissing my cell-buddy's statement. "Anyway, just be careful what you say and do around that nigga. Because a lot times the same nigga that will carry a tale to you will carry one about you. You feel me?"

"You already know I don't do a lot of talking to these jokers."

"What I tell you before? Every time you separate from someone more than ninety-days, you got to get to know them again. Especially up here, these motherfuckers got niggas acting brand new."

"Man, fuck these crackers!" I fired, ready to talk about something else. I mean, I wasn't racist or nothing, but I was definitely against anybody who was against me.

Redburn and I continued to chop it up until it was time to lock in for the night. In the cell, my cell-buddy basically confirmed everything Redburn had told me. The only thing he added was the fact that the women were bullshit for the most part. "We're a long way from Jessup," my cell buddy said afterward.

I continued to make my bed, but I know my cell-buddy was right. We were definitely a long way from the 'Cut' and annex. I had only seen a few women so far. But I hadn't been impressed once, and that was something that I couldn't say about the Jessup region. Even the white girls were dimes.

"You know it's fucked up when the only bad thing around is simply bad because there's no competition," my cell-buddy continued. "The only thing right up this bitch come out of the medical or case management department."

"I hear you," I mumbled, tired of hearing about the lack of pretty women from a dude that had a life-sized poster of R. Kelly on the wall. "You say you used to be in the Nation, too, right?" I changed the subject.

"Yeah, it wasn't for me though," he replied matter-of-factly.

"You know a brother named Little Muhammad?" I dismissed his disdain because being in prison for the last seven years had shown me a lot. I knew from personal observation that the Nation of Islam was a very strict organization that didn't bend its rules for no one or nobody. It didn't matter the street or prison's status they had, and that was something that I always respected. They weren't like all the rest of the religious groups, gangs or organizations. You couldn't be an FOI and still be hustling, using drugs, back-biting, killing your people, etc. Their laws were LAW! That was why a lot of guys used to be in the Nation. Hence, the fact that my cell buddy had made it his business to inform me that he was 'Sunni' Muslim the moment I stepped into the cell speaks volumes, although I could smell the smoke and jail-house alcohol in the air.

"Nah, I know Warren Muhammad and Sane Muhammad. I don't know no Little Muhammad. The only other Nation dudes on this compound are Robert X and Master GX. But that's it, and they both sleep on B-Tier with Warren Muhammad."

I continued to unpack. When some photos slipped from an envelope and I saw my brother Antauwn and his wife— Samone—dressed in all-red on their wedding day, I couldn't do anything but smile. That nigga had actually gone through with it. I mean, yeah, Samone was bad, that shit ran in her family.

But, Truesdales were players for life. Still, deep down I understood why Antauwn would marry Samone because wasn't nobody else going to put up with all the crazy shit that nigga did. Collecting junk off the streets, recycling and shit. I flipped through a few more photos, checking out the family. Moms and pops dancing, the kids playing, Detauwn and Antauwn bluffing. I got stuck on a photo of Tinika for a moment. *Damn, she is still bad.* I laughed and shook my head as I reminisced. Then, I stuffed the wedding photos back into the envelope and began to put my shit up.

***

One thing I had to learn quickly about North Branch was that no one was to be trusted. I mean, don't get me wrong. Redburn was my guy, but beyond that, North Branch was a predatory and parasitic environment. Everybody was on the come up. Even the guards and a lot of them motherfuckers didn't care who they had to take down to get to the top. I really wasn't feeling it and I spoke out because I knew that it was going to lead to some bullshit with the police. Which put me at odds with a lot of motherfuckers, especially the police. But I didn't give a fuck because at the end of the day, it was us against them. What tripped me out though was how the police pulled me to the side one day after lunch and warned me to mind my business. When I asked why I should do that, one of them told me that as long as they weren't bothering me, I didn't have anything to do with what was going on. I laughed and walked off because in my mind, I was thinking how the minute some shit went down, they punished all of us. They don't play the "You-ain't-got-nothing-to-do-with-it" then. But, prison had taught me a long time ago that you had to go through something to get to something. Frank used to always say that prison was all about test. You were tested when you spoke up, tested when you stepped out. Shiddd, he said you were tested when you sat down.

"Nobody takes a stand up here without a price," Redburn explained to me as we were walking back from breakfast trying to figure out if the tier was going to come together to make a stand about the constant disrespect. "Every stand had a price."

I knew Redburn was right. Respect isn't free in prison, not even from the officers. "I just don't understand how niggas can keep going for that shit!" I confessed, thinking about how everybody began rushing out of the dining hall when a young boy screamed at the guard about his tray ration. "These the same niggas that were breaking bad down Jessup, disrespecting all the women and everything. Now niggas get out here with these crackers and they got all the excuse in the world not to buck."

I really didn't understand it. The police were straight out carrying niggas—Gangs, gangsters and God-fearing men alike. Calling dudes 'niggers' on the compound and all that and nobody was doing nothing. That shit made me lose a lot of respect for guys. Especially every time I thought about how they used to act up in Jessup when they had all the reasons to chill.

I was reading the *Daily Bread*, working out and studying, trying to stay out of the way. But it was hard because that shit was right in my face. I started attending the Nation of Islam services, because they appeared to be the only brothers on the compound who felt like I felt and spoke out about it. That made the administration nervous. In fact, as soon as my name was added to the NOI count out, the tier-officer pulled me up and asked me why I wanted to attend the service. He said they only taught race-hate. I looked at this openly racist cracker and just laughed. Because if I didn't know anything else, I knew that there was a huge difference between speaking the truth and teaching hate.

My cell buddy always had something to say when I returned from service concerning the Nation's teaching. But, honestly speaking, it just didn't make sense to me that we would come out of one form of indoctrination—slavery— just to submit to another one. To me, being a Muslim seemed to be about more than just looking like an Arab, praying five times a day, and speaking Arabic. And the more I talked to serious Sunnis who truly tried to walk the Sunnah, the more they verified my beliefs. Besides, my cell buddy was one of the clowns who always knew something but never did anything.

Knowing and doing were two different things. Just like in the streets, you could quote all the g-codes and street laws you wanted. But if you weren't walking and moving out on them, then, they meant nothing! That's why I didn't pay my cell buddy mind. He could quote the Quran all day and he knew all the hadiths. But I lived in the cell with that nigga. So, I knew that he was only a Muslim on Fridays. Beyond that, he was faking.

In the cell, that nigga talked differently. He didn't study; he didn't pray. He didn't do anything; he just gives up and gives in to all his lower desires. For real, I felt like he was using the community for protection. But I kept my thoughts to myself because I'd always been taught to mind my business.

I did learn one thing from the nigga though. And that was that most guys who told me they 'used to be in the Nation' and were now a part of another religious community, were more often than not, now doing everything under the sun. In more ways than one, they were professing out of their mouths what wasn't in their hearts and that was 'why' they'd left the Nation. Because they knew that the Nation of Islam wasn't having that shit! And that's why I didn't respect most organizations in prison. Too many niggas be faking, talking about that straight up and down brotherhood or community shit only to slaughter each other verbally and in some cases physically. I despised that shit because I hate hypocrites.

"Man, I say we buck the trays. Don't go to lunch or dinner!" one brother suggested.

"That's easy for you to say. But, I don't got no commissary in the cell," my cell buddy lied.

"We got to do something. Niggas can't keep sitting back letting these bitches do anything," the brother countered.

Although I respected my cell buddy's Muslim brother's stand, I always found it funny how the first thing guys thought about when it was time to make a stand was hurting himself. But a certified revolutionary by the name of Shaka had schooled me about the need for strength to fight. "Don't ever go on a hunger strike in preparation for a war, soldier. That's how I lost my legs," Shaka warned me one day while I was pushing him around the 'Cut' yard in his wheelchair.

I had also learned that everybody just wasn't built to miss a meal. The administration knew it too. That was why and how they broke dudes. Shaka said, "You didn't even really know what you're made of until somebody withheld your food."

"What are we doing, yo?" I looked to Redburn because I know that he was experienced.

"Locking in for right now because they're watching us," Redburn said. "Let everything calm down and then after the shift change, niggas can get in the dayroom and put their heads together. We can also figure out exactly how shorty nem are trying to carry it, because we're not just jumping out there if these little kids not trying to work." Redburn explained and nobody opposed because they all knew that he was tried, tested, and proven several times over.

In prison, it did not matter if you were Democrat or Republican, black, Hispanic or white, religious or atheist, a gang-member, or what was now known as a 'civilian'. The police was the enemy and it was always us against them.

"Niggas be giving these crackers too much credit," my cell buddy mumbled as the cell door closed. Although I knew that it was more of a statement than question, I had to address it. Though it seems harmless enough, prison had taught me that harmless thoughts or people for that matter always ended up causing the most problems.

"Nah, the problem is, niggas don't give them enough credit." I looked out the cell door window as the officers strategically marched on the tier to secure us in the cells, before going to fuck with the young boy they really wanted.

Look at these weak bitches, I thought to myself, knowing my cell buddy couldn't fathom how far these crackers would go to keep us divided. *They don't ever step to no black man alone.*

"They're fucking with shorty now," I said to myself as six or seven guards crowded up outside the cell.

I stood there at the door and watched as the correctional officers pulled the kid and his cell buddy out of the cell for a retaliation cell search and began kicking their property out.

"Man, you ain't gotta do that!" the young boy shot to his feet.

"You better sit down, son!" one of the big crackers ordered, stepping out of the cell, blocking the doorway.

"I ain't your motherfucker son, nigga!" the boy retorted, trying to see into the cell.

"I am not going to ask you to have a seat again, boy," the cracker threatened.

"Man, he ain't gotta be throwing our shit around like that!" his homie bucked, getting to his feet.

The next thing I knew, they were jumping on shorty and his homie while they were in handcuffs. "Y'all some racist bitches!" I yelled out the door as they repeatedly struck the two defenseless Crips. Niggas were banging and kicking on the cell doors, going off. But they continued to jump on the two kids. I punched the door and walked away because it broke my heart to see that shit. "I hate these crackers, yo! I swear to God!" I fired, shaking my head. A cracker to me was a racist white man. Nothing more, nothing less.

Chapter Four

The Streets Aren't the Only Thing That's Gangster

"Look at this hoe ass nigga." Jamaine hit the blunt and smiled as Shaun's chump ass boyfriend popped up in the doorway of Shaun's crib. "This nigga know I'm still stabbing that pussy and can't do nothing about it." Jamaine hit the diesel and passed it to one of his little protégés.

"That nigga a curved. Yo, let you mush him out here and I know he had that wretch on him." The little protege hit the diesel.

"Yeah, that nigga shouldn't never pulled me up about that bitch!" Jamaine spat just as Shaun's boyfriend jumped off the steps and whipped out a huge ass .44 Magnum. "Oh shit, nigga, watch out!" Jamaine warned, pulling his little protégé in front of him just as the first shot went off.

Jamaine and his little man went down and took off running with Shaun's boyfriend hot on their ass. *Doom!* The deafening sound of the .44 Magnum went off again and Jamaine felt the turbulence of a bullet whizz past his head just before the wing-mirror on the truck he was running past exploded. *Doom!* The cannon went off again and Jamaine saw the back windshield of the car in front of him burst before quickly cutting in between the cars. However, Shaun's boyfriend wasn't letting up.

Somewhere around Baker and Rosedale, Jamaine and his protégé got separated. Jamaine could not believe that he might die over some pussy. His mother had warned him time and time again about sleeping with other men's women, but he refused to listen. Now his ass was on the line and he was being hunted like prey.

Doom! Doom! Jamaine kept running for his life. He was scared as shit. *Doom!* Jamaine didn't stop running until he finally made it to Hook's grandmother's backyard. Then, he started running his hands all over his body, patting himself down, checking for bullet wounds. He just knew that he'd been hit. Shaun's boyfriend had been right on his back. His heart was pumping so fast that he felt woozy.

"Oh, I'ma dog this nigga!" Jamaine said to himself once he realized that Shaun's boyfriend had missed.

Jamaine said a silent prayer and got himself together, then he made his way around to his cousin Tierre's house. "I need to use the phone, yo!" Jamaine said the moment Tierre opened the back door. "A nigga just tried to kill me."

"What?" Tierre stole a quick peep outside before quickly securing the back door as Jamaine headed straight for the phone.

Jamaine knew that he couldn't call Paul-Paul because they weren't fucking with each other like that. Paul-Paul had changed his number the last time he'd gotten jammed up on a domestic violence charge and asked Paul-Paul to turn in a pistol to keep from going to jail on some back-up time. So, he called his man, Jeff Ebb-Banga because he knew that Banga was down for whatever. "Hello, yeah, what's up, nigga? This 'Maine," Jamaine explained the instant Banga got on the line.

"Where you at, yo? I need you, big boy," Jamaine continued. "Nah, yo, this nigga just crank on me over some pussy!" Jamaine explained. "That's my word."

Banga gave Jamaine directions to his location. "That's what I need to hear. I'm on my way." Jamaine hung up the phone. Thuglands wasn't more than ten minutes away. Jamaine gave Tierre his car keys and took her car because he didn't want to go back around near Shaun's house.

***

"Yo, I swear to God. I always thought Shanna Brooks was going to be your wife. Everybody did. Especially considering how bad she was," Jamaine admitted as he and Banga sat outside of Shaun's house on Rosedale hoping to catch a glimpse of her punk ass boyfriend. "That's your ride-or-die right there. I couldn't even imagine you seriously fucking with another bitch."

"You ain't lying," Banga smiled at the thought of Shanna. They didn't even make women like her anymore. "That's my baby right there. She had a nigga hooked from the moment I saw that stinky walk." He confessed, knowing that there was something special about Shanna. She was the only woman who'd ever truly made him feel like a king. "Then her birthday is in March too."

"Hold up, yo!" Jamaine suddenly cut Banga off as a U-Haul truck turned on to Rosedale. "Who the fuck is this?" Jamaine wondered as the U-Haul truck slowly drifted down the block. "It's three o'clock in the morning."

"That nigga probably went and got some help," Banga rationalized, reaching down between his legs to pick up the sawed-off shotgun off the floor as Jamaine kept his eyes on the U-Haul.

"That ain't him," Jamaine realized as the U-Haul truck drove past Shaun's crib.

"I was ready to go work." Banga sat the sawed-off back on the floor and relaxed just as the U-Haul truck stopped and began to back up.

"Hold up, Maine." Banga watched the U-Haul Truck back completely up to the front door of the house they were sitting on. "You see this shit?" Banga stole a look at Jamaine to make sure that he was seeing exactly what he was seeing. "This nigga trying to move in the middle of the night?"

Jamaine couldn't believe it. Shaun's boyfriend was really trying to disappear into thin air. "Oh, I got to get this nigga."

"Is that him?" Banga inquired, picking the sawed-off up again as two guys climbed out of the truck in overalls.

"Nah," Jamaine shook his head as the two movers made their way to the back of the U-Haul.

"So, what do you wanna do? Wait these niggas out and follow them?" Banga looked at Jamaine again.

Jamaine kept his eyes on the house. He didn't know what to do. He wanted Shaun's boyfriend bad, but the nigga was a no-show. "We should grab these niggas. They probably know where he's at," Jamaine suggested just as he spotted Shaun's boyfriend cautiously hop off the back of U-Haul to help extend the ramp across the steps. "Hold up, that's the nigga right there!" Jamaine exclaimed, picking the tech up out of his lap, cocking it back.

"Smeggie?" Banga said as though he knew the chump.

"Who?" Jamaine questioned.

"Smeggie," Banga repeated. "That was my son at one time. He bitched up on me though."

"Oh yeah?" Jamaine looked at him curiously. "You know Shaun too?" Jamaine asked, surprised.

"Yeah, I know Shaun really well. I used to fuck with her sister Chanae."

"You used to fuck with Chanae?" Jamaine questioned like he didn't believe it.

"Yeah, why?" Now Banga was curious.

"Oh, we're going to have to talk about that," Jamaine said. He couldn't wait to pick Banga's brain and get word to Dakaron. Especially since Chanae always tried to act like her shit didn't stink. "What's up with yo, though? You say he bitched up?"

"Oh, this hoe ass nigga did more than just bitch up. He *performed*. I'm talking about yo really put on a show at the police station after we got booked. Yo cried for every bit of eight hours, bruh. Talking about how Shaun is going to leave him and shit. It got so bad that the police cut the radios off and called homicide because they couldn't believe that this nigga was acting like that behind a simple gun and weed possession."

"Wow!" Jamaine said. Dudes never ceased to amaze him. "Hold up, is that the situation where you and the dude got hemmed up in your car up the village and he told the folks everything was yours? The shit you got hanging up on the wall at your mother's dealership?" Jamaine remembered reading about the incident and how the dude admitted to the smoke and phones the police had taken off of him and still got let go.

"Exactly, that's Reginald, the one my brother slapped up–"

"And the bull-dyke chick recorded it on her phone." Jamaine took the word straight out of Banga's mouth. He heard the story many times.

"Right, that was yo cousin. This nigga, you—" Banga paused as if he couldn't even find the words to describe what he was trying to say.

"Anyway, you can sit this one out. I owe that bitch. And an Ebb always pays his debts."

"Shiid, nigga, you don't got to tell me twice," Jamaine agreed with quickness. After all, retribution was retribution. It doesn't really matter who dealt the final blow in his eyes. Just so long as it got delivered.

Banga adjusted his baseball cap as the wise words of his uncle—Kerwin—echoed in his head: "Take notes, nigga!" Banga grinned, opening the door to slip out the car. It was time to go ring a nigga's bell.

Jamaine sat there in silence and watched closely as Banga moved like a pro, creeping up the block, out of sight, to get into position.

Jamaine began to wonder if bosses felt what he was feeling as he sat there patiently waiting for Banga to get his opportunity to knock Shaun's boyfriend's head off.

Suddenly, Banga sprinted across the street and ducked in front of the U-Haul truck. Then, he slipped around the side, crouched down and slowly began moving towards the rear of the U-Haul.

"Why would I carry the heavy stuff? That's what I paid you for." Smeggie bounced out the house joking with one of the movers with a plush teddy-bear in his arms, and Banga instantly stopped and pressed his body up against the U-Haul with the sawed-off across his chest.

Jamaine didn't know if Smeggie felt Banga's presence or saw his shadow. But whatever it was, it drew his attention and made him shift the teddy-bear to his opposite hand, so that he could peep around the side of the U-Haul, and that was all Banga wanted. Banga leveled the sawed-off shotgun with Smeggie's head and pulled the trigger. It was the nastiest thing Jamaine had ever witnessed. Sure, he'd busted on a few niggas. Even when Dak and Frank were home, he'd seen them stretch a nigga or two out. But he'd never actually seen a motherfucker's whole head explode. That shit almost made Jamaine throw-up.

As if that wasn't enough, after Smeggie's body collapsed and was hanging over the ramp with the teddy-bear, Banga grabbed him by the collar of his shirt and yanked his body to the ground. Then, he stepped over top of him and shot him twice in the chest before picking up the teddy-bear and slowly walking back to the car, as the movers ran off to get help.

Jamaine was fucked up. He'd never really witnessed a nigga get finished. Usually when he pulled the trigger, he didn't stick around to see what the end results were. But Banga was a fucking savage with it.

"I hope there isn't any blood on this teddy-bear." Banga climbed into the car, looking at Jamaine. "I wanna give it to my daughter." Banga laid the sawed-off on the floor before reaching up to pull the sun-visor down and click on the light. "What are you going to do, sit here all day?" Banga stopped checking out the teddy bear to stare at Jamaine as though he was crazy. "Drive, nigga! You sitting here looking like you're stuck on *stupid.*"

Jamaine started the car and pulled off. "Yo, you dogged that nigga!" Jamaine finally spoke, barely slowing down to make a right at the top of the block.

"I told that bitch that I was going to see em' for that shit he pulled." Banga began wiping the teddy bear's face off as Jamaine hit Bloomingdale and stepped on the gas.

Jamaine barely heard what Banga had said. His mind was still back at the murder scene. Banga had slaughtered ol' boy close-casket-style. "Maine!" Banga snapped, getting his attention. "Slow down, nigga, you running red lights and shit! You know they got them traffic cameras." Banga reminded Jamaine. Banga knew that they needed to put some distance between them and the crime scene, but he wasn't trying to have his picture taken doing it.

"I got it!" Jamaine declared, slowing down. However, within seconds, Jamaine's foot got heavy on the gas again.

"Yo, Maine, don't fuck around and get us pulled over, nigga! You know we got the guns in the car!" Banga warned, looking around the deserted streets for any signs of law enforcement.

"I got this, yo!" Jamaine repeated.

Banga watched Jamaine closely. He was sweating and shit. His hands were squeezing the wheel. His eyes kept going out of focus. "I aint goin' to tell you again to slow down!" Banga threatened once Jamaine's foot began to get heavy on the gas-pedal again and the car was flying through the city streets like they were in a high speed chase. "You acting all spooky and shit."

At that moment, Jamaine looked Banga straight in the eyes. "Do you know that we can get twenty-five years to life for that shit?"

"Pull over," Banga demanded. "Yo, Maine, pull the fuck over!" Banga repeated as Jamaine kept driving.

Jamaine attempted to say something, but Banga had heard enough. So, the moment Jamaine pulled over to the curve, Banga ripped the back of the teddy bear open, stuffed the sawed-off inside and got out mad as shit that he had to fuck his daughter's teddy bear up. But he decided to take his chances on foot.

"Banga! Banga!" Jamaine climbed out of the car and stood in the doorway with his arms up. "Banga!" Jamaine yelled one more time. "You tripping, yo!" Jamaine got back into the car and pulled off. If Banga wanted to walk around with a murder weapon stuffed into a teddy bear, that was on his dumb ass.

***

The whole atmosphere up Cumberland made a nigga sick. First, I was a long way from home. So, the only people who came to visit me were my parents, my brothers, my grandmother, Sweet Pea, and my ribs. Secondly, the police just keep trying a nigga. I mean, it was still the more I tried to stay out of them racist bitches way, the more they kept asking for it. And it wasn't that I'd never experienced racism before. I'd been in three major race incidents on the streets and had been called 'nigger' a number of times fucking around with them white girls down South Baltimore. But it felt different up North Branch. The hate felt pure and deeply rooted. You could literally feel it on the daily basis. Not like the ignorance of South Baltimore when I first started hustling down there. I mean, these Cumberland crackers went out their way and worked overtime to keep us in our place.

When I wasn't working out extremely hard, trying to keep my body strong, I was reading or studying the law, trying to keep my mind strong. I had learned so much from being in prison. Like how listening was more important than talking.

I also learned how we all had two gifts in common: our mind and our time; furthermore, how most of us wasted them both.

"You can go ahead and head back to your housing unit, Truesdale!" I heard an officer instruct over the tier speaker and instantly knew who it was.

I was standing at the door of my cousin Little Phil's homeboy, Terrance—another Park Heights legend—trying to make sure that he had everything he needed because he'd just come back in the system, from out of state.

"Go ahead, before you get yourself caught up," Terrance encouraged, but I waved him off because I knew that I was good.

"Man, I ain't paying that bitch no mind. He don't even work down here. This is my job. I'ma tier runner!" I assured, knowing that my regular tier-officer was just a control freak. "Are you sure you don't need nothing else?"

"Nah, I'm good, bruh. Just get somebody to call my mother and let her know that I'm back in Maryland."

"That's done," I assured him, grabbing the mop to begin mopping again.

I finished mopping the whole tier, put my last load of laundry in the washing-machine and headed into the empty day room to jump on the phone like I do every day after I finished working. When I picked up the phone and noticed that there was no dial tone, I flagged one of the regular officers down in the bubble and pointed towards the phones, signaling with my hand for him to turn them on.

"What seems to be the problem?" My normal housing unit tier officer opened the window slot of the control center above.

I took a deep breath and stared at him for a moment because it was always some dumb shit with him. "I'm trying to get the phones turned on."

"Oh, you're fired!" He grinned, as if he'd finally gotten me.

"Fired for what?" I inquired knowing that I hadn't done absolutely anything wrong.

"For hanging on doors up and down the tier all day," he explained.

"Man, I wasn't hanging on nobody's door. I stopped at one door because the man just came back from out of state and needed to know about the visits and stuff."

"Yeah, well, you're still fired for disobeying a direct order!" he declared.

This has to be a test, I thought to myself. Because since leaving the supermax, I'd been fighting my greatest enemy—Self—and winning. I'd check my ego and keep my pride under control. "A'ight, I'm still trying to get on the phone before I get back."

"What part of being fired don't you understand, bud?" He hit me with the racist acronym for 'black uneducated dog.'

"That ain't got nothing to do with my job. I'm down here doing my recreation, period."

"And you're still not getting on the phone."

"Let me get an A-R-P then." I requested the administration remedy paperwork we used to make complaints against the staff, although nothing ever really happened. It was either that or a new case.

My tier officer turned beet-red and disappeared for a moment, then he came back, stuck his hand out of the slot and flung the ARP papers at me. "You can take that A-R-P and shove it up your ass, boy!" he fired, slamming the slot.

I stood there as the papers landed all over the place. I tried to get him to come back to the slot, so that we could talk like men because I had never disrespected him. But, he only came to the window to hold up his middle finger and shake his dick at me. I tried to get some assistance but all the other officers acted like they were either with it or scared to go against him.

I strolled back to the building in a daze. I was fucked up that the officer had disrespected me like that, especially since

I'd been chilling for real. I didn't know what to do. I wanted to go home so bad, but at the same time they had already taken everything from me. All I had left was my respect and I was ready to kill and die for that. When I walked into the building and saw Sgt. Ferris, I knew that I might be good because he was straight up. He wasn't a get-with who based his attitude on that of other officers who were around. Sgt. Ferris was his own man and I could respect that despite the fact that we played for opposite teams.

"Can I talk to you for a minute, Sergeant Ferris?" I walked up to him as he was exiting the control bubble with the bad little, young girl everybody knew that he was fucking. I'm not even going to front. Every time I saw her little sexy ass and smelled that Berry Vanilla Perfume she wore; I wanted a taste of her ass.

"What's going on, Truesdale?" He stopped and his girl followed suit.

Damn, that's a bad white bitch! I thought before focusing my full attention on Sgt. Ferris. "Nah, I'm trying to holler at you about Officer—" I went on to lay out the entire situation that had happened while I was at work and Sgt. Ferris assured me that he would look into it and make sure that I kept my job.

"What about an apology?" I forced the main issue. I remembered, at the end of the day, even if I lost the job, I was cool because my mother always made sure I was good. But, I couldn't exist without my respect. Not as a man.

"Let me talk to him. If what you said is true, then, I don't see why he shouldn't offer you an apology," Sgt. Ferris explained and that was all I needed to hear. Because honestly, I don't want to write an ARP complaint, especially since my old cell buddy Moon from Cherry Hill used to always say that it was a form of snitching.

Chapter Five

Being Gangster a Thing Now

"You sure you want to take this?" Freaky Black paused to give Jamaine time to consider before handing him the contract money. "Because I ain't just laying back. I'ma be hunting this nigga too. And if I get him before you do, then, I'ma hunt you next."

"I'm good, Unc." Jamaine smiled and reached for the money without hesitation. He knew that the death of his cousin—Fish—was personal. But he also knew exactly where to find the nigga who was responsible. So, in his mind it was easy money.

"The murder game's a different game, Jamaine," Freaky Black pulled his hand back and continued to school Jamaine because he wanted him to understand what he was getting himself into.

"So, once you take this bread, it's business, shorty. My relationship with your aunt don't mean anything. We're no longer family until this shit is done."

"I'm telling you, Unc, we're good!" Jamaine reaffirmed.

"A'ight," Freaky Black nodded. "You got seventy-two hours to bring me that nigga's head." Freaky Black handed Jamaine the twenty grand and prayed that he wouldn't become a liability over a hit. Because he wouldn't have any problem putting him in the dirt.

Jamaine accepted the money with a greedy smile. "I only need twenty-four." Jamaine stuffed the money into his pockets, nodded, opened the passenger seat door and climbed out of Freaky Black's Benz into the pouring rain.

Jamaine quickly jogged back across the street to the waiting truck as Freaky Black pulled out into traffic.

"It's on, nigga!" Jamaine exclaimed, hopping into the truck, shaking the cold rain off.

"So, we're taking hits now?" Banga started the truck up.

"Nah, nigga, you're taking hits," Jamaine corrected. "I'm just collecting the money and putting my name on the hit," Jamaine clarified. After he'd seen Banga's work with Shaun's boyfriend, he came up with an idea. And since he didn't really have the plug he once had because of Dak, he couldn't really get that kind of weight he needed.

So, he decided to use Banga to expand his business and create a new empire. Hence, the first murder-for-hire deal. "I'ma line 'em up. You mow 'em down. That way the sponsor doesn't know you and in the future you won't know them."

Banga stared at Jamaine for a moment. They still hadn't really discussed Jamaine's panic-attack during the last incident. But Banga was strapped for cash and Jamaine knew it. Shiid, after all, he had four kids to feed. "So, what's the take?"

"Fifteen stack," Jamaine lied. "And we're going down the middle on everything."

'Well, in that case, your ass is going to do more than just sit back and direct traffic, you can bet that. You're going to throw a Molotov cocktail or something!" Banga said, slowly pulling off. "And go ahead and separate mine from yours, nigga!"

"We can do that shit once we take care of this bitch." Jamaine waved Banga off, knowing that he couldn't pull the money out in front of him before separating his from theirs. "You sure you know exactly where this nigga at? 'Cause I got seventy-two hours to get this nigga. Twenty-four, if we want some future hits!" Jamaine said to get Banga's mind of the money.

"I told you I used to fuck his sister. So, as soon as it came out that money was on his head, he ran straight to me and told me the entire lick. Them bitch ass Midway niggas were hating on Fish, but it was niggas in his crew that set the whole shit up."

"Yeah, well, when Freaky Black finds out who pulled them strings, that's going to be more money for us. Right now, he just wanted the niggas who put Fish to sleep," Jamaine explained. "And I'm starting to see why they call you Banga, nigga. You been running through everything. sister, wives, baby mothers. Everybody!"

"Look who's talking," Banga said, making Jamaine laugh while they continued on the way to the spot where Banga had stashed the little kid who'd killed Freaky Black's cousin.

***

"Redburn! Redburn!" I yelled out the back window at the top of my lungs. "Redburn!" I was heated. Nah, I was livid. The bitch ass tier officer had just cracked real slick at my door during his account.

"Yeah!" Redburn finally answered and I could tell that he was half asleep.

"Ayo! Make sure you come to the day room, it's important!"

"A'ight," Redburn got out of the window. My mentally dead ass cell buddy watched me like a hawk.

"You got to chill, Dak, you know these people be pressing charges."

"Man, I don't give a fuck about none of that shit!" I fired, looking at this house-nigger. He had something to say about everything except how these bitches were treating us. "Did you hear what that bitch said to me? Huh?"

"Yeah, I heard him. But even still, yo, just write his ass up," my cell buddy rationalized.

"Yo, I'm not trying to hear that shit for real!" I dismissed him and continued pacing the floor. "I'ma crush this bitch, watch!" I fired, pacing the cell floor as my mentally-dead ass cell buddy kept watching me. *This nigga don't even realize that he's a slave*, I thought as my mind went back to exactly what the tier officer had said to me at the cell door.

"I see you went over top of my head, Truesdale. I guess telling on A-R-P's wasn't good enough, huh? Well, since you want to be a snitch so bad, run and tell this. I don't give two bits about you or any of these other officers who you can convince that you're anything more than just another nigger. You heard me, boy? This not down the road in Jessup. You niggers won't get no special treatment up here. And you're still fired!" I played this cracker's word over and over again in my head. He had to answer for that.

"What's up, yo?" Redburn stepped to me the moment I entered the day room.

"I need a joint," I said, knowing Redburn knew that the one I kept stashed in my neighbor's cell had gotten knocked off during the last shakedown, after he had beaten a New York Blood—until his head resembled a big apple—for something that had happened out Cherry Hill.

"What's up?" Redburn looked around. I knew knives were sacred to him. He only pulled them out when it was time to catch a body and there were no other options.

I explained the whole situation to Redburn, starting from the incident at work when I was standing at Terrance's door. Redburn felt my pain and ambition to answer the unforgivable disrespect. He just didn't feel like I should take it too far. "Just beat the brakes off of that bitch when he comes out that bubble for lunch."

"Nah, yo." I shook my head in disagreement. "I gotta put that knife in this cracker," I explained, ready to make it to take it you the next level.

"Look, you know that I'm not going to deny you no knife. I still got that hatchet you like." Redburn revealed, making me picture the barbed wire-wrapped, flattened out staple-blade with the toggle-styled handle he had just gotten from an Indian we all called, 'Comanche'—the only certified gangster I knew with multiple earrings. "But I'm telling you, yo, if you fuck around and kill this pig, you're going on 'B.T.K.' status," Redburn said, referring to another South Baltimore head-buster who'd beat a guard to death in the Maryland State Penitentiary and never touched the compound again.

Redburn's statement made me think for a moment. I thought about my ribs —Ta'nyah, Dooda, and all the rest. I thought about Delmonte and A'myiah. I thought about missing them grow up. More than that, I thought about my mother. I didn't want to die in prison, stuck behind the door even though I already had life. Even though they said it was over for me, I felt like there was still a way out. *If I kill this cracker, that's certain death*, I admitted to myself.

"A'ight yo, but I'm telling you now, if I don't whip this bitch the way I want to, when I come back from behind the door I'ma put that knife in him."

"Say no more." Redburn smiled.

***

Everything seemed to fall right in place. I mean, it was almost like the stars had aligned. Redburn stayed in the shower until the tier officer exited the control bubble for his lunch break. I peeped the move and signaled for Redburn to get out of the shower and head towards the door so that the officer up in the bubble would think that I was trying to get in the shower and open the door.

I heard somebody say something about being next for the shower, but I was stalking my prey. So as soon as the officer in the bubble opened the door, I shot out of the day room and met my target right on the tier. "What were you saying this morning?" I stepped straight into his personal space as a shit-eating grin spread across his face. *Oh, he thinks I'm sweet. He thinks I'm one of them prisoners with a loud bark and no bite*. Whatever he thought though, he thought wrong.

"You heard exact–" He began and I made him swallow the rest with a nasty overhand. To be honest, I was disappointed. I mean, I'd thought that big cracker had some guff up in him, especially, after he came past the cell like he was the big bad wolf. But when I laid into his chin, I instantly knew that it was made of glass because he went straight out.

When he hit the ground, I just started stomping the fuck out of him like I was in *Hammer Jacks*. I bullshit you not, I woke this cracker up and put him back to sleep at least twice. The next thing I knew—I was being tackled, choked, kicked and punched by a torrent of officers.

However, before they could handcuff me, I saw Redburn slamming one, slugging another and it was on. I must say, a lot of dudes surprised me. Because within seconds, more than half of the day room was on the tier putting in work. It was almost like they'd been waiting for somebody with enough grit to kick shit off.

I saw niggas beating guards with everything from broom sticks to telephones. One crazy dude was running up and down the tier, macing all the officers with their own mace. It was pure chaos. The thing I remembered seeing before the guards overpowered the tier was a bald, chubby, D.C, joker slamming a laundry cart on a guard's head.

After the guards gained control of the tier, they began yanking us to our feet one by one, forcibly dragging us off the tier.

"Put that nigger's head down like a dog!" I heard one of them crackers order as the guy beside me was snatched to his feet. I saw another guard pushing his head down as his arms were being forced upward behind his back further than they were designed to go. I thought they were going to break, but I didn't expect anything less. It was common knowledge in the system that when you stuck the police, they always stuck back at some point. Even though it was like cowards.

Each of us were led to the nurse's station where the nurse made jokes and ignored guys' pleas for help as our pants and shorts were snatched down for their amusement and hidden lust. "Look at the size of the crank on that motherfucker!" I heard the old white nurse lady say as the officers yanked down the sweatpants and draws of the guy standing next to me. I looked at the old, white, hairy-faced nurse and couldn't tell if she was more full of lust or race hate.

Still, most of us got off easy. It was the guys who refused to take part in the uprising that got the royal "Cumberland' treatment. They were marched out of the cells bare footed— each man's chest against the back of the man in front of him. Some were dragged across the paved yard outside the building and made to lay face down on the cold, rock-sharp concrete in nothing except boxers with their hands zip-tied. Even the most retained, passive boot-lickers were hit with batons, pepper-spray, and electrified riot-shields; all while under the threat of death for any sign of resistance. The most vicious attacks took place inside the dog-house-sized cells on defenseless elderly inmates outside to the presence of the camera. Guys were choked out, sexually assaulted and some more shit. They complained about not receiving medical treatment nor being evaluated despite the fact that there were clear signs of injuries. In fact, they said that they were only allowed to be examined by the nurses for about twenty, maybe thirty, seconds so that the abuse was not recorded.

I remembered standing in the door listening, thinking to myself how cowardly the guards were when we were kicking their asses. They were begging for mercy and they outnumbered us five to one. Yet, they chose to jump on some old, defenseless men because they were solid and refused to give up any information.

Chapter Six

Got to B-More Gangster

"That's it baby," I kept my eyes glued to my former judge, Octavia Bowman, as she slowly ran her fingers through the hair of the woman kneeling in between her caramel, toned legs, passionately eating her pussy and continued to leisurely stroke my hard dick.

"Now, take your time and carefully use the tip of your tongue to gently caress my clitoris. Good girl, just like that!" Judge Bowman exhaled as her head fell back. "Ooooo, baby, just like that."

I couldn't believe that I was actually about to fuck a judge, let alone one who'd presided over my case in the past. I squeezed my dick and bit my bottom lip to make sure that I wasn't dreaming. Judge Octavia Bowman was a bad mother fucker too. I thought back to when I first saw her sexy ass sitting on the bench. I couldn't see her body. But I could definitely tell that she had them motherly hips with one of them nice ol' asses. And I wasn't disappointed. I had already watched the little Florida stripper chick devour Judge Bowman's pretty pussy and I couldn't wait to get my taste.

"Open your mouth and curl your tongue for me. I am about to cum!" Judge Bowman instructed sternly.

"Yes, Your Honor," the stripper chick complied a split-second before Judge Bowman began squirting into her mouth.

"Oooooh, baby, get it all! Ohhh yes, good girl—" Judge Bowman shook, and shouted as her body locked up. "Come here," she commanded, pulling the stripper chick into a kiss by the rope tied around her neck. "I love the taste of my own cum," she mumbled reluctantly, breaking the kiss.

"Now, crawl over there and suck Mr. Truesdale's dick for me. Get it real nice and wet too. I want it to slide right in this tight pussy."

"Yes, Your Honor." The stripper turned around and looked at me with pure lust and hunger in her eyes as I continued to stroke my dick.

"Get 'em, girl." Judge Bowman slapped her across the ass and she instantly started moving. "Get ready, baby boy," Judge Bowman cautioned as the stripper began to slither towards me almost as if she was in a sexual trance, and I never took my eyes off of her. I had always known in my heart that judges and schoolteachers were freaks and I was ready to live out my fantasy.

"Get up!" Judge Bowman ordered all of a sudden, banging her gavel." Get up, Dak! Get on point!" She began banging the gavel uncontrollably until my ears began to hurt and dick started to get soft. "Dak! Dak!"

The loud shouting of my name pulled me up out of my sleep. "What the fuck!" I sat up and instantly got mad when I realized that I had actually been dreaming.

"Dak! Get up, baby boy, get on point! Dak! I know you not sleep over there!" My old head—Black Dana—continued to call my name and pound on the damn wall.

"Come on, Dana, yo!" I shook my head mad as hell. *This old nigga just fucked up a vicious ass wet-dream.* I thought about the threesome I was about to have with my former Judge Octavia Bowman and the bad ass Florida stripper chick. "You done already had me up all night." I reminded him that he'd already talked my head off, about how fucked up the annex was now, how young niggas talked too much and the police knew too much, which led to him and his cell buddy—my man, Hot Rod—having to tighten up a few kids behind a female he was fucking. "I'll holler at you when I get up." I flipped my pillow over and laid back down on the cool side. I mean, it was good to see my old head. But we'd been talking since they brought him on to the tier earlier in the day.

"Are you not listening, baby boy?" Black Dana questioned sarcastically. "I said Redburn just yelled over here across the lawn and said it's like two hundred C.O.'s in front of the building in full riot gear."

"Now?" I inquired because it had to be every bit of two o'clock in the morning.

"Yeah, baby boy, now!" Black Dana confirmed, getting my attention.

I stumbled out of the bunk quickly to clean house and make sure everything was put up and put up good. The guards had been on some bullshit since we had taken them to task and handed their ass to them. At one point, it had gotten so terrible that we'd been forced to orchestrate a hunger-strike to get comprehensive outside investigators to start coming in despite the myriad of allegations. This was after we had managed to keep slipping the handcuffs to punish something because they made it seem like they weren't the real perpetrators. As if they weren't constantly doing little bitch shit, like destroying our mail, fucking with our visitors, playing with niggas' food, throwing empty bag lunches into the cells to make it look good for the camera.

After getting the cell in order, I laid back down and waited to see what was going on. I was really beginning to get tired of being in prison. The constant drama, close family members dropping like flies, seeing my daughters growing up without me. That shit was killing me softly. I mean, regardless of how hard I tried, there was just no way that I could be a real father to them from behind prison walls, especially not on those nights when they needed me the most.

Then, there were the courts—or rather the justice system—turning a blind eye to the truth, playing with my freedom and Frank's. But Frank had amended both of our respective post-conviction petitions with all the stuff Antauwn had gathered from China Doll, and he just felt like it was no way the courts could deny us. I wasn't so sure. They hadn't blindfolded *Lady Justice* just so she wouldn't see color and wealth when she was balancing the scales of justice. They did it so that they could live by their own set of rules.

"Truesdale, step to the back of the cell and kneel down facing the wall!" A huge white boy popped up and pressed his face to the outside of the cell door's window.

"For what?" I challenged him to ensure that the scare-tactics didn't work on gangsters like me.

"I won't ask you again!" he spat, looking through the window like he'd love to get a piece of me. "Failure to follow orders will be dealt with as a sign of aggression," he added, looking over his shoulder.

"Open the cell."

"Yeah, whatever!" I said before complying. I wasn't stupid. I knew that the element of surprise was the best way to prevail on the enemy, but they'd come in full riot gear, ready to do battle and I'd never allow them bitches to get a free one on me; at least not if I didn't have to.

"Remain facing the wall!" the same white boy commanded, entering the cell with about six other WWE-sized goons as a sign of power. "Okay, get to your feet!" he instructed. "But continue facing the wall."

My heart was pounding, but again I complied. I felt a lot better being on my feet. But, I didn't feel safe. Especially not being cornered in a cell, out of the sight of any cameras with six or seven WWE-sized white boys, who'd probably just love to put the 'smackdown' on me. "What's going on, man?" I could sense their anxiousness and decided to break the silence to let them know that I wasn't going to be a problem. I mean, don't get it fucked up. I would defend myself to the death up in that motherfucker if I had to. But, I wasn't dying to get my ass kicked by a bunch of hillbillies who had it out for me anyway.

"Just follow the orders!" he fired and I heard one of his buddies mumble something about 'giving him a reason.'

After being stripped-searched and damn near forced to bend over and spread my ass cheeks, which always made me feel degraded and humiliated, I was marched outside and stuffed on the first of two buses along with a few other well-known, usual suspects who were being transferred. A lot of niggas were playing the guessing game, speculating, trying to figure out where we were going. But I didn't give a fuck. I was just happy to be leaving Crackerville. I had not seen one sister working up in that motherfucker since I'd arrived more than a year ago. Now, wasn't nothing wrong with a bad ass snow bunny, and North Branch had a few: Moulden, Barnes, Young and this little bitch named Coke who I know was nasty with all this colorful shit tattooed behind her ear. But there wasn't nothing in the world like a fine sister, especially a chocolate one. I mean, just their skin tone was intoxicating.

"I think we're going to the supermax," a wild knife-slinger who'd recently received life for stabbing a police K9 to death during a cell-extraction said to nobody in particular as the last man boarded the bus.

"Man, we're probably going to that new spot everybody keep whispering about," said a Pan-African, jail-house-revolutionary by the name of Afrikan James, who was behind the door for cutting the head off of a goose at MCIJ in Jessup.

"I wasn't talking to you, nigga!" Rockwell Jones said and everyone on the bus got quiet, because everybody on the bus knew that Rockwell Jones and Afrikan James couldn't stand each other for various reasons; the main one being their ideologies concerning the value of black life.

"I hear you, brother!" Afrikan James fell back with a smirk as the bus kicked into gear and the chit-chatter quickly picked back up.

As the bluebird pulled off, I blocked everybody out and began to daydream that I was on my way to be released. I knew the chances of ever seeing the streets as a free man again were slim to none. But I'd never admit that to nobody besides myself. For some strange reason, I began thinking about Chanae, wondering what she was doing or where she had gone. It had been a long time since I'd done that because I'd already made peace with her absences, even from my memory. Prison had shown me that a lot of the people I thought were down for me were just business associates in business relationships. Meaning, as long as I could give them something they wanted or produce what they needed, they were there. When I couldn't, they were gone. I learned and now understood that real love was forged through actions, not feelings; through everyday sacrifices; through the journey we shared, the pain we endured, the distance traveled and the joy we felt. All that other shit was rhetoric, and serving time showed me the difference.

When we came into the city limits and I saw all the school kids coming from school, I instantly began thinking about my ribs and felt a sense of strength. I thought about how blessed I truly was, despite all the bullshit I've been through in the last few years. I thought about all the good men that languished in prison alone. Men who had something to say that would never be heard. Men who had lessons to teach that would never be taught. Men who just needed to be loved.

Yeah, even after all my friends had turned their backs on me, I still had so much to be thankful for and believe in. There were so many people who gave me strength. Not just physical strength, but the strength that kept the walls from closing in; the strength that kept your body strong and your mind sharp. The strength that carries you though when there's nothing or no one else left. And I needed that because I had experienced and witnessed some things that would've broken lesser men.

I smiled to myself as the bus drove through the city streets going nowhere fast. I heard guys on the bus talking about everything from the school children's fine mothers to the new cars cruising by and it made me remember a time when I wanted to go home for all the wrong reasons. To all the wrong people. But I was tired of lying for people who were unworthy. If truth be told, there were a few people outside of my mother, who'd never lied to me or let me down.

"Ayo, C.O.! Turn that joint up for me!" Rockwell Jones exclaimed and bobbed his head as one of the well-known prison anthems began to play on the 92Q three o'clock mix. "This my shit!"

"Ayo, Rockwell!" somebody shouted from the back of the bus. "What's your life like, nigga?"

"Oh, mine is real, everything is signed and sealed!" Rockwell Jones replied, making me smile as everybody, including the bus driver, got ready to rap along to the first verse.

". . .*They got you stuck in the can / White man got you fuckin' your hand / Your wife on land fuckin' your man / What you know about no parole / Life in the hole / Life's cold, you be eatin' them swags / Guards on the nightshift they be beatin' you bad / The hardest nigga turned bitch, be sleeping with fags—*" I can't lie, even I joined in because my shit was signed and sealed too.

It was about four-thirty when we pulled into the dark ass Baltimore City Supermax underground tunnel and stopped, which always had me nervous because a nigga had gotten slumped down there.

After going through the 'Simone Says' game again, we were ushered to our cells. Since I'd already been in the supermax before, I felt right at home. I hollered at a few regular officers like my baby Montgomery—the baddest black beauty in Baltimore City—and Cookie Monster's retarded ass to find out exactly what pod Bugeye was on.

I knew his crazy ass was down there because his incident was the talk of the prison system. After all, this crazy nigga had jumped over the visiting room counter in the 'Cut' and attacked his baby mother because she'd spent all his lawyer money. Cookie Monster was known to spin a nigga with the quickness. But she don't play with me because she'd been sweet on my cousin Little Phil as far back as I could remember. So, once she told me that Bugeye was on E-Pod, I immediately cracked to move up there.

"Boy, just 'cause I used to chase your cousin doesn't mean nothing," Cookie Monster twisted her pretty lips up.

"Used to?" I said, as if she had just forgotten that fast that Little Phil was the first thing she inquired about, and she could do nothing but smile. "I heard that."

"Bye, Dakaron, my shift is over." Cookie Monster spun on her heels, waved over her shoulder and headed for the exit.

"Oh, that's how we carrying it now?" I called out behind Cookie Monster's red ass.

"Montgomery, put him on E-pod for me." Cookie Monster disappeared.

"I got his little bad ass," Montgomery assured, showing off her pearly white smile. I swear she was the definition of dark and lovely.

Montgomery came through for me big time. Not only did she make sure that I got moved up on E-Pod; she also got me moved right next door to Bugeye. I was so happy to see my nigga that I didn't even clean the cell up. I just jumped in the vent and started running my mouth. Bugeye reiterated a lot of the things Black Dana said. Jessup was fucked up, watered down and clowned out.

I was surprised to learn that L.A. was on some gang shit, especially after all the talks we had, and all the loyal soldiers we personally knew that had been misused, abused or thrown to the wolves. I mean, I wasn't one of those 'self-righteous' dudes who were prone to condemn other niggas' failures while excusing my own. But damn, if you were going to put it all on the line for niggas, at least do it for dudes who weren't quicker to take oaths than honor them.

"What's up with my rap buddy?" I questioned honestly, though I already knew how Frank was carrying it.

"Frank is still the same," Bugeye replied. "He fuck with who he fucks with. You know he's Muslim now, right?"

"Yeah, he wrote me and told me that he took his Shahada," I admitted. "I ain't feeling that shit though. A lot of them niggas be faking and hiding behind the community, looking for protection."

'Yeah, but you know Frank don't make any decisions lightly."

"True, but I still don't like him fucking with all them off brands," I explained before Bugeye and I continued to talk.

Bugeye also told me that word on the wire was that Pole had tried to re-invent himself at the new jail and ended up getting stabbed up again. "That nigga a pin-cushion now, yo." I shook my head.

"Don't it always seem like the same niggas getting stabbed over and over again?" Bugeye questioned.

"Hell yeah," I agreed without hesitation because it was the truth. Most dudes that got hit in prison stayed getting hit. Just like most of the dudes who did the pushing stayed pushing. "It's like them niggas can't sense danger or what not."

Bugeye and I talked until the breakfast tray hit the slot.

***

"So, you're telling me that I can't get my personal property?" I questioned with a lack of understanding the next morning after banging and kicking on the door to get Cookie Monster to the cell.

"Look, it's coming from up top, so it's out of my hands," Cookie Monster explained again.

"So, am I just supposed to not wash my ass!" I started getting more frustrated with Cookie Monster by the moment. She kept acting like she didn't have any idea about the injustice. She claimed she didn't know where my property was. She couldn't give me any names. But I know that at the end of the day, it was always 'us' against 'them'. I didn't care how much she loved my cousin. She would be loyal to her livelihood just like I would be loyal to mine.

"You know I got you," Bugeye volunteered.

"Man, I want my shit!" I snapped thinking about all the good men who'd been on the bluebird with me and weren't fortunate enough to have a solid homeboy in the supermax to look out for him.

"I'll see what I can do. But, like I said, from what I understand, you're not staying," Cookie Monster said.

"Come on, Cookie Monster, man, give me something," I pleaded, knowing that if anybody could find out what was happening, it was Cookie Monster. I mean, I didn't get caught up in all the prison rumors and daily jailhouse gossip, some of which would have me dead sometime ago. But, I knew that Cookie Monster was bad, and I knew that my cousin had given her the game. And that alone was enough to set her apart from the rest and put her in positions to run circles around the lames who outranked her in the supermax.

"Boyyyy!" Cookie Monster shook her head and smiled because she knew that I was hip to how she had them supermax clowns chasing after her.

"Excuse me, Sergeant Cookie," another officer interrupted before Cookie Monster could commit, and I looked over her shoulder to see the love of my supermax life—the one and only Ms. Martin looking fine as ever.

"Yes, Officer Martin?" Cookie Monster turned around.

"The captain just called for you. I think the guys downstairs are bucking about their property," she explained, and I instantly thought about Rockwell Jones getting everybody riled up.

"Okay, give me a sec." Cookie Monster turned her attention back to me. "Look, I gotta to go but I got you. That's my word."

"Bet." I nodded, immediately focusing on Ms. Martin." How're you doing, Ms. Martin?" I smiled. *Damn, she is still bad than a motherfucker!* I admitted to myself. There was just something about Ms. Martin's plain Jane, natural beauty that truly set her above all the rest. "I missed you," I confessed honestly.

"You see, girl, they go up in the mountains. Then, they learn to appreciate a sister." Cookie Monster teased.

"Don't do that, you know I love black women to death, Ms. Martin."

"Truesdale, please." Ms. Martin waved me off. "I can't tell you love us to death the way you got everybody beating and banging on these doors first thing this morning." Ms. Martin touched her ponytail. "You probably yelled out the window downstairs too," she added.

"I ain't have nothing to do with that!" I lied.

"Well, lover boy, I got to go. I'll be back as soon as I can to talk to you about, ummm, your property," Cookie Monster winked.

"Thanks," I winked back understandably as Cookie Monster stepped off.

"Do you need anything else, Mr. Truesdale?" Ms. Martin asked, raising her eyebrow. "Cause I don't want to get in this bubble and sit down and you start zapping out again."

You just don't know, I thought, licking my lips. "Nah, I'm good," I replied, wishing I had the opportunity to pin her ass down somewhere and tear that pussy up.

"Good." Ms. Martin left me standing there in the door.

Damn! I had to tip my hat off to Ms. Martin's old ass. Even in a loose fitting uniform I could tell that she had a petite body and a nice ass.

After gawking at Ms. Martin until she left the pod, I started thinking about how I would run all up in that old ass.

I bet that motherfucker super tight! I hung my superman-issued jumpsuit up to cover the window, grabbed the toilet paper and laid down real quick to beat my dick. I thought about Chanae, China Doll, Tinika and even Venus for a moment. And I'm not even going to 'lay' there and lie. I even thought about some of the women in my life who were like family and sisters. In the end though, I settled on a memory of fucking Ms. Glover in the staff bathroom in the middle of her shift while Ms. Hopkins looked out for us.

It'd been years since I had heard about or seen Ms. Glover. But, as I laid there reminiscing, slowly long-stroking my dick, I remembered the situation like it was fresh. I had snuck over to Ms. Glover's section and caught her and Ms. Hopkins on their way to lunch. Which meant that we could probably steal a quickie. Ms. Glover stalled at first, but once I started talking about eating her pussy while she sat up on the sink, it was over. The next thing I knew, we were locked in the staff bathroom fucking like crazy.

I bent Ms. Glover over the sink and hit it from the back. Then, I sat her up on the edge and tried to knock the bottom out of her pussy as she wrapped her legs around me and moaned my name.

"Ahhhh!" I grunted and nutted into the toilet paper as my body jerked repeatedly. "Damn, it felt good," I admitted out loud, getting up to clean myself up, wishing I could taste some pussy right now.

The first female I put this backed-up, penitentiary-pipe on is in serious trouble, I thought.

I never got a chance to get the scoop from Sergeant Cookie because right after lunch, I was pulled out of the cell, strip-searched and marched outside to a waiting bus, where I was shocked to see news cameras and reporters.

"Do you have anything to say about being declared one of Maryland's most dangerous and disruptive prisoners?"

Damn! It's Tasha Nelson! I thought to myself, instantly recognizing the fine ass, chocolate news reporter from

WBAL. I had to bite my tongue and turned my head to keep from saying something stupid, because real gangsters weren't ever dying to be in the spotlight. I stole one more look at Tasha Nelson and boarded the bus. *That's crazy! She's even badder in person.*

I took a seat where I could keep my eyes on Tasha Nelson as reporter after reporter tried to get a comment out of someone. But nobody volunteered; niggas just kept their head down because they knew better. That was until this giant, 7'2 goof-ball who should've been in college somewhere came out of the building and spat in a reporter's face before making a scene.

"Ayo, you dumb ass shit!" someone exclaimed to the tall joker once the police were able to get him on the bus.

"Man, fuck them *Fox* bitches!" he spat. "They got my cousin Smurf from Popular Grove caught up!"

"Ayo, does anybody know where the fuck we're going?" I looked up at the sound of Redburn's voice and smiled.

"I heard somebody say we're going to the feds like them D.C. niggas," someone replied.

"How the fuck they going to do that? Niggas ain't even got no fed time. And it's mad joints still opened in Maryland!" another dude fired.

"Man, we're not going anywhere but Hagerstown," I assured as Redburn took the seat beside me.

"I don't know, shorty." Redburn got comfortable "You see them folks in them tan uniforms," he turned my attention to three white guys standing off to the side. "They're federal marshals."

Redburn was right, which meant all the speculation could be true.

Before long, the bus was crowded with several certified niggas. Suf'yan, Skinny Pat, Jungle George, Big John, Fat-Rat, Lil' Player, White Boy Do-Dirt, Baby Joe, Goo, Aaron Holly-El, the old nigga Doogy I'd gotten into it with in the 'Cut'; New York O.J., Whitey, and my old neighbor Jodie

Hill. I had stopped calling him Homicide since he'd been smart enough to sever ties with them Blood niggas and stop letting dudes misuse him.

I can't lie—despite the circumstance, it felt good to be counted amongst the elite. I felt privileged, honored even, especially when niggas started talking about taking over the spot we landed at.

"Okay, listen up, gentleman," one of the federal marshals got everybody's attention after the last man was strip-searched, and shackled. "This is a thirteen-hour bus ride. We're going to a federal holdover in Ayers, Massachusetts, right next to Boston."

"What about my TV and shit?" Holly-El questioned. "I just bought—"

"Look, that's all I got for now." The marshal held up his hand to cut Holly-El off. "Sit back and enjoy the scenery," he added before walking back up front to secure himself on the other side of the caged-gate.

"Niggas with the feds now?" the tall dude proclaimed excitedly.

"Niggas that off the chain that the state can't even handle them? Yo, I can't wait for my man to hear this shit! I'ma take a flick and write *You don't have to get caught up under the RICO Act to see the feds no more, all you got do is go hard on these bitches*!" he continued and damn near everybody joined in. But, I still thought that it was a bluff tactic. I mean, there was no way that we were going to the feds. Out of state, maybe. But the feds, shiid. I'd like to see that.

***

"I love you too ma," I said, ending the five-minute phone call. I didn't think the shit was a joke anymore. We had arrived at a spot called 'Devens' in Massachusetts as promised and been given new federal registered numbers and all that. The spot was so high-tech that they had showers in the cells, right next to the bunks. That fucked me up.

The food was lovely too. So lovely that Redburn refused to eat because he thought they were trying to poison us. I took my chances though. If I had to go, I would rather go enjoying myself.

As it happens, out of ninety-seven of what was considered the worst prisoners in a state of emergency, sixty were sent into the federal system and the other thirty-seven ended up in various state joints throughout the country. My mother had just informed me that we were all over the local news.

"Yo, yo!" I hollered out as I came back onto the special housing unit tier to get Redburn's attention.

"Yeah, yeah!" Redburn came to the door and called back.

"I just got off the phone with 'One Love'. She said niggas all in the *Baltimore Sun* newspaper and shit!" I yelled down the range as the Marshal handcuffed my cell buddy, White Boy Do-Dirt before calling to have the door opened.

"Yeah, I'm hip! My daughter said the governor behind the shit! Yo trying to get reelected!"

"What are you doing down there?" I inquired knowing he hadn't eaten in two days.

"Working out!" he replied.

"Man, you are crazy as shit!" I fired, stepping into the cell with Do-Dirt after the door opened. "There's no way in the world that I could go without eating and still be working out!"

"It's mind over matter!" Redburn assured just before the cell door closed down. I couldn't do nothing but smile because I knew from the North Branch hunger strike that he was right.

Chapter Seven

Gangster's Ain't Never Be Picking

"Yeah, nigga, I told you that I knew what the fuck I was talking about!" Earny-Perny exclaimed from the back seat of the car when the two white boys exited Paul-Paul's spot. "I'm on this type of shit for real! That's why I said you should've been fucking with me. I know everything about Paul-Paul's operation, where he's getting his work from and who he's hitting off."

Jamaine remained silent and kept his eyes glued to the two fly looking white boys Earny-Perny had identified as Michael Beers and Tyler. He didn't really want to bring Earny-Perny into he and Banga's business, but had been forced to after he and Banga tried to grab Vinny and Slick Webb—Paul-Paul's Sandtown plugs—and ended up wrapped around an oak tree in a bullet-riddled truck. Earny-Penny was the only person Jamaine felt like he could trust at the moment and decided to take his chances. So, he told Banga to come on, and ran for Earny-Perny's house because he knew that as soon as Vinny and Slick Webb got to a phone, the whole Sandtown would be hunting them, and Paul Paul couldn't—nor would he—spare him for his betrayal.

"Which one is Mike?" Banga questioned, looking back over his shoulder from the driver's seat. "The one with the goldish hair?"

"Nah, that's Tyler. Mike's the Jon. B looking one," Earny-Perny replied as Michael Beers and Tyler climbed into a tinted-out F-150.

"And you say these white boys getting it, huh?" Jamaine finally spoke up.

"Yeah," Earny-Perny nodded. "Them niggas been copping from Paul-Paul every Tuesdays like clockwork since I can remember," Earny-Perny revealed.

"So, what are we going to do, bruh?" Banga inquired. He didn't seem convinced.

"We're going to see what these white boys got going on." Jamaine explained. "If what Earny-Perny is saying is legit, then we'll double back next Tuesday and catch them niggas together."

"Hold up, yo." Earny-Perny slid forward and leaned forward in between the seats. "Are you going to get Paul-Paul too?" He looked at Jamaine strangely. He'd always thought that Paul-Paul and Jamaine were like family.

"I ain't got no picks, nigga! Anybody can get it!" Jamaine retorted, thinking about the sucker shit Paul-Paul had told Dak concerning him, when he was still over the jail. "You got a problem with that? 'Cause you're in it now." Both Jamaine and Banga turned around to look at Earny-Perny.

"Nah, I just wanted to know." Earny-Perny sat back and kept his thoughts to himself as the black F-150 pulled off.

What Earny-Perny didn't know was that Jamaine was secretly on some sleeze-ball shit and he'd turnt Banga into his number one cruddy-buddy.

"Good," Jamaine acknowledged before tapping Banga's left, signaling for him to follow the white boys.

First, Banga followed the F-150 to a garage located in Hollontown. Then he followed them to a spot over in Westport, where Earny-Perny seemed to take issue with Mike tongue-kissing some black chick. "I'm just saying I don't like that shit!" Earny-Perny fired even though he admitted that he loved white girls. Banga cut his eyes at Jamaine and stayed on the whites until they hit the highway as Earny-Perny tried to justify his feelings.

"Ayo, we can't keep using cars off of my mother's lot to pull these licks," Banga interrupted. Earny-Perny's little history lesson was starting to get on his nerves. "Soon, we're going to have fucked around and used every car on the lot," Banga continued to tail the white boys at a safe distance.

"We can just double back and use the car again," Jamaine suggested. "If it ain't broke, don't fix it."

"Are you not listening to me, bruh? Imagine if somebody gets onto that shit and the people take my mother's dealer's license and shut her lot down. My uncle and them will go nuts," Banga rationalized.

"Man, ain't nobody thinking about no shit like that," Jamaine argued. "That's the best idea niggas ever came up with."

"I'm telling you, bruh, we got to come up with something else. I think Tammy knows I had something to do with that Durango getting totaled down Sandtown. Kevin told me she said something to him," Bango explained, making mention of his sister and her husband.

"Anybody could've stolen that truck, dog," Jamaine challenged.

"Man, don't nobody play with my family, niggas not crazy. They know how we get down." Banga saw the F-150 switching lanes and looked up to notice the Glen Burnie exit.

"A'ight, we'll come up with something," Jamaine submitted. "We'll just work momma lot in the meantime."

"In the meantime, my ass!" Banga snapped. He knew that Jamaine hated to hear the truth. "After we get this joint back to the lot, that's dead!"

Banga stayed with the F-150 until it made a left on Delaware Avenue, in a quiet part of Glen Burnie. Banga circled the block and pulled up down the street just as Tyler climbed out of the parked F-150 and disappeared into a house.

"Write that address down too," Jamaine instructed Earny-Perny. "We're going up in all these nigga spots."

"You think these white boys dropping off work all across town like that?" Banga still wasn't convinced.

"I don't know, but we're going to find out," Jamaine replied.

Banga kept his eyes on the F-150, wondering how many stops the white boys planned on making before they reached their final destination. "We're goin' to have to fuck around and kill these white boys, watch!" Banga spat.

"As long as we get the money, it's all good," Jamaine declared, glancing out the passenger's side window. "Oh shit, yo, look out!" he warned, spotting a spaced-out looking white boy, with long hair quickly approaching the rear of the car, aiming an AR-16 in his wing-mirror.

Banga looked back just in time to see Tyler, the golden haired white boy with the crew cut from the F-150, running up on his side of the car before the first shot rang out.

Jamaine took cover and yelled for Banga to pull off repeatedly as AR-16 bullets tore through the car from both sides.

"I'm trying, nigga, I'm trying!" Banga finally got the car started and pulled off. However, as he sped down Delaware Avenue, Michael Beers stepped out of the F-150 aiming what looked like an AK and instantly opened fire. Banga wasn't a master behind the wheel like Jamaine, but he wasn't a slouch either. So, after swerving into a few parked cars, he jumped the curve and went flying down the sidewalk, across the well-kept lawns until he hit the corner.

"Fucking white boys!" Banga shouted, checking the rearview mirror. "I can't believe this shit!"

"Them white boys had some heat too," Jamaine admitted, looking back out the bullet-shattered windshield. "You can get up, Earny-Perny, we're good. They're gone." Jamaine was thankful that the white boys had been rookies.

"Earny-Perny!" Jamaine repeated, finally looking at him. "Did you hear me, nigga? Get your scared ass up!" Jamaine grabbed his shirt.

"What?" Banga saw the look on Jamaine's face and knew something was wrong.

"I'm going to kill them fucking white boys!" Jamaine fired seriously.

Jamaine's statement made Banga take his eyes off the road real quick to steal a look into the back seat. "Fuck!" Banga snapped when he saw Earny-Perny's sprawled dead body. He knew they had to get the hell out of Glen Burnie because there was no way that he could afford to get pulled over and have to explain why there was a body in the back seat of a shot-up car that was registered to his mother's dealership.

Chapter Eight

Out of Gladiator School N2 the Gangster's Den

It took me two weeks to leave Massachusetts. I went from there to Rhode Island to Brooklyn, New York in one night. I was on the second load to leave. Redburn had been on the first. In my travels, I got to see a lot of shit. I saw motherfuckers ice-fishing. Got a chance to see Ground Zero, the famous New York lights and the phony ass Statue of Liberty. I was realizing that there were lots of things that I had never gotten to do or see before the system had taken away what little freedom I had. I promised myself, although I knew that changes were slim to none, that if I even managed to gain my freedom, I would never fall victim to the system again. I'd rather be carried by six.

"Ayo, this is my first time going on an airplane," I admitted to Suf'yan as we made our way through the terminal towards the tarmac surrounded by Federal Marshals, after arriving at the New Jersey airport.

"Mine too," Jamaine Holt from Edmondson Village disclosed, although I wasn't talking to his receding hair ass.

"It's just like riding a rollercoaster," Suf'yan smiled. We were on our way to an Oklahoma holdover spot. There, from what I understood, we would be separated and shipped all over the world. Texas, Louisiana, Florida, Colorado, Kentucky; everywhere. "Your ears are going to pop a lot though."

We boarded the airplane, took off and started tripping on the flight, knowing it could very well be the last time that we ever saw each other.

When we stopped at the Pennsylvania Airport to pick up some more passengers, this one wild ass nigga with long dreads boarded the plane calling out snitches and suckers alike. I looked over at Suf'yan who was seated across the aisle from me next to Jodie Hill, then told Skinny Pat to check the nigga out. All the marshals appeared to know him.

The dude took a seat right on the row in front of me and began telling some Crips how one of their homies had 'jumped on his case'.

"Log on to www.rats.com," he suggested before explaining how the site exposed snitches from all over the globe.

After the bathroom break rush, the wild dude with the long dreads ended up sitting right next to me. "What's up, slim?" He raised his head slightly to acknowledge my presence "What spot you coming from?"

"Oh nah, I'm coming from the state." My response appeared to make his face twist up in thought, which was when I noticed that he had a missing tooth.

"From the state?" he repeated curiously before I explained.

We went back and forth and it turns out that he was what they like to call 'a homie in the feds'. His name was Mark, but everybody in the streets called him 'Fucka'. At first, I thought the nigga was playing. But, Suf'yan had actually heard of slim. He was a 'Langdon Park', Northeast, Washington D.C. legend.

"Niggas said you were dead, young," Suf'yan disclosed as he continued to ramble on and on about how humble, yet violent Fucka was.

"Nah, slim, I'm still the last of a dying breed." Fucka smiled. "Me and a lil' homies named L.A. from Greig Street out in Seat Pleasant fucked a Crip nigga around something terrible down there in Big Sandy behind some money. That's how I ended up in the A-D-X. I'm on my way back from court now." He explained before going on to ask Suf'yan about some chick named Lil' Nea Nea from Oxon Hill they both knew.

"You know Lil' Nea Nea still the baddest thing that come out of Oxon Hill. "Suf'yan smiled.

I didn't know exactly what Fucka and his lil' man L.A had done. But I knew that shit had to be serious for them niggas to end up in the federal supermax. That was where they housed niggas like Anthony Jones, John Gotti and Larry Hoover. Old-school gangsters who were not to be played with. Niggas who had never bent the rules.

Fucka was tripping off of our situation and how we'd ended up in the feds. He put us up on the 'BWI'—Baltimore, D.C. Car and broke the whole fed shit down for us. The East Coast was holding it down when it came to that knife play. "Ain't nobody fucking with the homies when it comes to slinging that knife, slim," Fucka assured as the plane landed.

"How far we got to go now?" I questioned curiously.

"We're here, slim," Fucka disclosed.

"Man, I'm talking about going to jail," I corrected myself.

"I know," Fucka smiled, showing his missing tooth again.

"What? You mean we're at the jail?" I asked to be sure.

"Yeah, the plane pulls right up the spot."

Damn! I looked out the window because I couldn't believe it. The motherfucking plane pulling right up to the jail was some serious shit. "Ayo, what the spot like? How do the phones and stuff work?" I couldn't wait to tell my brothers what was going on.

"Oh, y'all niggas ain't seeing no g-pop, slim." Fucka shook his head. "Why you the think y'all in them black boxes?" He gestured towards the movement-restricting black box connected to my handcuffs.

"You didn't notice we're the only ones with them joins on. Look around, homie," he instructed, and I did.

To be honest, I never really paid the shit no attention because I'd been so used to wearing them back in the State. But, as I looked around, I began to notice that we *were* the only ones wearing them. It all started to make sense. Now I knew why the Marshals kept us away from everybody like we were in protective custody or something.

"So, where we going?" I asked.

To the SHU. Y'all on high alert," Fucka replied.

"Man, fuck that SHU shit, young!" Suf'yan fired. "I'm trying to call my aunt."

"It's going to be like that until y'all hit the compound. But don't trip, slim. Just try to get on the side where all the bitches at. That way, y'all can talk to them through the toilets or freak off out the window with them," Fucka said as a bull-face female marshal stepped onto the plane and started calling all of our names.

***

Skinny-Pat and I landed in a special housing unit cell together and instantly began comparing notes. From what we gathered, it seems as if the FEDS wasn't much different than the state in a lot of instances. I mean, the money was plentiful, the guards were corruptible and basically whoever was on location first had home-field advantage. I loved the fact that they 'respected' the shooter-knife slinger in the FEDS just as much as I loved that niggas were on the paperwork heavy, because it keeps suckers in their place and rats at bay. The few things that I didn't like though, was the fact that you couldn't have naked pictures or girl books. Which was funny considering that they'd try to stuff flaming homosexuals into the cell with men and allow homo thugs to walk around hugged up freely with boys. The shit was backwards to me. But the state wasn't much better. I mean, there were new rules in place to stop us from kissing, hugging or even touching our women and it always made me

74

wonder what the prison industry was really promoting. I also hated the fact that because of the gang shit, niggas in the FEDS didn't let suckers be suckers. That was really new to me. I came from a place where there were two kinds of guys in prison: gangsters and suckers. Maybe that was one of the reasons why Baltimore and D.C. niggas stood out so much in the FEDS.

Over the next few days all Skinny-Pat and I did was work out and talk. Skinny-Pat even began training me a little on the boxing tip and I felt like I was back in the basement on Beehler Avenue going toe to toe with my cousin David. We were in the middle of the cell, going over combinations when Jodie Hill and Suf'yan stopped by to inform us that they were hitting general population after sitting down with the SHU lieutenant.

"Man, get that nigga to come over here. We're trying to come off too." Skinny-Pat spoke up for both of us and Suf'yan went to get him.

When the lieutenant showed up, Skinny-Pat and I immediately began to make our pleas, explaining our situation. The lieutenant said that the Maryland Department of Corrections–DOC had put all kinds of stuff into our base files. They claimed that we had assaulted staff, corrupted female officers and were smuggling in everything from drugs to cell phones to DVD players for both personal and financial gain. Which now explained why all the marshals kept asking us if we were the Maryland state troublemakers.

The lieutenant gave us his word that he would push to get us released from the SHU as long as we promised to keep our heads down. We'd have promised that nigga our souls as long as we got off, even if we had no plans of ever giving them to him.

"I'll let you know something before the day is out," he assured us before taking his leave.

I didn't know what Skinny-Pat's chances of going off were. But, I knew the SHU lieutenant was bluffing about me. After all, I had damn near six years of unfinished Maryland lock-up time just like everybody else who had crushed the police up North Branch.

For the rest of the day, Skinny-Pat and I chilled and waited for the lieutenant to come back. We tripped off how cunning the federal administration was, though. By allowing each state, race and gang to knowingly sit together, cell together, and even openly 'set' trip. The feds had basically taken the 'divide and conquer' game to another level. They had niggas so focused on each other that all they had to do was sit back and watch niggas slaughter one another.

"That bitch ass nigga spent us, dog!" I fired when it was no doubt that the SHU lieutenant wasn't coming back.

The next morning, me and Skinny-Pat were in the cell, getting it in when we were told that we were going into federal population. All I kept thinking was that, if it was official, niggas were federal gangsters now. The escort marshal explained that the Oklahoma Transit Center was what they called 'neutral ground' as far as cell buddies and things went.

"In here, I don't give a shit if you're Aryan Brotherhood or a D.C. Black," he made mention of a legendary beef to let us know just how serious he was. "You don't like the bedding arrangements, then you take your ass back to the SHU."

Me and Skinny-Pat ended up on the tenth floor, in the same unit. However, this time, we were assigned to different cells.

After we tossed our shit into the cells, we headed straight to the phones. A cool ass Chinese-Vietnamese dude named Tony from Chinatown, New York, explained how to work the pack number system and operate the phone.

The only person I got through to was Saprina—my cousin Andre's ex-wife—and as always, the sound of her voice made me smile. That was my baby and I prayed to one day find a woman of her caliber; a woman with a heart half her size and beauty as distinctive.

I hipped Saprina to what I knew so far and assured her that I was okay. Then, she got on me about finally being able to get my GED. She knew that I'd been studying behind the door, taking myself to school because she was sending me schoolwork and college lessons.

"If I get this GED, it's going to be because of you," I admitted, making her giggle.

"When you get it," Saprina corrected, "it's going to be because of the work you put in. I can only send you the work. I can't help you nor make you do it."

"I heard that."

"I am still tripping off you being sent halfway around the country though," Saprina said, "and you can work out all day. Because you have a shower in the cell," she quoted a portion of the first letter I'd written to her from Massachusetts. "You always make the best of everything," she added.

Saprina and I kicked it until the fifteen-minute phone call came to an end. She promised to call One Love—mom— and let her know what was going on for me. "I love you, family," I said sincerely.

"I love you too," she replied with her soft voice and just like that I toned back into the prison environment.

While Skinny-Pat finished up his phone call, I sat on the steps nearby and observed the surroundings. I didn't know who my cell buddy was yet. But, I knew he wasn't black because of all the long hair I'd spotted floating around in the toilet bowl.

"Where are you from, homie?" Tony strolled up and sat down on the steps beside me.

"Baltimore," I said, sizing him up out of pure instinct.

"What about your man?" He nodded towards Skinny-Pat.

"Washington D.C.," I revealed as Skinny-Pat hung the phone up. "Why? What's up?" I stood up. I was starting to get curious now.

"Nah, it's not anything like that," Tony assured. "My man Chen was right though. I thought y'all were from New York."

"Chen?" I repeated as he got up and waved about four dudes over.

"What's up, Dak?" Skinny-Pat shot over to me in a flash.

"I'm not sure," I admitted, stepping off the steps as the group of guys approached.

"Y'all from the district, slim?" the little dark-skinned, big-eared one inquired with a curious smirk.

"I am," Skinny-Pat confirmed without hesitation. "What? You be in the city or something?"

I checked out the rest of the group as Skinny-Pat and the little D.C. homie and Tony's man, Chen from New York really got a kick off of how I pronounced 'dog' like dug.

I found out that my cell buddy was the infamous Alberto Prez, a dangerous Mexican hitman for a notorious drug-cartel. "That motherfucker got a hundred bodies under his belt, slim," Nardo explained, directing my attention to a four-foot, long-mustachioed, bubble-bellied Mexican at the card table talking shit. "He plays like he's laid back. But, that nigga sneaky as shit though. I was out west with him when they brought the MS-13 dudes a move."

Me and Skinny-Pat continued to hang out with the East Coast homies and jumped back and forth on the phone for the rest of the day. We even got a little work-out session going with Nardo and another D.C. homie named Andy who was cut the fuck up and made me want to get my weight up.

"Ayo, what's the name of that workout you and Chen were doing?" I asked Tony, checking out the large green dragon tattooed across his back as we headed towards the cells to lock in for the night after getting out of the showers.

"Burpees," he replied, looking back.

"Yeah, you're gonna have to show me how to do them joints," I said.

"You know I got you," Tony assured.

***

Another week passed in no time. The FEDS were funny for so many different reasons. One reason in particular was the TV situation. For instance, there were five televisions stationed throughout the unit. There was one for sports and another for movies. The other three were actually designated for Blacks, Whites, Mexicans—the three dominating forces of the federal system. The funny part was the fact that if you walked into any of the respective TV rooms on any given day, you would see the blacks watching *Charmed*, *The Big Bang Theory*, *Telemundo*. The white boys would be watching *The Wire*, and the Mexicans watching *BET* or the *Sons of Anarchy*.

"Say now, celly, let me look at you for a moment," my cell-buddy, Alberto Prez—who'd barely said two words to me the entire time we'd been in the cell together—stepped to me the moment I walked out of the TV room.

"What's up?" I eyeballed him curiously. I was still picking up on the Texas lingo. 'Say' was like, "*Hey, look!*"

"The blacks aren't letting the Mexicans get on the phones." Nothing on his face moved except his mustache. "We're all men, amigo."

"What the fuck you telling me for?" I snapped instantly, noticing that the Mexicans had strategically surrounded the black TV room.

The next thing I know, three or four Mexicans started going off in Spanish. I wasn't sure what they were saying. But, I could tell by their body language that they were leaning.

"Hold up, yo, check this out. Don't be pulling me up about no fucking phones, nigga!" I barked on them. "I don't even know them dudes. I just came from the state—"

"Listen, I'm speaking for your peoples," Alberto cut me off with his thick Mexican accent. "The blacks have been on the phone all day. Now we want our turn," he warned. "If not, then nobody's going to be using their phones."

Is this nigga threatening me? I stared at Alberto longer than I had to before I replied. "So, what are you saying?" I challenged. I didn't give a fuck how many bodies his little, butter-ball ass had on the streets. We were in prison now and when it came to hand-to-hand combat, I was as vicious as they came.

"What's up, slim?" Skinny-Pat, Andy and Nardo rolled up right on time.

"Nah, this little nigga talking some shit about the phones!" I revealed and Andy took off for the cell.

From there shit got crazy. Everybody started grabbing any weapon they could get their hands on. Motherfuckers had chairs, brooms, buckets, whatever. The whites and Indians cleared the floor and huddled up together to give us space to work and the stage was set.

I weighed the odds; we were about twenty-five strong. But the Mexicans still outnumbered us 2 to 1. Yet, most of them were old and out of shape.

"Fuck them wetbacks, blood. You know I'ma squabble with you," said Tiny-Lee, a dark-skinned, Fifty-fourth Street Brim with long braids. "I can't stand them marks." He flashed a gang sign.

I looked around as Nardo and Alberto made their way to the center of the unit to negotiate. All that Los Angeles gang-banging shit was out of my league. I knew nothing about it other than what I saw dudes doing back in the Maryland prison system, and I wasn't impressed. So, I damn sure wasn't about to ride behind it. I was going on GP, gangsta protocol, alone. Because, to be honest, I was still fucked up that my cell buddy had singled me out for the Mexicans.

In the end though, after Nardo and Alberto Prez finished talking, the Mexicans got their wish and it was over. I learned my first valuable lesson about the Feds though. When it was some race shit, there was no such thing as neutrality. Everybody had to go. And the opposing team always honed in on the niggas they thought were the biggest threats.

Chapter Nine

Gangster Documentation

"Truesdale! Grab your sheets, leave the mattress. You're transferring out!" One of the marshals unlocked the cell door around 5 a.m. before stepping off.

I was already on point. So, I jumped down, covered the cell door up like I was using the bathroom and shook the infamous Alberto Prez awake. "Get up and put your shoes on, bitch!" I fired when he opened his eyes. "I know you didn't think that you weren't going to answer for that shit you pulled last week?"

I went to all the homies' doors to let them know how I'd carried out my plan to see my cell buddy before I left, so that they would be on point. Especially Skinny-Pat because everybody knew that we'd come from the state together. Plus, I wanted to brag about using the new skills I'd learned. Like I said, Alberto Prez may have been treacherous on the streets. But, on the inside, in close quarters, where weapons were limited, skilled hands always reigned supreme.

I met up with Suf'yan and White Boy Do-Dirt in the bullpen and found out that they were leaving too. Dudes were tripping off how much we all fucked with each other; because in the feds, everybody plays the race card. In fact, from what I gathered, every single state except Maryland and Louisiana threw their white homies to the wolves. Meaning, the Aryan Brotherhood, Skinheads, Dirty White Boys or Peckerwoods. I knew it was only like that for us because, in the Maryland prison system there were no color lines. I mean, niggas weren't color blind. Men just respected men.

We sat around the bullpen, listening to guys trade war stories until they processed us. I found out that Suf'yan and I were going to the same location. Do-Dirt was going to the spot called 'Big Sandy' out the in Kentucky somewhere. We gave Do-Dirt some love and told him to hold it down before parting ways. I was still tripping off the fact that we literally stepped out of the jail onto an airplane. I mean, our feet never touched the ground.

After landing at a small Louisiana airport in Pollock, Louisiana, we were driven to the nearby USP-Pollock. Once there, we were strip-searched, interviewed and screened for housing. Half naked photos were taken—allegedly for our tattoos. But I wasn't so sure. Then, the marshals warned me that, 'If I was a snitch, it would be best for me to check in because as he said, 'Baltimore was on that paperwork heavy'. I smiled and assured him that I was way too cool to be hot. My gangster history was well documented.

When we finally hit the yard, it blew my mind. I mean, first of all, the marshals just walked about the twenty of us to a door, pushed it open, pointed out each housing unit and told us to get out. And I'm not over exaggerating when I tell you that there were at least a thousand niggas on that yard surrounding the door. When we stepped outside, they were hurling all kinds of questions; asking niggas what state they were from, what they claimed, and if anybody checked in, etc. You had brothers looking for everybody from family members to Gangster Disciples.

I saw a group of neatly dressed, well-organized brothers and instantly knew that they were Nation of Islam members. Anybody who'd ever been to prison could always spot an FOI, especially the serious ones. They stuck out. They weren't loud or anything. They just looked different, even though they wore the same standard prison-issued clothing. They were clean, and sharp. They conducted themselves differently. They moved, talked and acted like they had somewhere to go, even though they were in prison like everybody else. They reminded me of the old school gangsters—Preserved and hard, like they'd been carved out of stone. But, that wasn't what made them so noticeable to me. What always drew my attention was the fact that, despite the small number of members, the ranking members were fearless, yet very respectful, almost as if they knew that whoever or whatever was backing them was stronger than anything else in the world.

"Any Crips traveling with you, Cuz?" a big Terry Crews-looking banger asked as we strolled down the pathway like we were on an assembly line.

"I don't know you," I hunched my shoulders and kept moving.

"This shit crazy, young," Suf'yan mumbled just enough for me to hear him and I had to agree.

"I ain't never seen no shit like this," I confessed while looking around. "Niggas clocking us like new merchandise, yo."

"Where y'all from? Baltimore?" a slim, older guy questioned with a thick country accent.

"Ain't no question," I confirmed.

The old-head looked over his shoulder and yelled into the crowds. "A Yeyo! Will! I think y'all homies over here!"

A few seconds later I saw the crowd part and couldn't believe my eyes. It was my nigga Willie Bates. One of the old North and Long gangsters who'd laced my boots growing up. "Little Dak, what up?" Willie Bates threw his hand up and a smile instantly spread across my face.

"You, old man!" I said before we shook hands and embraced like long-lost brothers.

"Ahhh, it's good to see you," Willie Bates confessed as we broke the embrace.

"Likewise." I stepped back and took a good look at him. "You've got all fat and stuff."

"I know," Willie Bates admitted, rubbing his stomach. "When the hell did you get fed time, Jack? Last thing I remembered you and Frank blew trial behind that stale was nigga *Hoe-nique*. So, when the homies said your name, I was like 'I only know one Dakaron and he got state time'."

"It's a long story," I explained, not wanting to go into it now.

"Don't worry. We'll rap about it later." Willie Bates nodded. "Right now, let's get off this yard. The Vice Lords are supposed to be hitting one of their own coming off the bus."

Damn, I thought. *No wonder why whoever was on location first had the drop on a nigga.* "So, they already know a nigga coming?"

"Yeah," Willie Bates nodded.

"The case manager gave me your name two days ago." the other homie volunteered.

"Oh, my bad." Willie Bates paused to look round. "This the homie Buckey Fields." He put his hand on the shoulder of a stocky, bald-head, bow-legged, brown skinned, pigeon-toed dude with a huge beard.

"What's up, slim?" Buckey Fields extended his hand and I accepted it.

"What's up?" I nodded.

"You probably don't remember me, but I was on the yard with your brother Antauwn out Lompoc back in the day."

"Oh yeah?" I thought back to some of the photos Antauwn had sent home from the feds. I didn't recognize Buckey Fields' face, but I definitely felt like I'd heard the name. "I think I remember the name from the back of a picture or something."

"Yeah, that's my man. I remember me, him and a dude named Skeet from V.A. got to pushing with the G.D.'s out that mothersucker."

"Hell yeah!" I exclaimed. "That's where I remember your name from too," I admitted as the situation of my brother and a few of his good men getting into it out west came back to memory.

"What's up with bruh now? What is he up to? I knew he out that mothersucker getting it." Buckey Fields balled his face up and poked his bottom lip out.

"Nah, he's chilling," I revealed. "He just got married to his children's mother. You know he lost his legs."

"What?" Buckey Fields spat.

"Yeah, wild ass nigga ran down on him and my cousin about a bitch," I explained.

"Damn, slim!" Buckey Fields shook his head in disappointment. "Make sure you give slim my regards when you talk to him."

"Will do," I assured.

"You already know Yeyo." He pointed to the familiar André 3000-looking homie. "You probably remember him as Lil' Ache from Murphy Homes though. The one Monique rolled over on," he added, instantly jogging my memory.

"I respect how you handle that shit," Lil' Ache confessed.

I didn't confirm nor reject Lil' Ache's comment. I just looked around uncomfortably and asked if this was all the homies.

"Hell no!" Willie Bates fired. "You'll meet everybody else later. Right now, we have to find out where you're living."

"B-Three," I informed.

'Yeah, I know, but the homies ain't really got no cells down there. So, let's go see what's up." Willie Bates started moving and we all fell in behind him.

"What you mean, the homies ain't got no cells over there?" I was confused. "If there weren't any beds open, why would they assign me to the unit?"

"Nah, its cells open, just ain't none of them homies. It's different in the feds, Dak. Everybody on homie time," Willie Bates explained.

"Oh, don't worry though, slim. Our homies don't go back up top, believe that!" Buckey Fields fired, walking beside me. "We'll check one of them farmers in first," he assured before turning to Suf'yan to ask where he was going.

"B-1."

"Oh, the homies got that mothersucker on smash." Buckey Fields nodded and I realized for the first time that he didn't curse.

"Homie good either way," Lil' Ache spoke up. "I hollered at Black Randy last night. So, if all else fails, he can put that farmer in the cell with him out."

When we got to the unit, I gave Suf'yan some love and told him that I'd see him later on before he and Bucky Fields headed for B-1. Then, Lil' Ache, Willie Bates and myself continued inside to find out what the sleeping arrangements were going to be.

To make a long story short, the Texas nigga who I was supposed to go into the cell with was on some real bitch shit. To be honest, I begged Willie Bates for a joint so I could tear the fur off his ass. I was dying to let them federal niggas know that I had arrived. But Willie Bates wasn't having it.

The dude Black Randy, who I found out was from Virginia, kicked his cell-buddy out and just like that, I moved in.

Lil' Ache and Willie Bates hung out for a little bit to make sure everything was good. Then, they said they would see me in the morning to make sure I had everything I needed.

The first thing I did after the homies rolled out was go through the bag they gave me to find some lotion. It had been weeks since I'd lotioned up and my skin was dry as fuck. Black Randy was tripping off me. Wondering why I hadn't waited to bathe in the shower. But, I wasn't paying his ass no mind. He hadn't been the one stuck in transit for weeks without basic necessities. Shiiid, it had gotten so bad once that I'd begun to use butter to lotion up, I'm dead serious, a nigga was walking around smelling like a butter-milk biscuit; fucking with that butter off them breakfast trays.

Black Randy put me up on the happenings. He said the Baltimore homies were well respected on the compound, but the D.C. homies had the yard. "Some of the homies are on that goofy shit too. So, watch yourself!" he warned before going on to explain how Willie Bates and them were carrying it. "Lil' Ache is the heart of the city. But ain't nothing on the yard moving without Bucky Fields though."

I laid back and just took in everything Black Randy was saying as I continued to lotion up and try to get a feel for the spot. One thing for sure: I wasn't going to make the same mistakes I'd made coming into the 'Cut' and the 'Annex' moving too fast.

This nigga Black Randy claimed to have cases in D.C., Maryland, Virginia, New York and North Carolina. Now, I don't know if he is bluffing or not. But his stories sound so authentic. I mean, he had the state lingo and everything down. All I kept thinking to myself as he talked was that this nigga was a true chameleon.

Chapter Ten

Gangster Assessment

Over the next couple of months, I got a little deeper into the life-giving, life-saving teachings of the Nation of Islam. I mean, I didn't join up or nothing. Gangs and religious organizations just weren't my thing because besides my cousins, there was only one nigga behind the 'G' wall who I wouldn't ever go against. However, I did begin to learn a lot more not just about the Nation, but also about myself. Furthermore, I finally obtained my GED–thanks in large part to Saprina. I also began to adjust to the federal system and its politics. Which was when shit jumped off; it quickly spread like wildfire. For example, a few weeks after I'd arrived, some homies were at a poker table, gambling with some farmers–out-of-towners. When one of them decided to punt-fake like he wasn't going to pay what he'd lost at the table in the end, the homies called a blitz and we ran the whole car–city off the yard. I'm talking about every single nigga with the last three digits of a 'Florida' register number.

I really got to know Lil' Ache and Buckey Fields and I could see why my brother fucked with and respect them both so much. Lil' Ache's hustle and ambition for freedom was unmatched. I swear, I only knew one other nigga with more hustle and drive behind the 'G' wall, and that was a Park Heights Gangster by the name of Shawn 'Goo' Garner. I fucked with Buckey Fields for real. He was a gangster of another kind who was always down to make the ultimate sacrifice when it came to the homies. And if he rocked with you, he would go against the entire yard. He kind of reminded me of my rap-buddy, Frank. Thorough, stubborn and loyal.

Of course, Willie Bates' ass was still a nutcase. I mean, this silly Negro still thought that he was in the streets pulling licks. He had a crew of homies called the 'BWI Boys' running around the jail jacking niggas for everything from commissary to drugs. They were even kidnapping niggas and making their families pay ransom though Western Union.

"So, what are you going to do if these folks let you go?" I questioned Willie Bates as we walked to the kitchen for lunch, talking about his upcoming parole hearing.

"You know me," Willie Bates replied and paused for a moment. "I don't know how to do nothing but play with that pistol."

"Man, don't go out there fucking with them streets," I cautioned, thinking about all the shit he'd talked when I first hit the yard about how he'd changed. He'd even asked me to forgive him for all the wickedness he'd shown me in the streets. "They're going to lay your ass down."

"Nah, see, I have finally begun to realize that the way I've been playing the game is dead. It's a new day. Now, don't get me wrong. I'ma always stick to the script because I know that those who forsake the old ways for the new know what they're losing, but not what they shall find. Still, I'm not stupid. I know that any man who continues to cling to old ideas and fight to keep things the way they were in a changing world, will soon find himself in a world that no longer exists or worse. In the crosshairs of those who have evolved and want to see change."

I looked at Willie Bates and thought about what one of the Nation of Islam brothers had said at the last service. *"We're enemies to ourselves by circumstances because we have been taught and trained by an enemy to hate ourselves and kind."*

"I hear you." I knew Willie Bates had a point. Things were changing. I was starting to see it myself. The death of the old give birth to the new. Still, I was old-school and I would break before I'd bend.

"Look at little Jamaine," Willie Bates continued, "he's out there taking hits now."

"Man, don't even mention that slimy ass nigga!" I fired. Willie Bates laughed. I had absolutely no respect for Jamaine. He'd left Frank and I for dead. Then, he had the nerve to be running around telling niggas I was his brother.

"You know what's funny? When y'all little niggas were young, I always looked at y'all like the Godfather brothers. You were Sunny all day long. Stubborn but honorable. Frank was more like Michael, loyal and patient. But I always saw Jamaine's little sneaky ass as Fredo. Ambitious and selfish!" Willie Bates explained. "So, I ain't surprised that he didn't have any do-right in him."

I kept my thoughts to myself because—truth be told—I was still hurt that Jamaine had turned his back on me and Frank. Especially after all the shit niggas had been through. We'd all worn the same clothes, slept in the same beds, fucked the same bitches and even shared the same toothbrushes. A motherfucker couldn't have even paid me to believe that Jamaine would turn out the way he did.

"Oh shit, yo, guess who my mother said asked about me yesterday?" Something I had forgotten popped in my head. Which was good because I wanted to change the subject anyway.

"Who?" Willie Bates asked as we got to the kitchen.

"Chanae" I revealed nonchalantly as my eyes locked on a white boy coming our way with a baseball bat resting on his shoulder, like he was waiting for the pitch. "She gave mom a number for me."

"You going to call her?"

"For what?" I played like I didn't care the same way I had when my mother first told me about the number. The truth was I'd lost faith in Chanae a long time ago. I felt like she only thought about me or reached out to me when some nigga broke her heart and she needed to be comforted or she wanted something. "I'm good."

"Man, you better call that girl," Willie Bates encouraged me, knowing how much I loved Chanae. "You know you want to."

"I didn't even take the number," I confessed honestly as the white boy began twisting and twirling the bat around above his shoulder. I wasn't a coat that Chanae could just put on whenever it got cold outside. It was all or nothing!

"Hold up, yo," I suddenly stopped in my tracks to let the white boy stroll by, so I could keep my eyes on him.

"Come on, man, I know you're not worrying about no damn white boy?" Willie Bates looked at me crazy, but I didn't trust any of them racist white boys. AB's, Skinheads, Dirty White Boys, none of them. "If that white boy would've hit you with that bat, I would've torn him up out here," Willie Bates assured.

"Man, if he would've hit me with that bat, it would've been nothing that you could've done to make me feel better. I would've hit one of them bitches on every compound I touched."

"You got a lot of compounds with no AB's, Jack."

"Yeah, well, I'd hit any white boy whose name starts with the letters A or B!" I fired seriously.

"I'm not messing with you today, Dak," Willie Bates said, pulling the kitchen door open so that we could go inside.

***

"Say, little Dak, the phone opened round?" I looked up from the chess board to see my guy Wash—a well-known, tall, light brown-skinned, New Orleans goon with long dreads—approaching.

"Give me one second." I held up a finger and eyed the chessboard again, looking for the best move. Quickly assessing the board, anticipating my opponent's next move, I decided to castle.

"Finish this for me, big boy!" I gestured towards the table smiling at Wash as he took my place.

I fucked with Wash for several reasons. Number one being because he was real. I was still tripping off the fact that his silly ass had made the cover of the New York Times Magazine as 'Hurricane Katrina's Most Wanted. The article talked about how dangerous he was. But, I knew this big goofy nigga. He was a jokester at heart.

I shot over to the phone to call One Love. It was a Sunday morning ritual that had begun at the start of my bid. "Hey, girlie!" I fired the instant my mother accepted the call.

"Good morning, baby!" my mother fired back as usual, making me smile. I could always hear the joy in her tone when she heard my voice. It didn't matter if it was seven in the morning or one o'clock at night, my mother was always happy to take my call.

"Who are you calling baby on my damn phone?" I heard my father in the background and shook my head. He played about a lot of things, but my mother wasn't one of them.

"Timmy, get out of my face and go do what I asked you to do please." I listened to my mother and father go back and forth for a moment. It always amazed me how after over thirty years they were still so in love. "Get your crusty lips off me, Timmy, you know your son on the phone!"

"How many times is he going to call? Didn't he just call here Thursday?" My father sounded jealous.

"You better leave my baby alone."

"What he say, Ma?" I asked as if I hadn't heard him clearly.

"Don't pay your father no mind. That fool just talking out the side of his neck, baby."

I took my mother's advice and disregarded what my father was saying because I knew how he was—tough love all day every day. "What are you up to already, Ma?" I laughed because one thing I knew about my parents was that they were up at the crack of dawn. Especially One Love; she don't care what was going on; she lived by the early-bird-got-the-worm motto. To be honest, I couldn't ever remember actually seeing my mother lying in bed. And I was almost never up before her.

"In here cleaning up, listening to my oldies, waiting for your fatherhere to get out of my house," my mother replied and my Pops immediately went off in the background.

"Whose house?" I heard my father's question. "This is my house! I pay all the bills up in here! Who bought all this furniture, huh? Living room sets, dining room table? Silverware?"

"Timmy, please, you ain't pay a bill in twenty years!" My mother retorted, giggling. "You ain't got no damn money."

"What?" My father lost it. "Who ain't got no money?"

My father began going on and on about stuff that I personally know that he hadn't paid for. But my pops was crazy like that and my mother loved him to death. "Timmy, just go to the market and get my eggs and stuff please!" my mother pleaded again.

"Dakaron?" I heard my father call my name. "That's my son on phone?"

"Timmy!" my mother whined.

"Give me the phone, woman!" my father demanded a second before he was on the line. "Dakaron!"

"What's going on, daddy?"

"You okay, boy?" Pops inquired.

"Yeah, I'm good, daddy." I smiled.

"That's good. Now listen, son, this is your mother, not your girlfriend. This is my wife, so don't keep calling her like she's your girlfriend. I'm in here trying to get some poontang. Don't you want a little sister?" My father joked until my mother was able to wrestle the phone from him.

"Don't nobody want that wrinkled up, old thing!" My mother got back on the phone.

"Daddy shooting blanks now anyway, Ma," I teased, laughing.

"You ain't lying." My mother laughed as my father mumbled something as his voice faded out.

"Anyway, I got some good news." My mother was excited, collecting her thoughts. "Frank called yesterday and said that y'all won the case," my mother disclosed and I began firing off a thousand questions that she couldn't begin to answer.

"Look, you know I don't know about all that stuff. Talk to Detauwn. He was over here talking to Frank too. So, call your brother. The only thing I know is, Frank said something about one hundred eighty days ago."

I spaced out for a second. It was on now. A nigga was about to see the streets again. I couldn't wait to shit on all the motherfuckers who've ever turned their backs on me or wrote me off because they thought that I was finished. All the hypocrites who loved throwing my name around or flashing my photo, like they were truly down for me when they weren't. A lot of them wouldn't even walk with me when the smoke was thick and I was challenging everybody from South Baltimore to Western Maryland, gunning for the crown. But, it was all good because I was gonna fuck the city up. Motherfuckers were going to regret the day they left me for dead.

I'm really going to bring it this time, I thought, *I'm going to make niggas hate for real.*

They'd already lied to me, conspired against me and tried to kill me. So I already knew who was who. That was why when I got back out there, I'd be extremely careful because prison had shown me that people feared exposure more than anything else.

It also taught me that weak and phony motherfuckers always wanted something for nothing. They wanted the love, the loyalty, the respect and the fame, all without having to put in the necessary work; all without having to make the needed sacrifices. They weren't ready to weather the storm. But, me and Frank had paid our dues. We had stood tall against all odds and now we were about to be back bigger and better than ever, ready to take what the streets owed us.

I thought about my daughters. I thought about the future. I no longer thought small. When you thought small, you moved small. Which meant you were no threat because you stayed in your place. But those days were over. That Dakaron was dead.

"Dakaron!" My mother snapped me out of my daze. "Did you hear what I said?"

"My bad, say it again, Ma," I requested.

"I said if any one of my children had to do that type of time, I would prefer it to be you," my mother repeated.

"Why do you say that?" I questioned, kind of hurt, not really understanding One Love's logic.

"Of course, I don't want any of my children to be locked up. But, you are my strongest child. I mean, even locked up, you don't do no whining or nothing. Now, when your brothers were in jail—" One Love began to explain the difference between me and my brothers. Both our weaknesses and strengths. She said Antauwn was like her— he could endure anything. He was compassionate and if all else failed, he'd be the one that held everything together.

I agreed. "What about, Detauwn, Ma?" I wanted to know more.

"That's your father," my mother revealed without hesitation and I could just picture the smile on her face. "He's going to do things his way. But he's dedicated to family, come hell or high water. He just has a funny way of showing it sometimes."

One Love and I hung out until the operator cut us off and the phone call came to an end. I hung up and headed to the cell with my head spending. *Home*, I thought. *A nigga was about to go home.*

When I got in the cell, I covered the window and did something that I hadn't done in a very long time. I got down on my knees and prayed.

***

"I see y'all got bruh working out now," I said, walking up on Suf'yan, Buckey Fields and another homie who looked like he was about to pass out.

"Yeah, his mothersucking, fat tail went up medical and found out that he might got diabetes," Buckey Fields said in between his set.

I shook my head. Not because he might be a diabetic. But because it always took the threat of death or bad health to get us to do what we already knew we should've been doing.

"Hold up," the homie leaned forward to place his hands on his knees humbly.

"Nah, young, come on. Let's go!" Suf'yan ordered, going straight into a squat-thrust.

"I can't breathe," he pleaded, looking to Suf'yan for mercy as he tried to catch his breath.

"Nah, scrap, ain't nobody tell your fat tail to be inhaling all those stir-fries every night!" Buckey Fields snapped, showing no mercy.

"Y'all seen Willie Bates?" I watched the homie do slow squat-thrusts.

"Yeah," Buckey Fields kept his eyes on the homie. "I think him and Lil' Ache over there near the football field." Buckey Fields did another squat-thrust as I stepped off and left them to it.

The last two months had passed in a blur. I mean, my public defender had never sent me a copy of the court's ruling, but it was definitely official. I had the newspaper article to prove it. The courts had vacated our time for an evidentiary hearing.

After making my way to the football field, I actually found out that Lil' Ache and Willie Bates had gone up to the gym to take some flicks for an internet dating website and hurried up there to join the them. Shiddd, I wanted to bag something nice too, especially since I was now on my way back to court.

I arrived at the gym just in time to jump in a few of Lil' Ache's and Willie Bates' fishing pictures. "I'm trying to get me one of them thick ass, dirty south chicks," I confessed after posing for the camera man. "I heard they're loyal as shit."

"Shid, that's all you need? Loyalty!" Lil' Ache said.

"I need a little bit more than just loyalty to have a good relationship," Willie Bates confessed.

After signing for the photos, I pulled Willie Bates to the side. I wasn't big on talking about my personal business. Shiddd, Suf'yan, Willie Bates and my cell-buddy Black Randy were the only ones who knew that I'd given my time back.

"What's up, Jack?" Willie Bates fixed his shirt.

I didn't say anything. I just handed him Chanae's letter. Then, I watched as he read it, wondering if it would make him cry also. I wondered what he thought about all of Chanae's pledges to never leave nor forsake me again. And I wondered what he thought of her apologies.

"So, what are you going to do?" Willie Bates handed the letter back. "You going to give her another chance?"

"I don't know, yo," I admitted sincerely because I honestly didn't know what to do. I really loved Chanae and all the feelings I'd buried deep inside resurfaced the instant I began to read her thoughts and that made me mad. Mad because I wasn't supposed to feel nothing for her anymore. At least that was what I'd been telling myself for the last few years. "Detauwn and Sweet Pea saying she only wrote me because she's locked up."

"She's locked up?" Willie Bates inquired and I nodded, remembering that I'd only brought him a portion of Chanae's letter.

"Yeah, she got a drug charge," I revealed, not really feeling the need to go all into how some lame she was fucking with had allowed her to get jammed up.

"She got that gangster shit from Shawnell," Willie Bates mentioned Chanae's mother proudly and I didn't even want to tell him that Shawnell was locked up as well. I didn't find anything gangster about a female having to step up and hustle because the father of her children was either gone or just simply wasn't worth shit. "The thing is, she wrote to you. That means she recognizes her faults. So, if you're asking for my advice, I say write her back and tell her how you really feel. Not none of the bullshit you are telling me either."

I stared at Willie Bates for a long moment. He was right. If I ever wanted anything with Chanae again, I had to tell her how I truly felt. How her actions or lack thereof had really affected me. "I'ma reach out to her," I confessed, knowing that the journey of a million miles starts with the first step.

Chapter Eleven

Introducing the 'G' Lock

"This fed shit some straight bullshit, young!" "Suf'yan exclaimed as I did my set of push-ups.

We were walking the track, doing twenty-five push-ups a set. "Why you say that?" I inquired, standing up as Suf'yan went down.

"Because homies trying to force you to deal with niggas you normally wouldn't deal with just because they're from Washington." Suf'yan extended his arms, took a deep breath and continued. "I'm tired of running to the yard every time a homie has an issue," he added before falling into his set.

I knew that Suf'yan was venting and I felt his pain. The so-called homie thing was definitely some bullshit. I mean just yesterday, I'd gotten into it with another so-called Baltimore homie about the same shit. We'd damned near come to blows behind his stupidity. "You can't let these crash dummies get to you, dog," I said, although I honestly knew that it was almost impossible. Especially when you considered the fact that a homie's actions could get you caught up.

"Then, niggas act like they got a problem about who I work out with," Suf'yan fired, coming up from his set. "To be honest, I wouldn't even be fucking with most of these niggas if I wasn't in the feds. You know me, Dak. A lot of homies not even my type."

Again, I nodded in agreement before going down for my set. Suf'yan was right. In the 'Cut' or 'Annex' a lot of homies wouldn't even be able to sit at the table with me, let alone walk the yard. Especially the homies that were running around on the dope-fiend shit, stealing, running up bills and whatnot.

"Again, homies talk that gangster shit. But, how many of these niggas ready to go for broke, young?" Suf'yan continued. "I'm not dying for these niggas!"

"Yeah, me neither." I got up so we could walk some more before the next set. "I'll back a niggas play all day long. But, I'm not going to battle for nobody but my rap-buddy." I spoke from the heart because Frank was the only nigga I'd gladly put it all on the line for. "This is why I'm glad it's not really a lot of Baltimore homies on the yard. The more homies, the more problems."

"My thing is: treat everybody the same. Niggas be letting homies get away with anything, especially if he goes for bad. But, let it be a homie who's not in the 'in' crowd who does something. A homie whose name don't ring. Niggas be ready to run him off the yard," Suf'yan explained.

"Yeah, you're right 'bout that. Homies do pick and choose who the laws apply to. But you know how it goes in the joint. That's nothing new. The strong get catered to and the weak get preyed on. We may not like it, but niggas made it like that, you dig?"

"True, but still, that's why I'm ready to go back to Maryland. Fuck this fed shit! All that fake homie, fake car shit!" Suf'yan fired.

"Like it or leave it, dog. It is what it is. The only way I'm ever trying to go back is for release or in a box," I declared, never wanting to see North Branch again. There was no doubt in my mind that the racist bitches up there would kill me the next time.

"Attention! All inmates, get on the ground! I repeat! All inmates, get on the ground or you will be shot!" The deuces suddenly sounded and everybody in the yard got on point, because nobody knew exactly what was going down or who all were involved.

"¡Atención! ¡Todos los prisioneros, tiren al suelo! ¡Repito! ¡Todos los prisioneros, tiren al suelo o serán fusilados!" The warning continued in Spanish to make sure everybody understood that the officer in the gun-tower that sat slam dead in the middle of the yard would shoot anybody who didn't comply.

"Attention! All inmates, get on the ground! I repeat! All inmates, get on the ground or you will be shot! *¡Atención! ¡Todos los prisioneros, tiren al suelo! ¡Repito! ¡Todos los prisioneros, tiren al suelo o serán fusilados!"*

"C-Yard, young!" Suf'yan said, pointing towards the baseball field as we squatted down on the track. "Niggas rocking by the bleachers!"

Whenever the deuces went off, everybody took precautions to protect themselves. At least until they knew for sure that it wasn't their homies rocking or some race shit jumping off. I mean, nobody was trying to get shot. And them fucking marshals that sat up in that gun-tower loved putting that AR16 on a nigga after that third warning sounded. The first two rounds were always rubber. Then, it was live ammunition. I'm talking about flesh-tearing, bone-breaking, limb-taking, 3½ inch hollow-tipped bullets.

I stayed down and zoomed in on the situation to make sure it wasn't none of the homies getting it in. "Ayo, ain't that your man?" I questioned, locking on one of Suf'yan's workout partners and his West Coast homie beating the breaks for another dude with padlocks strapped to the end of belts.

"Oh shit, young, that is Bozo!" Suf'yan confirmed as their victim took off running with Bozo and his homie on his heels.

"Get down! Everybody, get down!" Marshals ordered as they flew by in the same direction to assist the dude in need of major help, but Suf'yan and I continued to make our way over to the fence.

The homies had a motto—'Never get all the way down or cuff-up until the battle is over'—and I followed it to the letter. I wasn't about to be late or get tagged for bluffing like so many others who laid down on the ground in the heat of battle.

"Damn yo, they're dogging slim," I stated more to myself, as Bozo cracked the dude across the back of the head and sent him to the dirt, right in front of us on the other side of the fence.

I saw white meat hanging out the back of the dude's head a second before Bozo and his homie began to slaughter him with the padlocks. I'd heard about the damage the locks could do. Especially from guys who had bidded up in Hagerstown, Maryland. And I'd witnessed a nigga or two get slapped upside the head with a food can or some D-batteries. But man, watching Bozo and his homie beat dude with them padlocks gave me a whole new respect for putting that lock on a nigga's head,

They beat the dude until his eye fell out of his head. Until even his own mother wouldn't have recognized him, and all the marshals did was: stand back and pleaded with Bozo and his homie to stop.

"That nigga gotta be a rat or something for them to punish him like that," I tried to justify, shaking my head.

"*Boom!*" The unmistakable sound of the AR16 brought the yard to a dead silence as Bozo flew backwards.

"Oh shit!" Suf'yan and I exclaimed in unison as Bozo's body's bounced off the gate and hit the ground. I had been so engrossed in the beating that I'd forgotten all about the warning.

"What the fuck happened to the rubber bullets!" I heard someone shout. But, my mind was fucked up. It wasn't every day that a nigga got shot in prison.

I looked up at the gun-tower just as Bozo's homie took off running. I saw the marshal out on the landing, lining him up with the scope of the AR16 and yelled for him to get down. After all, they'd just bust his homie. The only thing that saved him was the fact that this cowboy-marshal came out of nowhere and tackled him to the ground.

"Yard is closed!" The order came over the loudspeaker as a pack of marshals rolled Bozo over on his stomach and handcuffed him.

"It looks like he only got hit in the shoulder," I said as they dragged Bozo off the yard.

"They're going to mess around and lock us down, watch, and I got a visit coming," Suf'yan whispered as we stood up and headed for the building. However, I wasn't so sure I agreed. It took a lot for the feds to shut the jail down. I mean, they'd put the clamps on certain cars, deadlock their cell doors or whatnot. But, there had been nine bodies in the last seven months, two of which were dropped on the same day.

"For some homie on homie shit?" I questioned because everybody knew that the administration didn't trip when niggas were cleaning house. In fact, they encouraged it. They only truly got concerned or nervous when it was a race war, or two cars were clashing.

"Nah, because that's the same racist white boy who just shot the BGF shot-caller last month," Suf'yan revealed.

"Yeah, it may be some shit behind that." I thought about all the mumbling I'd heard when the BGF dude got shot.

However, after Suf'yan and I separated and I got inside the unit, the range was still out and everybody was running around with suggestions. Which meant, anything could still happen.

I fell in with the homies and just began to explain what happened, when the range-marshal walked up and informed me that my case manager needed to see me.

I looked at Black Randy because I knew exactly what time it was.

"Don't forget the paperwork you got to turn in," Black Randy said, buying me some time.

"Oh yeah, damn." I snapped my fingers as if I'd just remembered, and followed Black Randy towards the cell.

"What you want me to do with all your stuff?" Black Randy asked the moment we entered the cell because he knew that once I went to see the case manager concerning court transfer, most likely I wasn't coming back.

"I don't give a fuck," I confessed before giving Black Randy some love. "Just make sure Suf'yan and Willie Bates good."

"A'ight, big boy, take care of yourself." Black Randy broke the embrace.

Smiling, I said, "I don't know how to do anything else."

I exited the cell with freedom in my mind. I didn't say too much to the homies. I just kind of breezed through, not really wanting to be bearing 'good news' in the midst of some shit about to go down. So, I just nodded to the homies and lied, telling them that I'd be right back with a hidden grin. However, when I walked into my case manager's office and saw the chaplain, I knew something was terribly wrong.

***

The death of my father crushed me. I never knew that a human body could produce so many tears. I wanted so badly for it not to be true. But it was and I never knew that I could experience such mental pain. I always 'tagged' myself as strong. But, when the chaplain told me that my pops had died of a sudden heart attack, all the strength I thought I'd built over the years crumbled. For the next few weeks, I was in a dream state. I wasn't eating or working out. I just walked around with the knife on me, waiting for the deuces to go off, praying that it was a homie. I wanted to butcher something. Black, white, Mexican, marshal, whoever. Even a homie on homie situation would've quenched my thirst for blood. I didn't give a fuck. The system had taken everything from me. And all I kept thinking about was how I'd come to prison as a child and allowed the system to turn me into a monster. Now, my father would never get to see me return as a man.

It took me some time to bounce back. It had been a long time since I'd felt pain that deep. Pain that burnt me at the core. Everybody was writing, reaching out, but none of that shit helped. My father was gone. The original gangster of all gangsters. The guy who would've walked into hell, covered in gasoline, and knuckled up with Satan himself about his family.

When I think about it now, it still hurts and I know that attending the Nation of Islam service was the only thing that kept me from just fucking somebody over. Because despite how I felt, I didn't just want to kill a motherfucker for no reason.

Chapter Twelve

The Gangster of All Gangsters

"Ayo, read that shit again," I encouraged Black Randy, hopping down off the bunk so that I could look at him and get the full effect the next time he read the poem. "That motherfucker mean."

"*My tear drops paint an image—and my canvas in simple life. Though seen through the eyes of the suffering, in the hood is where we earn our stripes, from hanging out and getting high, to honoring t-shirts and chalk lines, with a tilt of the bottle and a silent vow to ride. This is where it all ends, no compassion, just the sound of two souls clashing in a fatal shootout with only one person emerging as the deadly assassin, and still nobody rests, we just keep filling up caskets, and—*" Black Randy paused to flip the page.

"*My teardrops paint an image and tell stories of real life, now we can all brag about Phantoms, Bentleys, and new chains, but what about those mothers and fathers that shoot poison into their veins? Or the parents that stopped being there because of crack cocaine? What about that little boy who's been molested, or that new born child that's being neglected, or that sister that just contracted AIDS because she forgot to use protection. My teardrops paint an image, because nowadays, people would rather sleep in hallways than to pursue their dreams on Broadway. And teenage girls wanna imitate the things they hear their momma say, and wonder where their daddies have been for their past five birthdays. Shiiiddd—*" Black Randy looked up briefly to see if I was still with him as he flipped to the last page.

"My teardrops paint an image, one that some could hardly imagine, and that's why my pen speaks with so much passion, but when the world becomes too tragic, my tear drops burn, just like acid. My tears!"

"Yo. That. Mother. Fucker. Is like that!" I fired as Black Randy sat the papers on the bed. "Who you say wrote that again?"

"My sister Katina's husband, John Bravo."

"That's your sister that lives in D.C right?' I picked up the poem to read it myself

"Yeah, the one that's into real estate. The one who always send me poems and stuff from out in Adams," Black Randy confirmed.

My teardrops paint an image—I began to silently read when Willie Bates burst into the cell and scared the hell out of me. "Man, don't be bursting up in here like that!" I snapped, ready to curse Willie Bates' ass out.

"Strap up, homie, it's a work call!" Willie Bates ignored my statement.

"What's up?" Black Randy shot to his feet as I tossed the poem on the bed.

"Buckey Fields just got into it with one of them AB's," Willie Bates informed and that was all I needed to hear.

I immediately put my throwaway up, the joint that I basically walked around with, and pulled out my murder-weapon. I'd been dying to steam-roll a nigga ever since my father had passed away.

"Hurry up! The homies already on the yard. We're about to blow this bitch!" Willie Bates fired before taking off.

"Lock my shit up too," Black Randy instructed as I secured my locker.

I stuffed the leather baseball gloves into my back pocket, snapped Black Randy's combination lock on his locker and ran out of the cell behind Willie Bates. It was show time.

When we hit the yard, I could tell that shit was about to get funky because all the white boys were huddled up near the basketball court. I spotted Suf'yan and headed his way. We'd made a pact a long time ago that no matter whatever happened, we'd always ride that shit out together, side by side, win, lose or draw.

"These crackers want some work or what?" I pulled up on Suf'yan and started strapping my gloves on.

"We're about to find out. Here come Buckey Fields and them now," Suf'yan replied.

"Which one Buckey Fields got into it with?" I looked towards the basketball court.

"The chump right there with his foot on the basketball, cracking his knuckles."

Hitler, I thought, recognizing the large Nazi Swastika on the side of his head. Rumor had it that Hitler had '*kill one nigger before you die*' tatted across his back.

"He's the one pushing the issue. He accused Buckey Fields' little cousin of stealing some boots out of his cell."

I peeped at my watch. "What unit do they sleep in?" I inquired, knowing the activity move only lasted for ten minutes.

"A-four, I think," Suf-yan replied.

"Hitler's playing games," I assured. "It's fifty white boys up there. A nigga would be a fool to go in one of them crackers' cells."

"That's what I said," Suf'yan agreed just as Buckey Fields and them walked up.

"So, what's it gonna be?" all the homies seem to ask in unison as we gathered around Buckey Fields.

"Them crackers have one option. Back down or we're going to tear them mothersuckers up," Buckey Fields fired, and no more needed to be said.

We all made our way over to the basketball court and stood around Buckey Fields and his cousin as they got to the bottom of the situation. ". . .What I'm saying is you running around, putting a bad bone out on my mothersucking little cousin, like he's a thief," Buckey Fields argued.

"One of my brothers saw him coming out of my cell with the boots," Hitler retorted as Buckey Fields balled his face up and poked his bottom lip out.

"Why he didn't stop him then?" Buckey Fields wasn't buying it and neither were the rest of us. It don't make sense. The AB's and the D.C. homies especially didn't get along. And the hatred ran deep. So deep that any little infraction on either side was met with swift and deadly retribution.

"Man, cuz, this cracker lying, slim," Buckey Fields little cousin defended himself. "Tell that bamma say that shit to my face."

"The officer on the range saw it too," another AB added.

"When we start taking the word of the enemy as law?" I fired, unable to bite my tongue any longer.

"Like I said, my brother saw it and I believe my brother before I believe anybody!" Hitler spat on the court.

"And I'm telling you, I stand with my mothersucking family, regardless. Especially when I know that he didn't do nothing. So, the question is, where we at now?"

Hitler grinned. "I want my boots back and I want your cousin off the yard. If not, then I guess we have to go—"

Buckey Fields hit Hitler with a solid overhead that seemed to put his brain on freeze. I'd heard that Buckey Fields had quick hands, but what followed was a combination straight out of a Ringside Handbook. Buckey Fields walked up and down Hitler's body with a wicked head-body, head-body calculation before drawing what resembled a hunting spear, and opening Hitler's face up to the bone.

I froze up for a moment. I think everybody did. At least until Hitler fell on his back pockets.

"What y'all waiting for? Get them crackers!" Buckey Fields commanded, jumping on top of Hitler and everybody started pulling out.

It was like some shit out of an old prison movie. They rushed, we rushed. They swung, we swung. They wanted our lives and we wanted theirs.

The homies had some serious heat. I mean, the shit I was swinging looked like it was custom-made by a blacksmith. But, I'm not even going to front. The heavy-metal them crackers were holding really made them a 'nigger'-killing rock band.

I slammed my knife into the first AB I could reach—a big cracker who was about to sneak up on Buckey Fields. He looked up and groaned as if he wasn't even fazed. Then, the motherfucker charged me.

I'ma keep it real. I broke, I didn't flee though. I just gave myself enough cushion to regroup and position myself to stand off against a cracker twice my size in weight and height. You had to see this big cracker. Anyway, I yelled out to Suf'yan for assistance. The big cracker grabbed me by the back of my neck and howled like a wolf.

The next thing I knew, I was airborne. I looked over my shoulder just in time to see the cracker drawing his heavy-metal back under hand-style to slam it into my spine when out of nowhere, my cell buddy—Black Randy—saved the day with a 'Barry Bonds' type swing. I'm talking about this nigga lift his leg up in the air and everything before he swing.

Now, I didn't know where the hell Black Randy had gotten the baseball bat. But, when he smacked that big AB with that baseball bat, it was game over. From there, everything got cloudy.

I can't say what everybody did or who all stabbed who. And I definitely didn't know how in the hell I'd ended up on the baseball field. But, I can honestly say it was the most serious incident that I'd ever been in since coming to prison.

Them fucking AB's were relentless. They just wouldn't let up or lay down and we gave them crackers the business, too. Still, nobody escaped the yard untouched. Even a wild ass Southeast D.C. homie named Go-Go got snatched out of his wheelchair and rolled over by two AB's.

The marshals rushed the yard with riot-guns and started lighting our asses up with bean bags and dragging us off the yard, but they fucked up when they left me unattended inside the medical department, though. Because I quickly slipped out of the room and crept down the hall to where some of the AB's were waiting for medical attention.

"I think I killed one of them niggers," I heard one of the AB's bragging to one of his brothers as I dropped down and crawled across the floor.

I looked around for anything that I could use as a weapon and spotted a menacing looking scrub-brush with a pineapple-shaped head on it lying up against the wall just outside of the staff bathroom.

"Hey!" one of the marshals spotted me "Hey! Stop!" he yelled as I jumped up, snatched the scrub-brush and rushed inside the medical room, catching the AB's off guard.

Though they were all restrained, they instantly jumped up to defend themselves. But it was no use. I hit one of the AB's who'd knocked Go-Go out of his wheelchair. His head cracked open like a coconut, and I immediately spun and cracked the cracker next to him as he tried to run me into the wall with his body. Then, I just started punishing them crackers up in that bitch.

And I bullshit you not, the marshals only stood outside and begged me to stop saying I'd proven my point. I fucked them cracker over in the medical room until I was satisfied. Then, and only then, did I throw the blood-covered scrub-brush out into the hallway and surrendered.

When the homies saw me walking past, covered in blood with a smile on my face, they didn't even have to ask. They knew that I'd just put on for the city. They placed me in the tank across from Suf'yan and I could see blood slowly streaming down his face from a gash underneath his left eye. So, I mouthed to him what had just happened as he read my lips. Little did I know how much my actions would affect my stay in the Federal B.O.P.

Chapter Thirteen

Gangster Friday

"Tell bruh to stop crying. He know I got him damn." Jamaine ended the call before tossing the phone into the cup holder. "This nigga Banga a nuisance. Yo, sister keep calling me about his lawyer," Jamaine reached for the diesel. "Come on, nigga, pass the blunt."

Jamaine's girl's little brother and sidekick—a wild, fourteen-year-old knuckle-head everybody called Lunchmeat—took one more pull of the diesel and blew smoke in his direction. "Nigga, you're a nuisance with this weed," Lunchmeat joked.

"I'm serious, yo. I'ma change my number on his dumb ass in a minute."

"What about his lawyer?" Lunchmeat questioned curiously, ready to soak up the game Jamaine was always giving him.

"What about it?" Jamaine stared at him.

"Didn't you say, you're always supposed to hold a nigga lock-up down?" Lunchmeat watched Jamaine hit the blunt.

A thick cloud of weed smoke escaped Jamaine's mouth before he replied. "Not when you don't fuck with him for real." Jamaine looked over at Lunchmeat sitting in the passenger's seat. "Banga is just a means to an end, you feel me?" Jamaine explained, handing Lunchmeat the blunt.

"Yeah," Lunchmeat nodded understandably.

"Ain't nobody tell that simple nigga to keep going on missions with cars off of his mother's car lot," Jamaine assured. "That's on him."

Banga was the last thing on Jamaine's mind at the moment. The state was going to put that nigga up underneath the jail anyway. Especially once they started connecting all the dots. "Open the glove compartment." Jamaine watched as Lunchmeat did as he was told. "Reach inside and grab that cigar box," Jamaine instructed and again Lunchmeat complied. "Open it!"

Lunchmeat placed the blunt in his mouth and cracked open the silver cigar box to find a stack of large bills. "That's yours," Jamaine informed.

"Jazakellah, Ocki!" Lunchmeat lite up. There had to be every bit of one thousand dollars in the box.

"Move the money," Jamaine kept his eyes on Lunchmeat and pointed towards the box.

When Lunchmeat picked up the bills and laid eyes on the hidden nickel-plated .380, he looked up confused. "Remember why you told me that you jumped into the streets?"

Lunchmeat nodded. He remembered it clearly because he was reminded everyday he stepped out of the house.

"Tell me again," Jamaine ordered, instantly noticing the fire in Lunchmeat's young eyes. It was the same fire he used to see in Dakaron. The same fire he'd learned from Monique how to manipulate.

"I didn't jump off the porch for the same reason as most," Lunchmeat began. "I never been impressed by what niggas had. I was resentful about the shit I didn't have."

"Nah, man," Jamaine waved him off. "The other part."

'Oh," Lunchmeat smiled. "To take the crown from the niggas who don't deserve it."

"You ready to make your first run at the thorn?" Jamaine inquired but Lunchmeat remained silent almost as if waiting for directions.

"Remember I told you that you're going to have to run through a few pawns before you could get to the king?"

"Yeah," Lunchmeat took one more hit of the diesel, flicked the blunt out of the window and slowly picked up the .380 up.

"Well, you're about to knock over your first pawn today," Jamaine tried to read Lunchmeat for any signs of weakness. Seeing none, he continued. "After you do this, I'ma take you shopping and put another stack in your pocket."

Unbeknownst to Lunchmeat, Jamaine was parked up the street from the mosque on Liberty Heights, waiting for Freaky Black's right-hand man to show his face. As it turned out, he'd been the one behind his cousin Fish's death. He needed Fish out of the way, so that he could convince Freaky Black to go alone with his expansion idea. However, it backfired because his shooter had given his name up; now it was his turn to pay the piper.

"Here comes your man now," Jamaine looked as the mosque's double doors came open and people began to spill out of Ju'mah. "A'ight, that's him right there." Jamaine pointed. "The nigga with the loafers and yellow kufi on."

"That's a Muslim brother, Ocki," Lunchmeat declared, remembering his teachings about the sacredness of a Muslim's blood.

"Man, you keep letting your sister pump all that bullshit into your head!" Jamaine fired. "Don't you see me as a brother?"

"Yeah," Lunchmeat admitted honestly.

"A'ight then, trust me, I know a lot more than your sister!" Jamaine exclaimed. "That Muslim shit's bullshit! It's every man for himself out here in these streets. Don't ever forget that! Ain't no friends. Every nigga that ever ran with me is dead or in prison for life!" Jamaine explained. "Don't let that Muslim shit fool you. That nigga's not your brother. I'm your brother! I mess with your sister. I put food on the table. And I got your best interest at heart. Now what's it going to be? You want to stake your claim for the thorn or what?"

"What did he do?" Lunchmeat eyed the humble looking brother as he shook hands with other service goers and believers.

"He's the one that got Banga arrested," Jamaine lied.

"When you want me to get him?" Lunchmeat knew that snitching was a big no-no in the streets.

Jamaine had been on Freaky Black's partner for two weeks before Banga's dumb ass went and got himself arrested. So, Jamaine knew his routine now. He did the same thing every Friday after Ju'mah. He left the mosque, traveling on foot to his car a couple blocks over where he re-armed himself and headed for his wife's job. There he sat for a few minutes, making calls before his wife came out and they headed for the Midway Daycare Center to pick up their daughter.

"I got the perfect idea," Jamaine started the car and smiled, thinking about a move he and Dak had pulled off during the South Baltimore beef back in the nineties.

After circling the block to give Freaky Black's partner some time to finish standing around lolly-gagging, Jamaine slowly cruised down the street behind him as he approached the corner. "Get ready," Jamaine mumbled, pulling alongside his target.

"As-Salaam-Alaikum, Ocki! You wouldn't happen to know where Bell and Garrison is located, would you?" Lunchmeat greeted the brother out of the passenger's seat window.

"Walaikum salaam," he returned the greeting with a genuine smile. "Just keep going straight until you hit that second light up there near the school." The worst thing he could've done was take his eyes off of Lunchmeat to point in the direction he was referring to because at that moment, Lunchmeat extended the nickel-plated .380 out of the car window and pulled the trigger repeatedly.

"I got him, Ocki!" Lunchmeat looked back at Jamaine with a smile.

"Empty the clip!" Jamaine fired and Lunchmeat stuck the .380 back out the window and shot Freaky Black's partner in the chest until the gun was empty.

Still uncertain if the .380 had done the job, Jamaine backed the car up, looked around and rolled over top of Freaky Black's partner's body as he laid in the middle of the street, bleeding to death.

"You did good," Jamaine commended Lunchmeat, breaking the silence after he'd put enough distance between them and the crime scene. "But, always empty the clip. Always make sure the job is done, a'ight?"

"My bad, yo, I thought he was finished when he fell," Lunchmeat admitted.

"Don't worry about it. You'll get it right the next time," Jamaine smiled, knowing that he was going to turn his girl's little brother into a savage. "Where do you wanna go shopping at?"

"How many pairs of shoes can I get?" Lunchmeat asked thinking about all the girls at his school who were going to be on his dick when he showed up fresh every day for a few weeks straight.

"As many as you can carry," Jamaine assured. After all, now that Banga was out of the picture, he had an extra twenty stacks. "You earned it."

"In that case, let's hit the Plaze," Lunchmeat exclaimed. "Insha'Allah, they got them New Balance I been begging my sister for."

"The Plaze it is then," Jamaine hit play on the CD player and headed in the direction of their destination.

Chapter Fourteen

A Gangster's Migraines

The Feds had something for a nigga's ass. First, there was what was known as 'diesel therapy'. A little game the administrators like to play whenever you assaulted one of the staff members. Then, there was the 'Smooth Program.' An eighteen to twenty-four-month step-down program located in Lee County, P.A. Which was where most of us ended up.

Now, I'd been behind the door before. I mean, damn near half of the time I'd spent in prison had been in segregation. So, I was no stranger to solitary confinement. But man, I had to admit, the 'Smooth Program' was next level. I mean, the drab, dark cells were extremely hot, stuffy and small. There were no windows, no ventilation system and no fans. So, you smelled, heard and felt everything. It was a real madhouse and at least two guys had been found hanging from light fixtures in their cells. Perhaps it was murder or suicide, depending upon which cell-buddy you were conversing with.

Fortunately for me, they'd stuffed me and Suf'yan into the cell together because we were both a part of the ICC Program. Simply meaning, we are still state property. The only smooth thing about the 'Smooth Program' was the fact that the telephone rolled right up to the cell door. Beyond that, it was mayhem. Still, I loved the days when a lazy marshal worked the range—which was often—because Suf'yan and I got to play on the phone for hours.

By now, the state had appealed me and Frank's court decision and I was talking to Chanae on a regular basis;

119

especially since she was shut in the house on the home-monitor with nowhere to go. We were kicking it, playing catch up, ironing a few things out. We had a lot of teeth-pulling, tough conversations about how and who was at fault for all the disappearing acts. One thing was for sure, though: Chanae and I still had a lot shit to work through. But the love was there.

What tripped me out though was the fact that Chanae didn't want to be judged for her bullshit. However, the minute I started praising her for the work and time she'd put in, she loved it.

The kids were growing up so fast, and Chanae's brother was finally on his way home for the King's Court murder. Everybody kept asking me exactly when I was coming home. But I wasn't stupid. I'd seen too many good men go home and fall victim to that game. Not me! Not Linda's and Timothy's youngest son. You see, I haven't forgotten about all the dirt I'd done on the streets. And everybody knew I wasn't that clean behind the prison walls. So, I definitely wasn't about to let no 'so-called' friends who hadn't played fair the entire time I been down, get enough information to play me out of position and put me in the blender. That was how they'd gotten my man Flake when he went home; they played the celebration game and walked him right into the lion's den for two young lions to slaughter.

"Yeah, that shit sound slick, Dakaron!" Chanae challenged me when I spoke about not smoking when I got home. "You're going to be right out here partying like everybody else."

"I shook my head. *She thinks it's jail talk*, I thought, like my word hadn't always been my bond. "Yeah, we'll see," I mumbled, disappointed that Chanae didn't have any faith in me. Which only further confirmed for me that we really no longer knew each other. "You heard anything about Jamaine?" I asked for the sake of conversation, changing the subject.

"Like what?" Chanae answered my question with a question as if she could still pick up on when I wasn't feeling her response.

"Like what's up with him?" I fired rhetorically.

"Same old, same old. You know Jamaine, out there trying to fuck everything moving like the hoe he is. You remember Margaret, don't you?"

"Margaret?" I questioned as if I could forget my number one childhood crush. "Which Margaret?" I continued to play dumb as a vison of Margaret's pretty ass face popped up in my head.

"Don't play with me, Dakaron!" Chanae sounded offended. "You know exactly who I'm talking about. Margaret Blevins ass, Pooh sister. Who used to be with your little girlfriend, Tierre Richardson."

"I didn't never fuck with no damn Tierre," I lied, instantly remembering her and Chanae getting into it. "I mean, not like that," I tried to clean it up. The truth be told though: Although Tierre was my baby, on the low it was Margaret that I'd always really wanted. I just never crossed that line because she started talking to Jamaine and I was a loyal nigga.

"N-E-way, Jamaine mess with Margaret now," Chanae revealed and I instantly wondered how phony niggas always seem to have some of the realist women. "He got her little brother into everything but a hearse."

"Oh, he finally got serious, huh?"

"Please Jamaine ain't serious about nothing but himself. His nasty ass just stopped by here the other night like he was trying to fuck."

"Oh yeah?" I played it cool because I wasn't sure if Chanae was trying to get a reaction out of me or not.

"Mmh hmm, talking about he was drunk when I said something to him about it," Chanae added instantly, making me think about what Sweet Pea had said concerning Jamaine when I was still over the jail.

I'd actually thought Jamaine was still locked up for his second or third domestic, because that was the last I'd heard. "Oh, so he's home?"

"Yep, out on bail. But he's not going to last. He's out here doing the same shit. That's why he got Margaret's little brother with him all the time."

"Oh, Jamaine not going to put his hands on Margaret. He knows Pooh will crack his shit!"

"Pooh locked up," Chanae retorted.

"Still, Jamaine ain't stupid," I assured. "Plus Margaret ain't going for no shit like that anyway," I added just before the operator interrupted the call to inform us that it was about to end. "I guess I'll catch you next time."

"I love you," Chanae said and for some reason it just didn't have the same strength to it like it used to.

"I love you too. Kiss the kids for me," I said just before the phone went silent.

I sat there for a moment with the phone pressed to my ear. I couldn't believe it. Today was my birthday and Chanae hadn't even remembered. But I wasn't surprised. For the last few years, the only two women who'd gone out of their way to make sure that I felt special on my 'G' day were my mother and my baby Susan Kerin.

"So, did Chanae remember your birthday or not?" Suf'yan inquired, ready to cash in on his bet.

"Fuck no!" I fired, hanging the phone up. "I told you. Now you owe me a week's worth of snacks."

"That's crazy, young," Suf'yan shook his head.

"I'ma do something that I should've done a long time ago when I get home though," I mumbled more to myself than Suf'yan with my mind on something else.

"What?" Suf'yan stared at me curiously.

"Kill that bitch ass nigga Jamaine for all his betrayal," I confessed, walking over to my bunk to lie down.

***

When the folks popped up at my door and asked me if I was ready, I'm not even going to lie, I straight pulled a fireman. Meaning, I jumped out of the rack and cuffed up without putting that gun-toothbrush in my mouth or washing my face. Shiid, I was so ready to get going that I barely even gave Suf'yan some love.

It had been damn near a year since the State had decided to appeal my shit and the court had finally given its ruling. Now it was up to a circuit court judge to determine if Frank and I had enough evidence to warrant a new trial.

When I went to the records department, the marshals told me that I was being transferred back into state custody for good. I was avid; I couldn't get out of the feds quick enough. Plus, I was ready to hit the city and let niggas know that Dakaron was back better than ever.

"Go out there and mold you daughters, young, fuck all that other shit!" were the last words Suf'yan said to me as I walked out the cell with my breath smelling like animal ass.

After getting processed, I was escorted outside, uncuffed and handed over, then I was taken into state custody, driven to the airport and rushed onto a private plane.

"Sorry we took so long," the cool ass white C.T.E officer apologized to the pilot. "The jail gave us a hard time about custody." He winked at me.

I looked out the window and smiled as the plane took off because Officer Brown had stopped to treat me to something to eat.

It felt good to be returning home with all my shit intact. I felt like I was leaving a war zone, returning from 'Vietnam' or something. There weren't too many gangsters like me left. Gangsters who had taken their show on the road and stood tall the whole time. Gangsters who'd come back the same way they'd gone in. Gangsters who'd earned the respect of their captors, enemies and peers. Of course, I knew that a lot about me changed. Prison had that effect on everybody. But, when it came to that gangster shit, I was truly a notch above the rest and couldn't nobody take nothing from me. Because I always live my life with integrity rather I was running the streets or walking the yard. I choose family over friends, right over wrong, honesty over victory, fairness over bullying, and principle over profit. But, more importantly, I always chose honor over everything, even my heart, and that was something that most gangsters couldn't say.

"Where they got me going, Brown?" I questioned curiously.

"I believe city jail," he replied. "But we gotta go to D.O.C first to place you back into the system. Either way, you're going to be surprised at how much things have changed."

I asked Brown what he meant, but he only smiled and said that I would see. So, I fell back and continued to enjoy the scenery from the top of the world.

Chapter Fifteen

Gangster Message

"Run in there and grab Margaret some orange juice and a box of those blueberry muffins she loves so much," Jamaine instructed, pulling up outside of a convenience store on Lexington Street. "Get me a Pepsi too."

Lunchmeat nodded and climbed out of the car. It felt good to step out of the house with a pocket full of money and not have his hand out. To be able to buy what he wanted, whenever he wanted it, and look out for his brother Pooh. On top of that, all the bitches at school were on his dick now, especially the ones who used to turn their noses up at him. Now he was having all the fun, making them beg and plead to get a taste of his dick.

"That's all you want?" Lunchmeat questioned, holding the car door open.

"Yeah," Jamaine nodded and started going through his phone, checking the messages.

"I'm the topic in every barbershop and beauty salon, 'cause—" Jamaine hummed along to a G-Unit song as he deleted his only message and looked up in time to see Lunchmeat entering the store and smiled. His little ass was turning out to be a major asset to Jamaine's new line of work. Lunchmeat had already slumped three dudes for Jamaine for less than four stacks.

"What's up, Jamaine?" A truck pulled alongside Jamaine's car.

Jamaine instantly reached for his gun. "Don't be creeping up on me like that, nigga!" Jamaine smiled when he realized it was Banga. He'd heard Banga was home. But, he hadn't really had a chance to get up on him to see where his head was at yet.

"Ahhh, nigga, if I wanted you, you would've been got!" Banga laughed, climbing out of the truck to make his way around to the other side. "Where are you on your way to?" Banga approached Jamaine's car.

"The hospital—my aunt just had an accident," Jamaine lied.

"We need to get together and rap about a few things," Banga suggested as Lunchmeat came bouncing out of the store.

Lunchmeat saw Banga standing at the car and instantly wondered what he and Jamaine were talking about. Especially since he knew for a fact that Jamaine had cut him off.

Jamaine looked up at the sound of the passenger's side door opening and Banga made his move. He stepped back, whipped out a big ass Desert Eagle, aimed at the back of Jamaine's head and squeezed the trigger.

"Duck, Ocki!" Lunchmeat yelled as the sound of the Desert Eagle rocked the entire block.

Jamaine felt the impact of something smashing into the side of his head as his hearing went out. Banga began firing into the car repeatedly, striking Jamaine in his back, legs and arm as he scrambled across the armrest.

The only thing that probably saved Jamaine's life was the fact that Lunchmeat pulled out his weapon and started dumping unhesitatingly.

Banga stumbled backwards into the double-parked truck, ran back around it, jumped behind the wheel and peeled off, burning rubber all the way down the block.

"Get me to a hospital!" Jamaine cried out in excruciating pain.

Lunchmeat ran around the car to the driver's side and climbed behind the wheel as Jamaine tried to sit up straight in the passenger's seat.

"Ahhhh!" Jamaine groaned through clenched teeth, ripping his own shirt open to survey the damage as Lunchmeat pulled off. His whole body was on fire. He could barely move his arm, and his legs were out of commission. But, if the game hasn't taught him nothing else, it taught him to always keep his bullet-proof vest on.

Lunchmeat stole a look at Jamaine as he flung the bullet-proof vest on the floor. "How bad you hit?" He placed his eyes back on the road just as quickly.

'I don't know," Jamaine admitted. "But, the vest stopped most of that shit!" Jamaine thought back for a second. Banga had almost rocked him to bed. "The vest and you, nigga!" Jamaine added, knowing that if it hadn't been for Lunchmeat, his ass would've been toast because he never saw Banga coming.

Lunchmeat just smiled proudly. He was really becoming trigger-happy. And it don't matter who was on the business-end of his barrel. If they violated those he loved, he would mow them down.

"You know you're going to have to kill that nigga, right?" Jamaine referred to Banga. "He's not going to sleep on you again."

Lunchmeat simply nodded and continued to drive towards the hospital. He'd already decided exactly how to take Banga out of the game.

Chapter Sixteen

The Heart of a Gangster

My name was ringing bells over the Baltimore City Jail. Not only had my walk through the system been unlike any other. But it was also a known fact that I'd had something to do with Monique's death. On top of that, niggas thought that I was secretly one of the heads of the most treacherous organization in the State of Maryland because I went up against anything and stood off with anybody. There were so many rumors that the administration had to place me on administrative lock-up under investigation for a few weeks until things settled down.

Niggas really thought that me and Frank was about to come home on some 'King of New York' shit. Especially after Frank sent a picture of himself uptown, standing on top of a pile of old photographs with the words 'I'm back for everything you know' written across the back in bold letters. But the icing on the cake was when word began to circulate that I'd had something to do with Jamaine almost being taken out of stock.

It made me laugh though. I mean, yeah, I secretly wanted Jamaine's head. But it wouldn't satisfy me if I didn't take that motherfucker off myself.

As always, Sweet Pea was the first woman besides my mother to kick the visiting room door down. Me and Chanae were kind of at odds because she was once again pregnant. To be real, I didn't care that she was pregnant. I'd gotten past those issues when A'myiah and Darrien were born. What upset me though was who she was pregnant by. The same lame who'd left her for dead when she was down the Women's Cut. The same lame I'd heard all types of stories about. Stories about snitching, stories about homo-thugs and stories about how the beef he'd helped crook up got too heavy to stomach. Still, I hoped he was better at being a father than he was at being a gangster. Because if not, he really didn't have nothing going for himself.

". . .Don't make me get you put together out there, dummy."

"Go ahead and try it, nigga! See if your dumb ass don't get yourself fucked over!"

I was sitting at the grill, listening to two comrades—or rather so-called brothers—argue about some drugs, while I was waiting for the cell to open so that I could hit population

"Keep on running your mouth, dummy, and watch me get you mixed up!" These were the same kids who'd pulled up on me about clicking up when I first hit the section. The entire scenario made me shake my head. *Why would I ever want to be a part of some shit like that*? I thought. Some shit where my so-called brother would use his power and position to get me hit for saying no about some shit that we honestly weren't supposed to be doing in the first place.

When the cell door popped, I grabbed my paperwork and shit and hauled ass off the tier. It was time to hit general population and make my presence felt. Once my escort showed up and informed me that I was going on J-Section, I flung my little bit of stuff over my shoulder and started moving.

"Where is your mattress at?" the escort jokingly inquired.

"I don't sleep on one," I replied.

"I heard that, gangster," he smiled and I couldn't tell if he was being sarcastic or not. "So, you gave your time back, huh?"

"Yeah," I replied nonchalantly, keeping my answers short.

"That's a blessing. I hope you make it count."

I looked at him. C.O.'s usually didn't talk like that, especially the males. They were too busy playing tough, cheating or trying to act like they didn't care, but he seems sincere enough to ask a few questions. "How long have you been working over here?"

"Three years, give or take. I was over the pen first."

"Ms. Glover still work over here?" I got straight to what I wanted to know.

"You mean, Captain Glover?" he corrected.

"Captain?" I repeated.

"Yeah, Glover is a captain now, if we're talking about the same one."

"Real pretty eyes?" I said further.

"Yep, that's Captain Glover," he confirmed.

"Damn, I have been gone a long time," I admitted, instantly thinking about somebody else I needed an update on. "What about the one Haiti clown who used to run around acting like he was on the S-R-T squad? I can't think of his name."

"Oh, I know who you're talking about." He grinned. "He had one of those funny names that I could never pronounce."

"What's up with him? Is he still around?"

"Nah, he got caught up in that big gang indictment last year." He laughed suddenly.

"Why you laugh though?" I pried curiously.

He looked around cautiously. "You didn't hear it from me. But, he was a horse turn informant. The feds nicknamed him 'The Vault' in the court records because they said he used to smuggle the contraband in, stuffed inside of a ten inch, hollow-glass dildo. Everybody used to joke about Captain Glover breaking him in because rumor was, she may go both ways."

I'd heard the jail was off the chain, but I didn't know it was going down like that. However, I was smiling on the inside. Not only had the gangster ass Haitian nigga been exposed, but I'd just found out that my baby may be into girls and that shit just drove her stock up.

"I always knew that nigga was a bitch," I spat as we approached the section. "And I mean that in more ways than one," I added, thinking about the way he used to try to control Ms. Glover.

It took me a minute to be able to get on the phone, because the gang-kids were running shit. Not the way we used to run it the old-school though. The way where both men and suckers alike got what their hands called for. Times had changed and now niggas ran shit by playing games. Games like putting each other after one another to make the phone line so long that nobody wanted to get in it. But, I wasn't easily discouraged. At least not yet. So, I sat back and watched who was who just in case I'd to line these young niggas up in the future.

"So, where they got Frank at?" My brothers asked when I was finally able to get on the phone.

"Frank still down Jessup," I revealed, knowing exactly why. "I guess he wasn't trying to start all over again, you feel?" I threw Detauwn a hint because I knew that he was sharp enough to pick it up.

"Y'all getting ready to come home. Fuck he worrying about starting fresh for?" Antauwn questioned, making me shake my head. Sometimes I really wondered if he were adopted.

"Boy, you better watch your mouth!" I snapped, remembering that everybody was on the phone, including One Love.

"Don't tell his tail nothing," my mother chimed in.

"Sorry, ma," Antauwn apologized.

"Antauwn, you as slow as—I don't know what," his wife Samone took the words right out of my mouth and I could hear Antauwn laughing.

"Ohhhh," Antauwn exclaimed and I could just picture Samone's face as she had to explain to him what I couldn't.

Which was the fact that Frank was fucking a bad ass, West Indies-looking nurse.

I continued to kick it with the home front until the phone was about to hang up. "Give me my sugar!" One Love demanded and we both instantly began rapidly blowing kisses into the phone.

"Love y'all!" I yelled as the call ended.

I handed the phone to one of the gang-kids and went on about my business. I really needed to find out what was going on over the jail.

***

The next morning, I had my first face-to-face with the new lawyer—a young, smooth, up-and-coming white boy by the name of George Smith whose office was located on Charles Street. I have to be honest, I instantly dig his style. I like the way he approached the case strategically. But it was his undeniable hunger and ambition that sold me. I could tell that he was definitely going to be a force to be reckoned with in the courtroom because he was out to make a name for himself,

The first thing we got into it about was Elizabeth Franzoso, my trial attorney; he wanted to post-convict her for ineffective assistance of counsel. In fact, his words were, "We have to post-convict your tail attorney. She made a lot of mistakes." However, I disagreed. I felt like even in defeat, Elizabeth Franzoso was a pit bull in a skirt. Yet and still, in the end, George Smith made me see his point.

"At this point, it's her representation or yours," George Smith explained. "Trust me when I tell you, Dakaron, if she's as good as you say she is, she won't take it personally. After all, your life's hanging in the balance."

George Smith went on to lay out the state's position. It seems they weren't buying what Frank and I were selling and claim to have no knowledge of China Doll's involvement.

132

They were ready to deal, though. "They are willing to give you fifty and offer Frank thirty."

"What do you think?" I questioned, crunching the numbers in my head as my self-preservation instincts kicked in. Years ago, I wouldn't have even considered it. But, when a nigga was underneath a life sentence, fifty years didn't sound all that bad.

"I don't think the judge is just going to let you walk out of here," he admitted and that was one of the reasons I respected him. "Still, fifty years is a long time. Of course, D-O-C is going to take two months off each year, then there's your good time and the time you have in."

"Let me reach out to my rap-buddy and see what he thinks."

"I talked to Frank's lawyer this morning," he revealed. "And they assured me that Frank wants to battle."

"Then, let's battle," I said without a moment's hesitation. If my right-hand man wanted to take them to the war, then war it was gonna be.

George Smith and I hammered out a few more issues before he bounced. Then, I fucked around on post #14 for a moment, trying to see if I knew anybody in the visiting room. I'd just spotted somebody I thought I recognized when the C.O. at the post chased me off because the supervisor was coming. I was standing there pleading for one more quick look, when the supervisor came up behind me. I knew it was the supervisor without looking. You could always tell when brass showed up because everybody straightened up.

"Good morning, Captain Glover." The C.O. looked past me as if I wasn't standing there and I turned around and laid eyes on my baby for the first time since 1999.

"Morning," Ms. Glover replied, reaching for the log-book. She hadn't even realized who I was yet.

Damn, I thought, standing there lost in her beauty. *Tiphani Glover still a bad motherfucker.* I licked my lips and slowly scanned her from head to toe. She still had that intoxicating beauty. Her breasts looked heavier and her hips had filled out slightly. But, the most noticeable change was her ass. The phat motherfucker was sitting up and out, defying the odds of gravity and it took everything in me not to reach out and grab it. "How are you doing, Captain Glover?" I spoke up as she finished signing the log-book.

When Ms. Glover looked up and realized who it was, the sexy ass smile I remember so vividly spread across her face. "Oh my gawd, if it isn't trouble-starting Truesdale." She still giggled like a school girl "How are you doing?"

"I'm good, you know me," I replied as she sized me up. Probably reminiscing. I could tell that she was impressed. I told you all my shit was still intact.

"I heard you were back. I spoke up to get you off."

"So, we're not beefing anymore?" I asked curiously because that was one thing that had always haunted me. The fact that, Ms. Glover tagged me as a lame before I left the jail.

"That was on me," she confessed and I finally exhaled. "But we'll cross that bridge another time." She cut her eyes at her nosey ass co-worker.

I smiled inside because her statement assured me that she had plans of seeing me again. "So, they're just giving anybody rank now, huh?" I teased and she couldn't help but blush at the hidden suggestion.

"Don't play," Ms. Glover rolled those sexy eyes playfully and it felt good to be in her company again. "I earned my stripes."

I just smiled, shook my head and kept my thoughts to myself. "I need a job where I get some skates", I requested, feeling like I needed to move around.

"Boy, you just got over here, talking about a job." She smiled.

"Man, I just gave life back. I'm trying to stretch my legs."

"Yeah, I heard about you acting up in the system." She shook her head. "Last time I checked you were in the feds or something."

"Oh, you were looking a nigga up, huh?" I really felt like a big dog now.

"Wasn't nobody checkin' for you? Your name was in the papers."

"So, you got me on the job tip?"

Ms. Glover stared at me for a moment as if considering her next move. Then, she spoke with a flirtatious smile. "Have your tier officer call me after lunch. Being as though you got a little bit of experience in the system, I can probably use you on the inmate-counsel board. Especially with all these little kids over here acting stupid."

"Bet," I nodded, looking into Ms. Glover's pretty ass eyes.

I'm not going to even sit here and draw this shit out for y'all. Because y'all know what's about to happen next. A gangster about to get into position and get that old thing back.

***

"There's no mercy, no love and no friends in this game," Jamaine declared from his hospital bed. "Niggas more loyal to their barbers than anything."

As always, Lunchmeat sat there soaking the game up. He'd been hunting Banga for days. Waiting for him to slip up so that he could punch his number. Jamaine was his big brother and he'd kill anybody for him, friend or foe.

However, as it turned out, Banga had been arrested. He was picked up at hospital, seeking medical attention after having been shot in the hand during the gunfire exchange between him and Lunchmeat.

To make a long story short, someone had identified Banga's truck fleeing the scene. So, while he was sitting up inside the hospital receiving medical treatment, the cops obtained a warrant to search his bullet-riddled truck. There they found the Desert Eagle under the driver's seat that would later be linked to the bullets that were removed from Jamaine's body. After that, Banga's truck was towed to the station and he was taken into custody.

"I could've hit that nigga when he first touched down. But, I tried to play fair. But, it's all good." Jamaine shook his head. "I got niggas who love me in the system. Real, live gangsters!"

"You think he's going to get found guilty?" Lunchmeat questioned.

"Not if I can't help it," Jamaine replied. "They don't got nothing on him but a bunch of circumstantial shit. All he has to do is not cop out. I want that nigga home bad!" Jamaine snapped. "That nigga fucked up when he didn't finish the job. He should've killed me. I've looked up to a lot of niggas for one reason or another. Most I ended up surpassing or straight up murking. Not always by choice though. A lot of them nigga faltered in their own teachings. I was never one of those students who wanted his teacher's place. To be honest, I strived to be just like them niggas," Jamaine continued to lay it on thick.

"That's why I don't trust nobody but you. You're the only motherfucker I got faith in. Fuck the rest of these niggas!"

"Fuck the rest of these niggas!" Lunchmeat repeated with a proud smile.

"It's me and you against the game," Jamaine exclaimed. "And I'ma do right by you like a nigga suppose' to. I'ma push you to go further, encourage you to be better than I ever was. Because I want you to stand on my shoulders. I don't want you to be in my shadow the way niggas wanted me to be."

Lunchmeat just nodded. Jamaine was the only nigga who respected his mind and treated him like he deserved to be treated. "Me and you, big bruh!" Lunchmeat declared. "Me and you."

"Just stick with me and you'll be rich before all this shit is over with, watch what I tell you."

"I ain't going nowhere," Lunchmeat assured.

"That's what I like to hear." Jamaine cracked a smile because he knew that Lunchmeat was full of blind loyalty and he planned on using it to strike down all those who stood against him.

Chapter Seventeen

There's a Big Difference between Gangster and Gangsta

Fuck what you read in the English or Urban Dictionary. Being a gangster and being gangsta are entirely two different things. I mean, I was an old-school gangster through and through. But, I respected a lot of them new jack gangstas. Especially the ones who were cut from that old-school cloth. But, if I was being straight up, and I was because I always am, then I had to tell you earning the name 'gangsta' wasn't as hard. The price wasn't as big. To me it was a lot cheaper. Furthermore, it was like these kids were not built as strong and the heart was weaker. Being back over the jail made me realize that the game was in serious trouble. Not just the game, but the gangsters who played it. We were losing numbers big times. Some old school gangsters were playing by the new rules, some gave up and others just flat out—laid down in one sense or another. Then there were the former suckers from back in the day. So, what was once an abundant species was now barely holding on. I mean, only a few remain true to the game and most of them were still trapped in the system behind enemy lines.

With so few gangsters to learn from and no real gangsters to carry the torch, the new jacks—or rather so-called gangstas—were not getting the proper teachings nor guidance. So, the game as well as the jail were both in bad shape.

For several weeks, I tried to cope with the jailhouse politics, intense suckerism and male gossip because I was a changed man. But I knew that eventually, I was going to have to lay my 'G' down. I mean, I couldn't help it. For as long as I could remember, it had been like second nature. Especially in certain arenas, under certain circumstances.

I knew that there was a major difference between conforming and adapting. But the way dudes were whispering about rats and talking bad about men was really becoming too much. On top of that, I hated bullies, especially the ones I knew were now hiding behind the numbers.

Captain Glover kept telling me to stay focused on my freedom. She explained how much things had changed for the worst. But it was hard to sit back and watch a bunch of weak ass, pussy niggas from back in the day, breaking bad because they were now in position. I mean, these bitch ass niggas weren't loyal to nothing but the numbers. Yet, they had these kids so faked out.

That was another thing that I couldn't understand and would never respect about that gang shit nowadays. Anybody could join. Even bitch ass niggas could take the oath and be all that they never could be on their own. I felt like all the recruitment agents needed their asses kicked. And I always wondered if there was a penalty for that shit. Like if you bring a sucker in, y'all should both get dust off when he fucked up.

"That's why I don't even watch TV anymore for real," my crazy old cell-buddy mumbled as we waited for the cells to open for afternoon recreation. "It ain't nothing but gossip or somebody being opinionated. The news the same way too. They don't just report no more. They take a position."

To be honest, I wasn't paying his wild ass any attention. His old ass talked that shit about how much the game had changed. He complained about how things used to be and the whole nine. But I knew that he too had been down with that new shit until they sent him on a dumb mission he could not or would not complete. "Look at all the TV shows we like.

Damn near all the main characters are rats, snakes or suckers."

"Yeah, but that's TV!" I fired, remembering our conversation about cop shows.

"Until it's not," he challenged. "You even have these kids naming themselves after certain characters. That's why I said what I said about Chicago PD and all them other shows that glorify snitching."

"And like I said, snitching is snitching. But there's a big difference between a rat who has something to gain, and a civilian who gains nothing," I argued. "It's just as different as watching *Oz* and *Law and Order*. One is a show about dudes pretending to be nobody but themselves. I can watch that because I know exactly what I'm getting. It's that fake shit that drives me crazy!" I complained, wondering how I'd let my cell-buddy pull me into his bullshit again. I hated debating about nothing.

"That's why I told you that if anything happens to me, tell the police to read what I wrote."

"Yeah, a'ight," I waved him off just as the cell doors began to open for recreation.

"What are you about to get into?" my cell buddy questioned as the cell opened.

"I'ma go jump on this horn," I replied, already stepping out of the cell.

"Man, you stay on that phone." He smiled.

"Everybody in prison has a drug of choice," I retorted honestly. "Some niggas work out, some lame chase uncatchable women, some zapouts drive themselves crazy, some suckers gossip and some gangsters play the phone. You know the list goes on!" I added before dipping down the tier.

In the rec-hall, I jumped straight on the phone. By now, the gangs kids had noticed everybody who was somebody—especially in their eyes—showing love and paid their respect.

"Hold me down, Uncle Dakaron," one of the little kids who always played the phone after me requested as he stopped by with of group of his little home boys.

"I got you," I nodded "And what I tell you about that uncle shit?" I fired as he smiled and continued on over to his usual spot. "My nephew's in the streets."

Chanae picked up on the fourth or fifth ring. So, I knew she was probably still in bed. Which was another thing I always took issue with. I mean, you couldn't get anything done lying in bed all day.

"Hello," I spoke the moment Chanae accepted the call.

"Good morning," Chanae mumbled softly, still half asleep and even though her timing was off, the sound of her voice always gave me a feeling of joy I could never explain.

"It's almost one o'clock," I corrected.

"Oh, I went out with my brother and them last night."

"You love to play the clubs, don't you?"

"Please don't start acting like you didn't used to be up in the club real heavy." Chanae sucked her teeth and exhaled as if she wasn't for my bullshit.

Yeah, when we were hoppers, I thought but decided to keep my thoughts to myself for the sake of peace. "What's up with your brother?" I'd been so focused on my own case that I'd forgotten all about Chanae's brother hitting the bricks.

Chanae began to tell me all about her brother. It was good to hear that he was still standing and carrying his own weight. Especially in today's climate. I mean, it was like everybody was a part of something. There were only a few lone wolves left. "Why I think Shawn gave my brother some pussy last night." Chanae giggled.

"So?" I fired. "I don't see any problem with that. Let that man live," I suggested, thinking about knocking the steam off something when I touched down.

"So, can I have some of that when you get home?"

"Some of what?" I played dumb.

"Some of that dick, don't play!" Chanae fired straight shots.

"You got a boyfriend, remember?" I reminded her.

"Dakaron, please, everybody knows where my heart at!" Chanae snapped. "Plus, I ain't had no real boyfriend since you left the streets."

"Yeah, right!" I challenged. "I'll see what I can do when I touch down."

"I know you better act like you know," Chanae warned. "Then again, I'm not paying you no mind, Dakaron. You know if I want it, I can get it," Chanae assured confidently. "You couldn't deny me that dick if you wanted to."

I knew Chanae was right, but I'd never admitted it. The chances of me going home and not fucking Chanae and Sweet Pea were as great as me going home and not having One Love fix me a home cooked meal. "I got a woman, Chanae," I lied.

"And?" Chanae came right back and it made me shake my head. "Is that bitch going to fight for you?"

I always found it amazing how women were quicker to fight over men than for them. "I'm not messing with you today, Chanae. How's your grandmother doing? I know she happy about your brother?"

"Mmmh," Chanae mumbled. "Oh yeah, I almost forgot. I saw Jamaine the other day too. Did he send you some money?"

"Jamaine? Hell no! That nigga hasn't sent me a dime since I been locked up!" I declared sincerely.

"Oh well, he supposed to have sent you something, or about to send you something. Five hundred dollars, I think," Chanae explained and I had to laugh.

That nigga was crazy if he thought some crumbs would settle my stomach after all the work I'd put in, I thought. "Yeah, I won't hold my breath," I said, looking around the dayroom as Chanae continued on until my eyes landed on one of the so-called shot-callers.

I watched him shake hands with a few of his homies. Or rather more like have hand-sex with all the twisting, turning and finger fucking they were doing. I didn't understand it but then again, I didn't understand a lot of things that nigga did.

To me, a lot of dudes nowadays don't even know what leadership was or looked like. Because most of them were too busy trying to lead from the back. Some were even worse than that. Because not only were they broke, but, they were stupid too. Showing off gang-handshakes in public, wearing all types of evil colors on their person like it was a badge of honor, only to turn around and cry about somebody putting the folks on them when they go down. Especially when they realized that a broke leader couldn't feed them anything when he wasn't eating himself.

It was almost as if discretion was a thing of the past. Like letting everybody know your business was the thing now. Of course, I knew there was no such thing as a bad gang, only bad leadership. Still, it felt strange to sit back and watch the game I once knew and loved continue to deteriorate. It was like sitting at the bedside of your dying child. It made me wonder what happened to all the good leadership.

The leaders who were stern but fair. The leaders who possessed good judgment and executed justice. The ones who were good listeners and great advisors. The ones who led by example. Those were the leaders I respected. Now you had dudes leading niggas nowhere. Emotionally unstable, uneducated, untested suckers. How the hell are you going to be a leader of anything? Commanding men when you can't even read and write?

No wonder why all the gangs were in disarray. Why niggas were running around doing dumb stuff. Look at their leaders.

It made me think about something one of the Nation of Islam brothers quoted from the Honorable Minister Louis Farrakhan at service, "Men don't follow no punks'.

I tuned back into what Chanae was yapping about, ". . . Well, you know A'myiah can't do nothing without Sha'nyiah, Omar and NyDeer. Especially since all that stuff with little Curtis and—" Chanae continued on about what was going on in my angel's life. But, all I kept thinking about was how everybody was having children. Big Tiffany, Ebony, Shawn, everybody!

I closed my eyes and zoned out for a moment. I couldn't wait to hit the bricks. I was going to fuck the game up.

***

"I'm not playing with your lil' ass, boy! Don't take your bad ass to school today and watch what happens!" Margaret threatened as Lunchmeat climbed into a car with Jamaine and tossed the mail she'd given him into his lap. "Jamaine, please make sure he goes to school!"

"I got him, baby," Jamaine assured with a look Margaret didn't like.

"I'm serious, Jamaine!" Margaret declared. "I don't need the school calling my house!"

"Baby, I got him," Jamaine assured again.

"Thank you," Margaret rolled her eyes. "And for the record, I'm not your baby!" Margaret fired, slamming the front door shut.

"Man, your sister be trippin' sometimes." Jamaine thought about the fight they'd had and picked up the mail in his lap and began to open it. It was another court summons to appear at Banga's coming trail. This time they were threatening to issue a bench-warrant. Jamaine ripped the summons in half and tossed it out the window. He only went to court for two reasons and neither one of them were to help the state.

"Ayo, drop me off my girl house," Lunchmeat ordered.

Shaking his head as he started the car, Jamaine checked the rearview mirror and pulled out into traffic. "Y'all lil' motherfuckers are too grown today." Jamaine smiled, remembering how he used to be when he was coming up. "That's why your little ass missing school. You running around chasing pussy."

Lunchmeat just smiled. There was nothing that he could say.

"Your little ass got it easy, boy. I couldn't choose what I wanted to eat when I was growing up, let alone what I wore. That shit was like talking back. See, but now, getting your ass whipped is child abuse. That's why all y'all little motherfuckers out of control. Walking around with y'all pants hanging off your ass, doing what y'all want to do!" Jamaine explained.

"You starting to sound like my sister, Ocki," Lunchmeat teased and Jamaine couldn't do nothing but laugh.

'Nigga, where your little girlfriend live at?" Jamaine questioned, and Lunchmeat quickly gave him direction.

Chapter Eighteen

Gangster Mockery

When they called me for my visit, I already knew that it was Chanae trying to get back in my good graces. Especially since she's admitted that she'd basically abandoned me for nothing. Or should I say nobody. I went to get fresh. Shiid, a nigga still had his swagger. But I knew that her visit was going to cause friction between Sweet Pea and I. Not because we were together or anything. Just because she felt like Chanae got too much credit and too many chances to have done so much slacking.

Maybe Sweet Pea was right. Maybe I did give Chanae too much rope. But what could I say! I loved her and there was no such thing as a safe bet when it came to matters of the heart. You just put your heart on the line and took a gamble.

I walked into the visiting room, sat down to wait for Chanae and began looking around, sizing niggas up. Guys didn't even take pride in themselves anymore. I guess that was a new thing too. Looking bummy, walking around with knotty heads and stuff. And I could tell that nobody was working out because everybody was busted up.

"Dakaron!" Someone walked up behind me and laid their hand on my shoulder. "How are you doing, brother?"

"Ohhh, what's up, Azid?" I turned around to see the Osama Bin Laden-looking Russian and immediately shot to my feet to embrace him with a brotherly hug. Azid had been like an uncle to me since the day we'd meet at my first tier-rap meeting. "How's it going?"

"I can't call it, brother," he replied before hugging me again. "Who's coming to see a stinky Ku'far?" he joked.

"One of my daughters' mothers," I revealed, taking a deep breath.

"I am here to see the wife and kids," Azid confessed with a smile.

"Oh, I know, ain't nobody else coming to see you," I teased with a bit of seriousness. "But Allah has blessed you."

"Jazakellah, Alhamdulillah!" Azid mumbled off something in his native tongue. "Well, look, brother. I'll talk to you later."

"A'ight." I nodded and turned back around to sit down and found Jamaine standing on the other side of the visiting glass with a smile on his face.

"What's up, nigga?" Jamaine broke the silence but I was still astonished.

It had been years since I'd laid eyes on Jamaine. However, he was now standing right in front of me in the flesh, leaning his weight on a designer wooden-cane.

So many thoughts ran through my mind. It felt strange to be in the same room with Jamaine again. It brought back so many memories. It brought up so much pain, I stared at Jamaine the same way I'd stared at Chanae on our first visit. He'd been my right-hand man and she'd been my first-love and they'd both changed up and left me for dead at some point while the chips were down and the cards were stacked against me. Now that the cards were falling in my favor, they were back and that's the thing that was so hard to trust.

"Damn! What's up, nigga?" Jamaine repeated, holding his arms up as if to remind me that he was there.

"What's up, yo?" I took my seat and waited for Jamaine to take his. "What the fuck you doing down here?" I questioned curiously. "I thought you were Chanae."

"What? A nigga can't come to see his brother?"

Brother? I thought, staring at Jamaine. Jamaine had to be joking. "I heard that." I shielded my true feelings with a grin. "What's up though?"

"Ain't shit, just wanted to see my nigga," Jamaine went into this long story about how much he loved and missed me, etc. He started telling me all Chanae's business. Like who she was fucking and stuff. He also told me about the things I guess he thought I wanted to hear. He even offered me the keys to his empire. The funny thing to me was, Jamaine sounded just like all the other motherfuckers who'd left me for dead. They all had the same story. Made the same claims.

They all tried to convince themselves that they were real because they damn sure weren't convincing me. Because I knew for a fact that the truth was seen, rarely heard.

". . .Which brings me to this nigga—Banga," Jamaine mentioned his partner in crime. "You remember him, right?" Jamaine questioned but I only hunched my shoulders. "The nigga who was supposed to squash the shit about your brother? The nigga from Uplands."

"I'm not sure, but what about him?" I knew exactly who Banga was. He was the nigga who'd handed Detauwn my cousin Tony's shooter. The same nigga the streets were saying tried to put the dirt over Jamaine.

"That's the nigga that tried to wipe me down," Jamaine leaned close to the screen.

"Oh yeah?" I played along as Jamaine tried to read me.

"Yeah, yo!" Jamaine confirmed. "That nigga over here somewhere," Jamaine continued. "I still owe that nigga about that shit with Antauwn. I was rocking that nigga to sleep but he got the drop on me all about his little hitman operation."

Jamaine started asking me a thousand questions, trying to pick my brain to see where I stood. But if the last eleven years hadn't taught me nothing, it taught me how to conceal my intentions. It was a survival tactic I'd mastered. But, I could no longer hide my true feelings when Jamaine asked me to find Banga and bring him a move.

"You can't be serious!" I eyed Jamaine like he had horns coming out of his head. Why would I ever ride for or come to the aid of a motherfucker who had betrayed me?

"Come on, yo, Chanae said you were on the inmate counsel board. So, I know you can move around the jail."

I almost laughed. First of all, my focus was on freedom. That was my mission and that would not change for anybody other than my real family. Secondly, Jamaine was a piece of shit. The perfidious type of shit at that. "That's not happening." I paused to look straight into Jamaine's eyes because I wanted him to know how sincere I was about what was about to come out of my mouth.

"Ayo, I been wanting to tell you something for years. You're a fake ass nigga!" I fired and instantly saw the hurt on his face. "And you'll be lucky if I don't come at you when I get uptown," I added.

"Come on, don't look all surprised. You know that y'all niggas said fuck me after I got found guilty. Niggas ain't do shit for me the whole time I was down. Then—" I went on Jamaine up in that visit room as he sat there wishing we were still close.

After I finished venting, I got up and kindly left Jamaine sitting there looking ten-carat stupid. I would've never believed that the same nigga who used to hug the block with me would be the same nigga to stab me in my back. But, I should've learned my lesson from Monique.

As I strolled back to the section, I couldn't help but think that if Jamaine had done the things that he was supposed to do, when he was supposed to do them, then I would've done anything he'd asked for me, no questions asked.

When I got back to the tier, I shot straight to the phones. I couldn't wait to tell Frank about his nigga Jamaine.

"Hello," I spoke into the phone the moment Frank's sister accepted the call. "Meek?" I questioned to be sure.

"Yeah, what's up, Dakaron?" she confirmed and I instantly recognized her sexy little voice.

"Nothing, trying to catch up with Cuz," I explained.

"You just missed him," Meek revealed. "He told me what you said too." She giggled.

"Man, you know your brother plays too much," I defended and reminded myself to curse Frank out for putting my business out there. "You can't believe nothing that big head nigga say."

"Mmh hmm," Meek mumbled all enticingly and I had to bite my tongue because I didn't want to fuck Frank up behind his sister. Everybody knew that the nigga didn't play about his sisters. He was worse than Tony from Scarface. "N-E-Way though, when you trying to hook up with bro?" she inquired, knowing that she was the only one we trusted to talk on the three-way with.

"Tonight, if possible," I replied, wanting to get up with Frank asap. "When is he supposed to be calling back?"

"He said the first rec," Meek disclosed.

"A'ight bet. I'll call then."

"I'll be waiting," Meek assured me, and again I wondered if she was flirting or if it was just me. Prison had a way of making a nigga read into things.

"A'ight, talk to you later," I said, hoping I wasn't becoming one of those dudes who thought every female was on him. *I haven't been locked up that long,* I thought.

"Don't have me waiting for nothing."

"Never that," I smiled and hung up the phone.

Man, she's lucky she's Cuz sister! I thought to myself. *If she wasn't, I would've been all over her pretty ass.* She was chocolate too.

I bounced out of the dayroom and headed to the cell to change my gear. I needed to skate up to the gym to see if I could find Captain Glover. I had two things on my mind, and she was the only person who could clear my head of both.

***

"Sit still for a second, Truesdale, I need to talk to you about your tier officer, because I kept getting complaints," Captain Glover suddenly spoke up as everybody was departing.

"I'll holler at you later on, Dak," my man Azid nodded and followed all the other tier-reps out of the office.

I sat back down and watched as Captain Glover gently secured the door behind Azid before turning around to face me.

I sat there in the chair and slowly looked Captain Glover up and down. She was still a bad motherfucker. *Damn!* I thought, *I still couldn't get enough of her*. Every time I laid eyes on Captain Glover, I just wanted to have my way with her.

"Let me see it," I heard the latch of the door lock as Captain Glover smirked and leaned her back up against it.

I knew what time it was. Captain Glover was just as anxious as me. I stood up slowly and smiled. Then, I untied the draw-string on my sweats and pushed them down to my knees along with my black boxer-briefs. "That's, what you want to see?"

Captain Glover shook her head and simultaneously began unbuttoning her uniform. I just stood still and watched as she removed her uniform. When she intentionally turned around, locked her legs and seductively looked over her shoulder before bending over to push her thongs down to her ankles, I swear I was no more good. My dick started jumping around with a mind of its own.

Captain Glover kicked her thong, spread her soft, honey-roasted thighs and reached back between her legs to tease her own pussy for both of our pleasure. I closed the distance between us quickly.

"Uhh-uhn," Captain Glover straightened up and playfully mushed me in the face before walking back around her desk.

"You're going to eat this pussy today and that's all you're going to do," she explained, carefully sitting down in her recliner.

I stood there in a trance with my dick dangling in the air, leaking pre-cum, ready to pounce on Captain Glover, especially when she hooked her leg over the arm of the recliner and began to tease herself again.

"Mmmm," Captain Glover moaned before cursing loudly as I noticed her pussy getting wet and wetter.

"Come over here and eat this pussy," Captain Glover demanded and I was around the desk and on her in no time.

When I was younger, I didn't really even know how to truly appreciate a woman beyond their physical beauty. That's why I didn't judge the young boys today when they couldn't see past a woman's face and ass. Because I knew that they didn't understand the true value of a woman. Don't get me wrong. I loved dimes too–Venus, Chanae, Sweet Pea, Margaret, China Doll, etc. Y'all know my history. But still I understand now that physical attraction wasn't beauty. Beauty was how a woman walked, the looks she gave, the confidence she carried and the way she smelled. The most beautiful thing to me about a woman was a woman who was full of energy. And Captain Glover's energy was off the charts.

"Take your time, baby, you're going to be down there for a while," she coached, palming the back of my head as I complied.

I slowed down and began alternating between tongue fucking and sucking on Captain Glover's clit. I loved the way she gasped and shook every time I locked on that motherfucker.

"Ooooo," Captain Glover moaned, sucking in air through her clenched teeth as I used the tip of my tongue to tease her clitoris with a circular motion. I could already taste her cum and I wanted more.

"Hold up for a second," Captain Glover pleaded for breath.

I leaned back and wiped my mouth before using Captain Glover's pussy juice to stroke my dick. Let me slide it in for a second," I begged, never taking my eyes off of her tight, little pussy that was basically, hanging in my face.

"No, keep eating it!" she directed.

I stared right into Captain Glover's pretty pussy, I mean, it was literally sitting there, wide open in my face. I could make out the miniature juicy bubbles as it slightly opened and closed as if breathing. I gently kissed Captain Glover on her pussy lips and I swear the pussy kissed me back. Y'all might think that I'm crazy. But, that pussy was alive.

"Stop playing and eat this pussy!" Captain Glover ordered and I carefully sucked on her pussy lips. I felt Captain Glover's body shake and knew that I had her right when I wanted her.

Yeah, she could play tough all she wanted to. But, I knew that before I left that office, I was going to get up in that good, wet, phat, little, tight pussy and I couldn't wait to feel Captain Glover's pussy tightly snugged around my dick.

Chapter Nineteen

State Versus Gangsterism

When I walked into the Clarence M. Mitchell Jr., Courthouse bullpen and saw my nigga, I just threw him into a bear-hug and held on for dear life. There weren't too many niggas like Frank left. Niggas who'd held up when it mattered and stayed down when it counted. Frank was the only nigga who I could honestly say stayed real from the day we first met. Yeah, we didn't always agree with each other's methods, and oftentimes we'd damn near come to blows. But in the end, we were always loyal to each other and we always had each other's backs.

"You look good, nigga. Strong," I admitted, suddenly shooting Frank a body shot as we broke our embrace.

"You too, Cuz," he slipped the jab and quickly countered with one of his own.

"Okay," I backed off respectfully and used a wild outburst to disguise my pain. I didn't give a fuck how hard Frank hit. And that nigga definitely hit hard. I mean, I'd witnessed him stop grown men in their tracks and knocked the light out of a few niggas. Still, I'd never admit that he hit hard, never. "You still get them quick hands, Cuz. You don't hit hard, but your hands still sharp." I laughed.

"Come on, Cuz, you know my hands like that, stop faking!" Frank fired as we walked over to have a seat on the bench.

My nerves were on edge. I'd already taken two shits this morning and my stomach was still bumbling. Only this time, it was worse because I knew exactly what awaited me and

Frank. We'd already given these bitches well over ten years and from what my lawyer was saying, they don't feel like that was enough. In fact, they only came down ten years on the plea offer and I won't lie—It was hard not to accept. Even against Frank's wishes. But, like I said, Frank and I were loyal to each other. So, if he said all or nothing, then it was all or nothing, and besides, I didn't have another twenty-five, thirty years in me anyway.

"Did you see anybody when you came in?" I questioned, taking a seat.

"Nah," Frank replied. "But Moms and all them suppose' to be here."

"Yeah, that goes without saying." I assured, knowing that Frank's family was just as ride-or-die as mine. Especially his mother, Aunt Evon. "I talked to One Love and 'em last night."

"I did think I saw Day-Day though. You remember little East Baltimore Day-Day, don't you?"

"Which one? The one who told on his brother Eazy?"

'Hell no! Fuck I care about that sucker ass nigga for? I'm talking little crazy Day-Day from Flaghouse. One of the Fry Brothers."

"Yeah, that's my nigga! I remember his crazy ass spent all his suitcase money on everybody. Last I heard, him and his cell buddy killed a dude at the old jail."

"Yeah that's what I said," Frank admitted. "But I swear I think I just seen that nigga carrying this little girl."

I thought about what Frank said for a moment. It was always good to see good niggas make it back to the streets. "I hope it was him. But, yo, you gotta see Delmonte. She done gotten big as hell."

"She still feisty?"

"Just like her mother," I smiled at the thought of Sweet Pea.

"She was off the meat rack last family day," Frank appeared to laugh at a memory. "What's up with Chanae though?"

I almost asked Frank what was up with Meek, but I caught myself because that nigga wasn't stupid. He knew that the truth was often spoken in a joke. "She good, chilling. You know I decided to give her another chance." I watched Frank's facial expression change. "What, nigga?"

"I ain't say nothing, Cuz."

"You didn't have to. It's written all over you face, nigga!" I snapped. "If you got something to say, say it!"

"I'm just thinking about all the shit you said over the years, Cuz." Frank looked confused, shaking his head. "I wouldn't do it," Frank added but I knew he was talking about when my mind was still trapped in the world of the living-dead and I was thinking like a motherfucker condemned to die. However, now that we were about to return to the land of the living, I felt differently. I felt like there was still a chance for me and Chanae.

"A lot of things have changed since then. A lot of people too." I thought all the way back to when we'd first blown trial and got hit with the bench. There were times when I wasn't sure that we would ever make it back; times when I wasn't sure my heart would take any more. Like the denial of our appeal, the betrayal of my friends, or the death of my father. "But Chanae knows me,"

"She knew you, Cuz. Just like you knew her," Frank corrected.

"You can miss me with all the word semantics," I waved Frank off.

"Chanae knows me better than anybody nigga! And I know her ass too," I added defensively.

Maybe he's right. Maybe me and Chanae have grown so far apart that we don't really know each other anymore, I thought.

"All I'm saying is, the world is already betting against us. So much shit done changed and we haven't been here to change with it. And you know the system done fucked us up in ways that our family may not really understand. That's why I say you should start fresh." Frank explained his logic.

"Let me holler at Meek then, nigga." I smiled a split second before Frank shot to his feet and started going to my body.

Of course, after Frank wiped the smile off of my face and I was finally able to escape the parade of body shots and get to my feet, it was on: Frank and I went toe to toe.

I can't lie—we were getting it in. But, that nigga still hit too hard. So, I had to go for what I know. I scooped Frank's ass and wrestled him into a position where I had the upper hand before letting my hands fly. I had just gotten that nigga to where I wanted him when the grill opened.

"Lace! Truesdale! Let's go!" the guard instructed like he had an attitude.

"You lucky, nigga!" I fired, letting go of Frank's arm, pushing up off the bench. "I was about to fold your ass up."

"Nigga, you wasn't about to do shit but get your dumb ass tossed up!" Frank retorted, standing up, straightening his clothes out.

"Yeah, a'ight, let you tell it." I fixed my clothes and headed for the grill. "And I'ma still holler at Meek when we get up town, nigga!" I ran from the bullpen to get cuffed up as Frank began to sell me death about playing with his sisters.

It felt just like the good ol' days. When we didn't have a care in the world. Before all the money, power and ambition corrupted the crew and that bitch ass nigga Monique betrayed me.

***

I scanned the courtroom as we entered and noticed that the family was out in full force. Even Susan and my cousin Little Earl were in the building. But there was no sign of Chanae. *Where the fuck is she at?* I wondered.

"The fam on deck, Cuz," Frank leaned over and mumbled into my ear. "We're up out this bitch!"

"You better know it," I took a look around and instantly felt a sense of love. I thought about Chanae again. I didn't even know why I was surprised. She'd been letting me down for years. *All the mother fuckers who love me are here!* I told myself.

I scanned the courtroom until my eyes found Meek chocolate ass. Then, I smiled and sat down. The judge was already on the bench.

"Good morning, gentlemen," the Judge spoke up. "I'm glad that you finally joined us."

"We're glad to be here, Your Honor." Frank smiled and I nodded.

"Okay, now that everyone is present, let's begin," the Judge suggested and the court clerk rose to her feet and began reading our case into her record.

After going through the procedural history, which was basically when and how Darryl Diggs was killed, my lawyer went into how the trial had been unfair. Frank's attorney followed up. Then, the state had their say about how overwhelming the evidence was and the battle was on.

"Who was the judge that sat on this case?" The Judge interrupted the hearing as my former trial attorney— Elizabeth Franzoso—stepped down from the witness stand.

"The Honorable Priscilla Carter, if I am not mistaken." George Smith looked at me and I nodded. "Yes, Judge Carter," he confirmed before going on to lay out all the Constitutional violations that took place during my trial.

The battle went on for the next two hours. We presented evidence, affidavits and case law. Both Frank and I testified that we were unaware of China Doll's name or involvement in the case. But, I think the strongest thing was when Frank's former trial attorney—Chip Johnson—testified. That nigga went off on the state for withholding evidence that he was sure could've changed the outcome of our trial. I was, like, 'yeah' because all we needed to prove was that there was a 'possibility' that the outcome of the trial could've been different.

My position and Frank's was clear and simple. Jacqueline Shakur had fucked up and we wanted the case tossed. Fuck a new trial, niggas were trying to walk. The state felt different. They said that Ms. Shakur had no knowledge of China Doll's involvement. But, even if she had, the likelihood that her testimony would've changed the outcome of the verdict was slim. Therefore, they wanted the petition dismissed. In so many words. The state wanted me and Frank to eat the conviction and die in prison.

". . .I mean, this goes to the very core of the case, Your Honor. You heard Ms. Franzoso herself. Had she known this witness's name, she would have certainly called her to testify," my lawyer made his last stand.

"I second Mr. Smith's position, Your Honor. We have to give a jury the chance to hear what this witness has to say," Frank's attorney argued, "especially since she was in direct contact with the state's key witness before and after the shooting. We all heard Chip Johnson's testimony about how it came out at trial that the key witness had a motive to lie. So, it was Ms. Shakur's duty as an officer of the court to dig into this. Period!"

After hearing all the evidence, the judge decided not to make his ruling today. Instead, he set the court in recess for ninety days to give himself a chance to carefully go over all the testimony and review the newly discovered evidence. "Court is adjourned." The judge banged his gavel and just like that the hearing was over.

"All rise!" the bailiff instructed as the Judge got up to head back to his chambers.

I kept watching him as me and Frank's attorneys cleared the table for the next case. Frank said he was stern, but fair when it came to handing down the law. However, I'd heard just the opposite. Whatever the case was, we were going to find out in three months.

Chapter Twenty

It's a Gangster's World, Play the Rules

"The State of Maryland calls Jamaine Jeter." The courtroom door came opened and Jamaine limped in.

Banga ground his teeth and tried to keep a straight face as Jamaine limped down the aisle with his cane towards the witness stand for his attempted-murder trial. He couldn't believe it; Jamaine was a lot of things. But Banga would've never guessed that a rat was one of them. Not after all the work they'd put in together.

Jamaine walked up to the witness stand with his eyes locked on the prosecutor. It was clear by the angry look on his face that he didn't want to be there. To be honest, had any other state's attorney besides Jacqueline Shakur been trying the case, he wouldn't have even shown up. Even after they had contacted his parole officer and had her threaten to violate him for associating with a known felon. But Jacqueline Shakur was different. She didn't make an empty threat. She made and kept her promises. Especially against motherfuckers she wanted. And Jamaine knew that she wanted him because she'd actually told him so.

It had all begun back when Jamaine had tricked the jury into returning a not-guilty verdict. He had been clever enough to hide a water-pistol under her seat during a possession of an illegal firearm trial.

Jamaine's cousin's car had been pulled over and a handgun had been discovered underneath his seat. A handgun that Jamaine swore wasn't his. However, during trial Ms. Shakur pounced on the fact that there is no way for

Jamaine to be riding around in a car and not know that there was a firearm underneath his seat. That was all Jamaine needed to hear.

He convinced his lawyer to sneak into the courtroom during a short recess and tape a water-pistol underneath Ms. Shakur's seat. When the lawyer bucked, Jamaine told him that if they lost, he would accept whatever the judge handed down. No appeals or nothing. However, they didn't lose. In fact, they both won; the lawyer—a legendary case, and Jamaine a lifetime enemy. Especially after how during the closing arguments, Jamaine's lawyer kindly walked over to Jacqueline Shakur's chair and removed the water-pistol from beneath it.

"And Ms. Shakur wants you to believe that a person can't be riding around in a car and not know that there's a weapon beneath the seat." He would aid the jury and the rest was history. The local news media and newspapers embarrassed Ms. Shakur and from that day forward, she vowed to take Jamaine down. To make matters worse, he was able to convince a couple of women to drop domestic violence charges against him before she could get him in front of a jury.

"Please state your full name for the record," Ms. Shakur requested.

"Jamaine Joseph Jeter," Jamaine whispered.

"You're going to have to speak up, sir," Ms. Shakur ordered.

"Jamaine Joseph Jeter!" Jamine snapped.

"With the court's permission, I'd like to address Mr. Jeter as a hostile witness," Ms. Shakur requested.

"Granted," the judge agreed without a moment's hesitation.

"Mr. Jeter, I would like to take you back to May the eight, two-thousand-eight. The day you were shot. Would it be fair to say—" Ms. Shakur began to go into all the circumstances surrounding the shooting. She pounced on Jamaine about not coming forward. She said that he was trying to protect Banga because of some made-up street code, 'the no-snitching rule', as she called it.

Of course, Jamaine denied everything. However, he didn't play dumb. He professed to know exactly who had tried to kill him and why and he assured Ms. Shakur that it wasn't Banga.

"Believe me when I tell you. I know who shot me because I done already got his ass back," Jamaine confessed with an evil smile on his face. "It was over a woman. I was fucking his bitch."

"Are you admitting that you have committed a crime of violence, Mr. Jeter?" Ms. Shakur looked from Jamaine to the detectives sitting in the pew.

"I plead the fifth," Jamaine continued to smile.

Ms. Shakur knew that there was nothing that she could do and she hated Jamaine even more for it. She'd thought that she'd be able to get him up on the witness stand and back him into a corner, or at least get him to slip up and say something that she could use to convict Banga. But, her plan backfired and now Banga was going to walk.

"No further questions," Ms. Shakur reluctantly surrendered after strongly considering her next move.

"The defense has no question at this time for the witness," Banga's busy-faced attorney stood up and quickly revealed.

"You are excused for now, Mr. Jeter. But don't go too far!" the judge warned and Jamaine carefully got to his feet and slowly made his way back down the steps with his cane.

Jamaine mean-mugged Banga as he stepped down off the witness stand and made his way past the defense table. Banga eye-fucked Jamaine back for a moment, but he didn't want the jury reading into nothing. Jamaine knew what it was. Banga picked up his ink pen with a smirk and turned his head to pretend like he was taking court notes.

Crack! Jamaine swung the cane so fast that nobody actually knew what happened for a moment; then, the bailiff tackled him to the floor and began wrestling him into a pair of handcuffs as Banga's family came to their feet.

"Don't fucking move!" the bailiff ordered, placing his knee on Jamaine's back. "You motherfucker!" the bailiff cursed, jerking the radio attached to his shoulder towards his mouth to call for assistance.

Banga's family was going off, trying to get to Jamaine, threatening to kill him as the other bailiffs rushed into the courtroom to hold them off.

Once back-up arrived, the bailiff yanked Jamaine up off the floor and rushed him through the judge's chamber, though not before he got to get a good look at Banga who appeared to be resting on the defense table. He was out like a light. When it was all said and done and all the commotion died down, Ms. Shakur decided to use the incident to convince the jury to convict Banga of first degree attempted murder and get Jamaine for assault.

First, she tried to get Banga to press formal charges. Then she spent an hour trying to get the judge to declare a mistrial. Of course, both plans failed. After that, she decided to put Jamaine back on the witness stand. By then most of the spectators had been removed from the courtroom for security reasons. Especially Banga's sister because she promised to get Jamaine and she didn't care who was there.

"An Ebb always pays his debts," Banga whispered loud enough for Jamaine to hear as the guards ushered him by.

Jamaine ignored Banga and made his way up to the witness-stand. He'd already proved his point and made his position clear. Every time he got a chance to get at Banga, he'd take it.

"Please state your name for the record," Ms. Shakur requested and waited. Once Jamaine restated his name, Ms. Shakur asked the question everybody wanted to know: *Why did he attack Banga?*

"I don't know, you tell me. You seem to know everything else!" Jamaine replied sarcastically.

"Is it not true that you attacked Mr. Ebb because despite all your earlier reluctance, you in fact know that it was Mr. Ebb who shot you."

"Nah," Jamaine shook his head. "I told you, I knew exactly who shot me."

"Come on, Mr. Jeter, admit it. You attacked Mr. Ebb because you know that he's the one that shot you."

"No, I attacked him because you said he's the one who shot me," Jamaine corrected and Ms. Shakur didn't know what else to say.

By the time Ms. Shakur recovered and tried to trip Jamaine up again, the damage was already done. So, all Banga's attorney did was ask Jamaine one question. Did he see the person who'd shot him on the night in question?

"Take your time, Mr. Jeter," Banga's attorney encouraged. "Look around the entire courtroom."

"I don't see him and I know why," Jamaine assured.

"Are you sure?" Banga's attorney inquired.

"Absolutely," Jamaine confirmed and there was nothing else to be said.

***

"Ayo, if something happens to me, tell the police to read this," my cell-buddy instructed, pointing at the wall just above where he laid his head and I nodded. Lately, every couple of days, my cell-buddy got paranoid and began talking crazy.

When we got out into the rec-hall, I could instantly tell that something was up. The energy was off; dudes were not talking or moving around as much. Which was an instant red flag. Still, I played it cool and headed for the phone. I dialed Chanae's number and placed my back against the wall.

Chanae accepted my call and began going on and on about something I'm sure that I didn't want to hear. Anyway, I only heard half of what she was saying because my focus was on all the sneaking whispering and passing going on in the rec-hall.

I was about to tell Chanae that I'd catch up with her later when I realized that the static didn't have anything to do with me. At least not directly.

I saw three young boys roll up on my cell-buddy and start talking, which was odd because my cell-buddy stayed to himself, especially since he'd been betrayed by gang members in the past. I could tell that whatever the issue was, my cell-buddy was trying to back out. But from where I stood it appeared that the young boys were pushing the envelope.

I thought about trying to squash it but decided to mind my business. I hadn't made it through prison playing peacemaker. Plus, I knew my cell buddy kept that bone crusher on him. So, I just fell back and continued to listen as Chanae rumbled on in my ear.

I saw one of the young boys cut his eye at a shot-caller as if he was looking for his approval or encouragement. When my eyes followed, the shot-caller acknowledged him with a nod and the young boy continued to talk.

"Hold up, what did you just say?" I asked, not really sure I heard Chanae correctly.

"I said Jamaine got killed last night," Chanae repeated her statement, and the sound seemed to go out of the phone.

"How? I mean, who? What?" I honestly didn't know what to say. *Damn!* I thought. Jamaine was dead and I don't know how I felt about it. I was sure I wasn't hurt though. After all I'd wished him dead on several occasions. I had even secretly gotten '*Rest in Peace, Jamaine*' tatted on my trigger finger. So, I knew that I wouldn't lose any sleep.

"When did this happen?" I questioned.

"Shawn called me like three o'clock this morning. It's all over the internet. They're saying he got shot with an AK-47," Chanae explained.

"Don't nobody knew who did it?" My money was on the dude Banga. I'd heard about the courtroom incident and knew that he had been found not guilty.

"They say Margaret's little brother," Chanae revealed.

"Margaret's little brother?" I said, surprised. I remembered her telling me something about shorty running around with Jamaine, getting busy. But, I didn't know that he was out there murking shit.

"Mm-hmmm," Chanae confirmed. "They're saying Jamaine put his hands on that girl."

"Wow!" was all I could muster.

"They say that little boy shot Jamaine over thirty times."

"Shorty balled him up like that?" It was more of a statement than a question. "I told you he wasn't going to be able to do all that sucker shit with Margaret. Shorty cut different."

Chanae had just begun to say something when I saw the young boy hit my cell-buddy with a solid right. I'm talking about he brought that motherfucker back like a MLB pitcher and threw it right down the pipe. However, my cell buddy ate that motherfucker like a back-catcher and stood up like an umpire.

The crazy thing was, when my cell-buddy pulled out his knife, niggas started breaking out. Running every which way. Which I always found funny. Niggas would beg for war, talk all that gangster shit and then fold up when you gave them what they wanted. It always makes me think about this song that said. "Think it's a game till them things come out and your brains hang out—"

When my cell-buddy got to slinging that knife, he wasn't bullshitting on no level, he got to hitting everything moving. I pressed myself up against the wall and threw my hands up. I didn't want anything to do with the drama he was issuing. That crazy nigga stabbed every bit of four hoppers before chasing their shot-caller out onto the tier.

"Close the door!" somebody shouted the instant my cell-buddy was gone.

"Yo, that nigga nuts!" someone voiced as two older cats ran over to the rec-hall door and tried to secure it.

"You see that big ass knife?" another kid asked.

When it was all said and done, twelve dudes ended up getting hit, including my cell-buddy. When I was finally able to get back to the cell after being strip-searched and checked for wounds, I went straight to my cell-buddy's bed to read what he wanted me to tell the police to read.

I read it and had to read it again: *If something happens to me, make sure the police read this.* I burst out laughing. I couldn't believe this nigga. Here I was thinking all this time that he had really written something serious on the wall and all he'd done was write the same shit he'd told me to say.

If something happens to me, tell the police to read this. I read that shit one more time and started laughing again. Then, I began to cry. I guess I was hurt about Jamaine after all.

Chapter Twenty-One

Gangster's Forever

After sitting in the bullpen for what felt like eternity, talking about Jamaine and the new details surrounding if Margaret had actually been the one to kill him, Frank and I were finally escorted up to the courtroom to receive our decision. "It's go time, nigga, let's get it!" Frank fired, already moving.

It felt like niggas were walking the green mile. I felt a sense of both relief and heartache. To most people, prison had just been a brief moment in time. A place that they'd passed through at one time or another. Of course, there were those who are foolish enough to continue to make a career out of going in and out. But for men like me and Frank who've spent more than the last ten years of their lives behind the wall, it was more than just a moment in time; more than just three walls and a grill. There were memories of friends, and family to be left behind, sometimes the only family you truly knew and trusted.

Prison had basically forced Frank and I to grow up fast. It shaped us in so many ways and honestly taught us everything we knew about accepting responsibility and standing on our own two feet. However, prison had fucked us up too. Which brought me back to what Frank said: *"The world has changed, Cuz, and we weren't there to change with it."*

When we entered the courtroom, I couldn't help but smile. My army was out in full force as always. For a moment, I thought back to how packed the courtroom had been with well-wishers and phonies when Frank and I were in trial. It was literally standing room only. Now, it was only the real, the sincere, the loyal.

"Will the defendants please stand?" the Judge began after all the formalities. "Mr. Truesdale and Mr. Lace were convicted of the July twenty-first, nineteen-ninety-eight, first degree murder of Darryl Diggs in a nineteen-ninety-nine jury trial. On appeal that conviction was upheld. However, this court found that the State in fact, rather intentionally or unintentionally, withheld and suppressed evidence, thereby triggering a Brady Violation. Therefore, this court reversed, so that it could be determined if the said evidence warranted a new trial or dismissal.

The defendants are guaranteed the right to a fair and impartial trial under the due process clause, which is protected under the United States Constitution Sixth and Fourteenth Amendments. Having heard both parties and taking into consideration the actions and testimony of former counsel, along with reviewing all the facts.

I find that the State did act improperly in the pursuit of justice. And I further find that those actions unfairly prejudice the defendant. However, I do not feel that they rose to the level to meet the standard set forth in the—"

The courtroom began to close in and I instantly felt claustrophobic. I didn't really hear much after that. All I heard was *denied and remain in the custody of the Maryland Department of Corrections*. There was no way in the world that a jury would have convicted us had they heard China Doll's statement. No fucking way! I was lost. My eyes found the approaching bailiff and immediately went to all the old men I knew. All the guys I'd witnessed die in prison.

"Dakaron!" The sound of my mother's voice pulled me out of my trance. "Dakaron!" she called again as my eyes locked on the bailiff's service weapon.

It's not over! I thought, looking up. The fight isn't over, I told myself. All hadn't been lost. We'd been bested in battle but the war was still on.

"What I tell you?" my mother questioned, making me smile.

"Stand tall no matter what. Nothing worth having comes without a good fight," I confessed.

"Alright then, hold your head up!" she encouraged.

I tried to keep it together for my family as I placed my hands behind my back to be handcuffed. I didn't want them to see me break. But, the truth was, I was crushed inside. All the studying, presenting evidence, case law, etc. didn't amount to nothing; the courts did what the fuck they wanted to do just like a Nation of Islam brother had told me. *"You'll never get justice under a corrupt justice system,"* he'd warned when I was on my way back from the feds for court and now I know that he was right.

I'd wasted all my people's hard earned money on a lawyer and I could've learned the same shit for free.

I heard everybody telling me to stay strong and hold my head up as Frank and I were exiting the courtroom. But I refused to look. I didn't want to disappoint them. I didn't want them to see that my spirit was broken. But it was something about the way my brother Antauwn called my name that stopped me in my tracks.

Maybe it was the tone of his voice. Maybe it was the sudden gasp.

Whatever it was, when I looked back and saw my brother standing up, I was at a loss for words.

"We don't give up, nigga! You hear me? We don't lay down!" Antauwn shouted. It was obvious that he hadn't even realized that he was standing up yet.

"Oh my god, baby, your legs!" Samone exclaimed, holding her hand over her mouth.

'Oh shit!" Antauwn looked down and for a moment everything was forgotten. Even the bailiff relaxed his firm grip on my arm. Everybody started going off. My brother had his legs back. It was on now. There was no way that I could stop fighting after seeing my brother stand up for me.

"I love you, bro!" Antauwn shouted. "I love you!"

"I love you too, yo!" I shouted back sincerely as the bailiff began to push me towards the door again. *Damn!* I thought. *My brother got his legs back after all these years.*

"How long your brother been in the wheelchair?" the bailiff inquired after we exited the courtroom and entered into the maze-like back halls of the courthouse.

"Shiid, like eight, nine years," I replied, thinking about it. It was right after I'd gotten found guilty.

"Well, if that ain't a reason to keep going, I don't know what it is," he encouraged me.

I nodded because I truly believe that it was a sign. Today wouldn't be my last stand.

Chapter Twenty-Two

It's No Longer 'G' Season

The next few years went by in a flash. Frank and I tried to get back in court, but nothing was working. We threw all kind of issues at the wall, but none of them stuck. The court denied petition after petition. During this time, I began to really get more into the teachings of the Nation of Islam, trying to understand the essence of the meaning of the 'knowledge of self'. I was passing though one joint after another, wondering if I was going to die in prison.

I went from Hagerstown to Westover back to Jessup. This time I landed at MCIJ–my first medium institution since coming to prison. It was rumored to be the nicest spot next to the Playboy Mansion due to the countless women, soul food style grub and danger-free atmosphere. But I was disappointed to say the least. I mean, the food wasn't half bad. Plus, my black ass, New York homeboy 'E' from the Annex was running the ODR so I was good. And the women were definitely fine. Especially Henderson, pretty ass Sgt. Jackson, feisty ass Sgt. Lomax, Lt. Mobley, Nwosa, Cpl. Morton and this dark chocolate-pudding, African piece named Ebai, arguably the baddest chocolate on the compound.

I was also extra sweet on this sexy ass sergeant named Jamison. She reminded me so much of my old girlfriend Crystal from school. All the way from her innocent look to the natural beauty. Y'all know how I'm about women brave enough to go without make-up. I loved that shit just as much as I loved chocolate. And though I would never admit it, I couldn't decide who I was on the most—Jamison or Ebai—I mean, I loved chocolate but I craved peanut butter; so, I refused to choose. I couldn't. It was like choosing between two children. Like trying to decide which part of the Reese Cup was the best.

Beyond the women though, MCIJ was trash. The cells were dirty and roach-infested. Intel was overzealous and there were rats everywhere. I'm talking about the human kind. Then something was always messing up, breaking down, going out or falling apart.

There were times when the water would go off for two or three days at a time and they had the nerve to give us one 16.9*oz* bottle of water twice a day. They'd have us shitting in bags and pissing in bottles. And they called us animals. The only thing that kept me going was the fact that I was focused on going home.

I jumped in the Anne Arundel Community College, Graphic Arts and Design class. The instructor, Tariq Nuur was cool as hell and his clerks—big Hamza and Yuwkal— taught me enough to start my own web-design business. Which became a major plus when I volunteered for these two pretty, little, petite snow bunnies named Ms. Melvin and Mrs. Howell's Employment Readiness Workshop and got all the information and resources that I needed to get started.

I could still remember the first day I had gotten transferred to MCIJ from ECI. It was one of those pouring down, rainy, miserable days. But, I swear to you when that transportation van pulled up and two sisters in body-hugging uniforms stepped out looking and smelling good enough to eat. My mind instantly went to the gutter. I thought, *Double the Chocolate, double the fun*! They were both snicker-thick too.

Officers Komolafe and Cassie were their names. One had the most intoxicating eyes I'd ever seen and the other one had that walk. Y'all know the walk.

The road trip was long but welcomed, especially after being away from beautiful black women for so long.

When we arrived at MCIJ and got inside, I realized how much I missed being around my own kind, attitudes and all. I mean, there were lookers everywhere and I was locking in names: *Gangster Halsey, fine ass Thomas, Komolafe, hood ass Lt. Allgood, Sgt. Hickman. Sweet ol' Ms. Adelowo, Dwumah, Sgt. Roach, and Property Officer L. Lawrence.*

"Gurlll, if they think that I'm 'bout to take my ass all the way back out them mountains for his medical files, then they have another thing coming," Officer Komolafe argued when it was discovered that somehow my file had been misplaced.

"And I'm damn sure I am not going," Officer Cassie seconded.

"I'm just telling you what Captain Hines is going to say," the cute, little traffic officer informed. "You'll know how she is."

"Gurl, Hines better leave me the hell alone. I'm about to get off too." Officer Komolafe rolled her magnetic eyes.

"Officer Hemsley," another officer with short hair interrupted, "the sergeant on line three."

"Give me a second," the little cute traffic officer quickly disappeared.

I sat there listening to Officers Komolafe and Cassie go on about possibly having to drive me all the way back to Westover, Maryland until the cute little traffic officer popped back up with some good news. She had explained the situation to the sergeant and she was making some calls. After that, I was left in the hallway for about twenty minutes by myself.

"Does he take medication? If so, y'all won't have a choice but to take him back."

I heard someone inquiring about me a second before Officer Komolafe poked her pretty ass chocolate face out the door.

"You take medication, Truesdale?"

"Nah," I shook my head.

"Truesdale?" the same voice repeated. "I know that's not who I think it is."

My eyes locked the doorway until the familiar face appeared.

"Oh hell, no! I should've known that was your little bad ass."

"How are you doing?" I smiled.

"Boy, your little bad tail don't even remember who I am!" she fired.

"Of course, I remember you, Ms. Carter," I said just to let her know I wasn't slipping. I could've never forgotten her pretty ass face, sexy overbite and awkward walk. "I remember all the Annex dimes," I added, thinking about Officers Hilton, Taylor, Porter, Watkins and my baby Sellmen.

I sat there and talked to Sgt. Carter for a minute about how much the system had changed. Convicts and correction officers weren't cut like they used to be. Everything was fucked up. I got a kick out of how niggas made the police jobs so easy nowadays, and here I'd thought that I'd heard it all.

"A lot has changed since the annex, Truesdale." Sgt. Carter paused as if to let what she was saying sink in. "Remember how you used to say that there was nothing slicker than a dope fiend turned hustler?" she questioned and I nodded. "Yeah, well, now there's nothing worse than a dope boy turned fiend. They'll do anything for a high. And I'm talking about these young boys."

I just shook my head because I didn't know what to say. I'd heard stories about young niggas stealing, lying, cheating and scheming to get high, taking batteries out of the TV remote-control, dayroom clocks and shit. Real junky shit. But, I never thought I would be in a position to witness it first-hand. Still, I'd learned a long time ago that the most dangerous prisons were the lax ones with the most crash dummies and least consequences. Because, whenever there was a lack of real gangsters around to enforce law and order, the lines got blurred; this led to guys being unable to sense danger. Which made the respect factor low. So nobody was on guard about what they said or did, meaning there were no checks and balances. Which was why every so often, everybody got a wake-up call when the wrong toes were stepped on.

"Stay out of trouble and take care of yourself, Truesdale," cautioned Sgt. Carter.

"You too, and you definitely don't have to worry about me," I assured. I had a plan, and setting myself back behind a crush-dummy wasn't a part of it.

Once my medical file was faxed over and the paperwork was cleared up, I hit the compound. I lucked up and landed on the tier with my little cousin Lamarr McKinnon. Which was a blessing. Especially once I discovered how he was bidding. He was working, attending college, still standing, carrying his own weight. You know what my blood line bred.

Lamarr put me down with what was what and who was who. MCIJ was a lot like a city jail. The only difference was a lot of the kids I didn't personally know and had never heard of.

"Most of the officers are cool though," Lamarr went on. "I mean, there are a few who are so dumb that they make me wonder how they even got the job. All they know how to do is open and close doors. Some of them can barely even count. There are a few I go for though because they are stand-up and carry it like men—Sergeant Strong, Jamaican Lee, this cool cat named Jennings. I mean, I know they got a job to do, but I respect how they carry it," Lamarr explained. "There's this one chump though. Real cowboy type who likes to walk around with his hat cocked to the back like he's about that work. But, I know this joker don't want no smoke for real. I'm telling you, cuz, I can't stand this lame. He's worse than them intel motherfuckers. Bobby Hill and Apple, without the intelligence though." Lamarr laughed and continued. "I'd like to get him up that gym, put them gloves on and knock his dumb ass out."

"Yeah, there's always one of them," I revealed, thinking about all the wannabe gangster cops who I'd encountered over the years. The ones who came to work to have all the power and control they didn't have in the streets; chumps with chips on their shoulders. Chump like Tiphani or rather–Captain Glover's ex-boyfriend.

All I kept thinking about as Lamarr gave me the rundown was how it used to be that when you came into a prison, dudes would ask where you're from, see if you needed anything and introduce themselves. Now, from the way my little cousin explained it, niggas wanted to know what you were with and if you had some drugs.

At the end of the day, prison was prison to me and it didn't matter where I was housed. I was trying to get out. Now of course, some joints were better than others. For instance, like I said, Jessup had good food and great women, but the place was filthy. However, when you got up in them mountains, the spot was college campus-clean. But the food was garbage and the women were trash with few exceptions

One thing that was universal though–and don't let nobody tell you different–was the fact that most of the C.O.'s were some lazy motherfuckers. But again, like I said, I was focused on going home. So, nothing else really mattered. I worked out with my little cousin because shorty was a machine and attended my classes.

However, that didn't stop me from ending up on administrative lock-up after this crazy ass old head named Randy in my Graphic Arts and Design Class decided to walk out with an entire computer system. The entire class got shipped out. The administration even got rid of the clerks, too.

Chapter Twenty-Three

Gangster Land

"Ayo! Go to CNN! They're out there fucking the city up!" someone suddenly yelled out the door. By now, I was back out Cumberland, North Branch at that. Of course, I tried to buck. I even filed an ARP–administrative remedy policy and brought up the court recommendation not to be housed at North Branch. But, the administration said it was just that—a recommendation, not a court order. So they dismissed my ARP and shipped my ass back out Crackerville for security reasons. A lot had definitely changed since I'd been sent out of state. Most of the openly racist officers were gone and they'd brought in a few lookers—white girls who I wouldn't mind digging out.

I took my time changing the channel because I knew how dudes in prison always got hyped up about nothing, especially since we didn't see a lot of city news.

When I settled on CNN I instantly recognized the Mondawmin Mall Subway Station. I saw a bunch of Baltimore City Police goons in full riot gear and wondered if it had anything to do with what my niece had been telling me about a kid dying in police custody, during a rough-ride routine. There were high school kids across the street hurling rocks and bottles and I began to think about my daughters, especially A'myiah, she was in high school now and off the chain. In fact, she went to high school not too far from Mondawmin Mall.

Within minutes, things began to escalate. The riot police advanced on the young kids and I began to worry. "I know these bitches aren't about to hurt them little kids!" I snapped at the television as the high school kids took off running and the police officers gave chase.

For the next four hours, I sat on the edge of my bunk with my eyes glued to the TV, wishing that I was free. The entire city was going up in flames. I was scared for my family, scared for my children, scared for my mother.

I'd never witnessed anything that made me so afraid in my life. I'd cheered about the L.A. riots and laughed about 9/11. Maybe because I was still ignorant. Whatever the case, I felt differently now. I felt like I needed to do something. Yet, I couldn't move, not when they began destroying police cars, public buildings and private property. And definitely not when the young, wild rioters began to push towards my mother's house.

I was torn between my pain and my sense; between my heart and my mind. I wanted the system to hurt, not the people. I wanted the city to know our pain, not burn. Then, I wondered if there was ever a way to separate the two. The emotions and reactions?

"Where the fuck are the police at?" I cursed at the television when the rioters got closer and closer to my mother's house. I prayed because if I didn't know anything else, I knew that my brothers would kill or die to protect our mother, no questions asked.

I tried to get out of the cell to get on the phone. But, they locked us down. The whole city seemed to be on fire. Everything was burning, churches, businesses, cars, homes, etc. But, it wasn't until the rioters reached downtown Baltimore that the National Guard showed up.

That shit made me so mad because to me it confirmed something that I'd been hearing since coming to prison. And that was the fact that the people in control of the system didn't give a fuck about us. Us being the poor disenfranchised; Black, White, Mexican, etc.

***

Over the next few weeks, Baltimore City was the topic of every major news station. A lot of things came to the surface: The broken educational system, the corrupt justice system, the lack of resources, self-hate, suppression and destructive crab-like mentality. It was around this time that I began to realize that I really needed to change. It was also during this time that I came to terms with the fact that, if I wanted change, I not only had to be the one to change it. But, I also had to be the change I wanted to see.

Susan and I began to trade thoughts on the topic. Honest, open dialogue on the topics of racism and responsibility in American. I truly loved and respected this woman. Not only was her heart pure, but her mind was just as beautiful as she was. I knew that a lot of people didn't understand our relationship. After all, Susan was a white Catholic and I was what was commonly referred to as a Black Muslim. Because of my attachment to the Nation of Islam, a group of men widely criticized and even hated for their teachings of the truth.

Most people thought that the Nation of Islam and its supporters were racist. However, nothing could be further from the truth. To start with, if they cared to investigate they would soon discover that the Nation of Islam founder, Wallace Fard Muhammad, was the product of a Caucasian woman and black man. Which is why he'd come to give justice to both races.

Either way, I didn't give a fuck! If a person doesn't know the difference between speaking the truth and promoting hate, that was on them. Susan was my baby, and my family loved her to death, especially One Love. We read together, prayed together, dreamt together and desired to make the world a better place together. Of course, Susan was doing a lot more than me though. I mean, she was putting in work; her boots stayed on the ground. She was that message that she preached and she taught me so much about blossoming where I was. And the fact that she was so different was only part of what made me love her even more.

When Frank got us another hearing, I wasn't all that excited. I mean, we'd been down that road enough times for me to know that a hearing didn't really mean shit! Twice, the court had denied motions through the mail without a hearing. But, Frank felt like it was a solid issue. He always did.

I read over the argument at least ten times to get a full understanding. Apparently, our verdict wasn't truly unanimous because jury number one had never been polled nor had the degree of murder been stated. I honestly felt like it was a long shot. But Frank's theory on jury-polling seemed to support his argument.

I sent a copy of the petition to George Smith, my post-conviction attorney and he instantly got on board. He agreed with everything Frank had drafted up and explained that because it was two of us on the case, the issue would be even stronger. He even decided to take the case pro bono.

I got excited once Mr. Smith decided to jump on the case for free; that was really saying something. Still, I played it cool because I didn't want to get my hopes up too high. In fact, I vowed not to tell the family until I was sure Frank and I were going inside the courtroom.

The longer we waited, the more I wanted to get home because the joint was getting worse and worse.

Everybody was getting high, nobody was working out, dudes didn't care about their health or appearance no more, nothing. Even religion, particularly Islam–something that supposedly should have made you take pride in yourself– was almost like a reason to let go. Dudes were walking around busted up, dusty looking, all out of shape with bad teeth, eating themselves to death. I mean, damn near eighty percent of the general population were built like 'Donkey-Kong'. And the guards were even the worse. Half of them were barely able to respond to an emergency. It was comical watching those crackers running.

The entire system had changed. All the jailhouse lawyers were going home or dying off. The administration was giving out video games, MP3 Players, tablets, internet access and some more shit. Some prisons even had transgenders on the compound now. I'm talking about wide open trannies with breasts and all. It was crazy.

Now, I'm not saying that the system had not come up with things in the past to attempt to make you lose sight of the bigger picture. They'd just taken it to another level. It was almost like they were intentionally allowing us to have all the things that would turn us into zombies–video games, drugs, etc. But, I wasn't falling for it. Not Linda and Timothy's youngest son.

To make matters worse, there were no demarcation lines. I mean, it was nothing to see a rat, so-called gangster, tranny, gang-member and religious leader all hanging out together. And I didn't know if it was fearlessness, stupidity, or unconsciousness, but dudes didn't have any shame or discretion even when it came to their weaknesses. I mean, they did everything out in the open. Nothing was secret, nothing was sacred. Gone were the days when dudes tried to protect themselves. It was like everybody wanted to be known.

I couldn't count the times I'd sat next to a dude on the phone and heard him talking recklessly over the phone about street and jail business to their mothers, girls and friends. Some of them even talked about street and prison affairs with the guards as if being recorded on the phone wasn't enough. I still didn't know what part of the game was that. But that's another story.

Then, you had the lames who wanted to be somebody so bad, that they began writing their handles–names and gangs–on the backs of postage stamps. I mean, the fake shit was getting out of control. It had to be the music and drugs.

It made me sick to hear a dude quoting some gangster shit, only to be on the phone later on, lying to his family about some crumbs, producing nothing! Still, I tried not to hold dudes to my standards. I did hold them accountable for what they said out of their mouths though, because I knew that was the only way that they'd do better.

Chapter Twenty-Four

The Only Gangster I Love and Trust

I won't sit here and bore you with all the court hearing details. The back-and-forth arguments and testimony. I'm sure you're just as tired of sitting through it as me. Therefore, I'll just tell you the outcome. Me and Frank went up in that motherfucker and became free men. Yeah, you heard that right. Me and my nigga won! After all the appeals, petitions, court hearings and studying, we'd finally won. We walked into that courtroom and took our lives back.

It was a bright, sunny day when Frank and I stepped outside of the courthouse as free men for the first time in almost twenty years. September the sixteenth, two-thousand-seventeen to be exact. Chanae ran and jumped into my arms and began tonguing me down with so much passion, that my dick couldn't help but to get rock-hard.

"I missed you so much," Chanae declared.

"I missed you too," I confessed as tears fell from my eyes. I squeezed Chanae's wide butt and had to remember that the family was there. "I can't wait to knock that pussy loose," I mumbled under my breath, placing her back on the ground.

Come on now, y'all know damn well that I was going to wax that pussy. Sweet Pea's too! Especially after watching them both fill out over the years. They weren't the only ones either. I had my eyes on a few women I'd dreamt about fucking.

I kissed my mother, hugged my brothers and refused to let go of the kids. I told everybody how much I loved them. Then, I snatched Susan up off her feet and twirled her around. I could not wait to hang out with her and eat some ice cream.

Sweet Pea stood back for a minute and let everybody get their hugs and kisses. Then, she stepped toward me like she was still the baddest thing in the city and laid them soft, thick lips on me. Man, let me tell you, there wasn't nothing in the world softer than Sweet Pea's lips, and I'm not only talking about the ones on her face.

"When you get tired of that," she side-eyed Chanae, "make sure you come get some of this," Sweet Pea whispered in my ear before pulling me into a tight hug.

"Oh, I'll be there," I assured with a wicked smile.

"I know," Sweet Pea broke the embrace. "I'm glad you're home though," she added. "My brother said if you need something, let him know."

I stood there and watched Sweet Pea walked off. Shiiid, I couldn't help myself. Sweet Pea still had one of the nicest bubbles I'd ever been privileged enough to bust and I wondered if that motherfucker still tasted as good as it looked.

"Ayo, Cuz!" I called out to Frank as if that's where my focus had been the entire time. "Ayo, cuz!" I called out again as Sweet Pea continued to move in that direction. *Oh, she's showing off now*, I thought as Sweet Pea put a little extra twist in her hips.

I was about to call Frank again when I noticed Meek pretty, chocolate ass, signaling for me to hold up and I realized that he was offering prayer.

I nodded understandably, told the family that I'd be right back and made my way over. I hugged all of Frank's sisters and thanked them for their unwavering support, especially Frank's mother—Aunt Evon. She had been an O.G. since the day we got grabbed, pulling up on witnesses and all.

I stood there and watched Frank offer *Salat*. Seeing my man down on his knees, submitting to something greater than himself almost brought tears to my eyes again. We'd been to hell and back together. We'd stood tall, remained strong and stayed true to the game. We were hands down the two realest motherfuckers alive. But Frank was more than that. He was the true definition of a friend. He embodied brotherhood. I'm not saying he was perfect, nor without fault. But, when it came to that gangster shit, Frank had it in the bag.

It was not only in his eyes. You could see it in his walk. I used to think that I was something. But, when it was all said and done, I realized that Frank was my best example. He was the only nigga who I'd come up with, whom I could honestly say had been exactly who he'd presented himself to be. Everybody else had been faking.

"They can't keep a fighting man down, Cuz!" Frank came up out of prayer. "They can't keep a fighting man down! Not when Allah is on his side," he repeated before going on to shout something in Arabic that I believed meant 'God is the greatest'.

To people walking by, it may have appeared like Frank was crazy, but they didn't know our story. They didn't know our pain and they damn sure didn't know what we'd survived.

"I love you, Cuz," Frank and I embraced.

"I love you too," I countered as we stood there in the middle of downtown Baltimore, hugging like long lost brothers.

Frank and I had basically gone to prison as children and returned as men.

It wasn't long before the tears began to fall again. Nobody said a word. Nobody bothered us. They just let us alone and allowed us to take in the moment. When I think back to how we must've looked—two grown ass men, standing outside the courthouse, hugging each other, crying—I always laugh. Motherfuckers probably thought that we were punks who'd just gotten married or something.

"Y'all know I'm the reason y'all are home, right?" Meek informed Frank and I. We finally broke our embrace.

"Yeah, I heard that," Frank smiled.

"I'm serious. You know today is my birthday," Meek revealed. "I made a wish."

"Oh yeah, damn, sis, my bad. Happy Birthday, love." Frank wrapped Meek up in a bear-hug and began kissing all over her.

I winked at Meek behind Frank's back. Whether she knew it or not, her pretty, chocolate ass was on my wish list too.

Meek winked back.

I nodded and kept my thoughts to myself. For one, she had her son with her and secondly, I didn't want to have to fuck Frank up, especially after we'd just given our lives for each other.

After giving Frank some more love, I turned around and stared at the court building that had taken nineteen years of my life from me and changed me into a totally different man. While standing there looking at the building that caused so many people pain and offered joy to others, I vowed to never fall victim to the system again. I didn't want that kind of life anymore, especially now that I knew the effects it had on my family and community.

I wanted to finish my life as a free man. Not trapped off in some prison cell, fighting to keep my sanity. I wanted to watch my ribs grow up and do something more with their lives. I wanted to give my daughters away at their weddings. Beyond all that, I wanted to just live in peace, realize my dreams and be there for the people I loved the most.

"I'm gone, Cuz," Frank gave me one more hug and disappeared into a sea of family members.

"Dakaron, come on, let's go!" Chanae guided me towards a red car.

I paused to look at the sky one more time and sincerely spoke to Allah for the first time as a free man. "I got it now," I confessed as one gangster tear rolled down my face. *I got it*, I thought. *Message received.* God, self and family was all that mattered.

"Boy, if you don't come on!" Chanae warned, opening the back door of the car.

"My bad," I smiled and climbed in behind her.

"Where to, baby?" One Love asked, turning around as I pulled the door shut.

I could see the traces of gray hair spreading out across One Love's dreadlocks. I could also see the struggle and pain in her eyes. The pain that all black mothers who were used to bearing the burden of their children's misfortune carried. Still, she was beautiful both inside and out.

"Wherever you're going to be," I replied. I'd vowed to spend as much time with my mother as possible if I were ever released. Why? Because she was the only woman who'd *never* left my side the entire time I was away. Not even for a minute. "I just want to be with you," I added with a smile.

My mother was in a class all by herself, a beautiful Queen in her own right. Better yet, Black Diamond; she was unconditional love, honor and commitment all wrapped up in one. She was strength, dignity and grace at the core. Patience, humility and understanding at its best. In short, my mother was the closest thing to Allah that I'd ever had on the face of the earth. And I only prayed when I found a wife, she was as half as qualified

"Alrighty then," One Love said, spinning back around to get ready to pull off.

"Don't forget the boys!" Chanae reminded, wrapping her arms around me as if she was scared that I'd vanish if she let go.

I wasn't mad though. Shiid, I was holding on just as tight, though for different reasons. Reasons I won't speak about. "Yeah, Ma, don't forget my sons!" I laughed.

One Love hit the horn and I saw Darrien and Ahmad sprint for the car, arguing about who would ride shot-gun.

I kissed Chanae softly on the cheek and gently laid my head on her shoulder to stare at One Love. "I love y'all," I mumbled and felt something that I hadn't felt in a very long time, contentment.

"We love you too, sugar," One Love replied and I just smiled. It felt good to be back.

Chapter Twenty-Five

A Gangster's Worth

I'm not even going to try to bullshit you. Since coming home, I had gotten a lot of pussy. Don't judge me, I had a lot of catching up to do and it was like everybody knew it too. Women were throwing me pussy left and right. It was like everybody wanted to know what that penitentiary dick was hitting for. I was tagging new pussy and reacquainting myself with old pussy. Even a couple of my female cousins' and sisters' homegirls set the pussy out. And the shit they were doing now, the tricks they had, was fucking my head up. I mean, I was far from a virgin when I fell for the murder back in the nineties. But man, these women were turning me out. They were doing things that I'd never even read about in freak novels.

This one Jamaican chick whose name I won't reveal—because I know her son's father reads my books—took me to her house, tied me to her bedpost and damn near sucked me to death. I swear to God, this woman gave the best head I'd ever had in my life. She had this thing she could do with her tongue that drove me nuts. Not to mention, her deep-throating skills. Lord have mercy!

I finally got to really tear Captain Glover's pussy out the frame too. I'm not even going to mention Sweet Pea. But y'all know I got my hands on that again. I even got to finally get at a few of my childhood crushes and wet-dreams but, I can't lie though, the surprise came when one of my nieces, paired me with one of her little friends—man, let me tell you!

Whoever said young girls weren't about their business must've been referring to them as 80s babies. Because this little eighteen-year-old girl fucked like a grown-ass woman. On top of that, the pussy and ass was so good and tight that I had to question her sexual history.

The problem was, I didn't need no little girl chasing me around. And this little girl was sprung after the first time I threw her the dick. It got to the point where I had to tell my niece to stop bringing her young ass around.

Babygirl did have this move I loved though where she would plant both of her feet beside my hips, squat down, froggy-style on the dick and ride me out of my mind. I loved looking down, watching that tight, little, phat pussy slide up and down my dick like a back-catcher's mitt as my toes curled to the breaking point.

I know you're probably wondering where Chanae was during all this. To be honest, we were going through it. Everybody seemed like strangers. Even the people I'd known all my life. The world I'd left was a lot different from the one I returned to. And that was fucking with my head.

Everything I thought I'd do now seems impossible. All my plans, my hopes, my dreams and my visions now seemed like a natural defense method to survive unnatural circumstances. What frustrates me the most though, was the fact that instead of talking to me when there was an issue, Chanae would talk about me to Shawn or Ebony. So we are always beefing.

Don't get me wrong, there were good times too. But after being gone for so long and having learned so much about just how sneaking, selfish, conniving and disloyal most women were, it was hard to trust Chanae. I definitely respected her though.

I not only respected her for being there throughout the years, but I respected the way she always made herself available to me no matter what–especially in the beginning. It didn't matter it if was for mail, phone calls, court dates or visits. If I needed Chanae, she was there and I couldn't say that about a lot of women. Not nowadays anyway. They just weren't built like that.

The longer I was home though, the more I began to think about when Chanae was there and when she wasn't. That always made me question *why*? And the answers always reminded me that I didn't owe Chanae anything other than genuine love and friendship.

I also began to go to the Nation of Islam Mosque up on Garrison Boulevard. So, the more I encountered women, the more I realized that Chanae had been more of a good friend to me while I was in prison than a good woman or wife.

She'd never had to sacrifice, not once. She basically was able to have her cake and eat it too. She'd give herself away countless times and disappeared at times for years.

"*You* left me, Dakaron! *I* didn't leave you—" Chanae would argue and I knew that she was right. Guilty or not, I had intentionally jumped into the streets and played a game that was impossible to win at. Still, it was hard for me to come to terms with the fact that sometime during my bid, Chanae had given up on me, on us.

I always thought about the young boy she'd said was just cool. Or the older chump she professed to be hers. Then, there were the dudes she thought I was in the dark about, and finally, the guy she refused to stop dealing with, when I'd given her an ultimatum. But, that was just the tip of the iceberg. What was really drawing a rift between us was Islam and evolution.

Chapter Twenty-Six

A Gangster's Work Is Never Done

. . .That means no more g'tting' high, drinkin' 40s / So I get back lookin' type slick again / Fake niggas jump back on my dick again / Nothin' but love for those that know how it feel / And much respect to all my niggas that kept it real—

By now, I had been in the streets well over three months. Christmas had come and gone and I still hadn't been able to get a job. Frank and I had taken a plea, so my record was haunting me. It was like despite what I'd learned and all the resources I'd gathered in ERW class, there were no second chances in Maryland. Add that to the fact that I had a felony murder conviction of my record and it got much tougher. It was enough to stress me the fuck out. That, and trying to get to know and re-know my family again.

The only blessing was that I wasn't on papers. So, I don't have some hard up, career-chasing, parole officer breathing down my back every step of the way like a lot of guys.

Another struggle I was having: was staying away from the game. And it was hard. Even after spending almost twenty years in prison. I mean, to have to sit back and watch kids as young as my daughters drive around in the latest whips was painful. On top of that, they were reckless, showing off all their wealth, disclosing all their business. So, I knew it would've been like taking candy from a baby, if I decided to get back on my robbery shit. I almost went looking for Willie Bates but Frank talked me off of the ledge.

It was during this time that I also found out that Venus and Monique had a seventeen-year-old son named Venique, who was off the wall. Chanae said he had a notch or two under his belt and A'myiah said he ran with a wild crew called the 'Young Cruddy Buddies.' From what A'myiah explained, they basically had South Baltimore under control.

The streets weren't like they used to be. There was no honor, no loyalty and no rules. Being conniving was the thing now. All the unwritten laws had been forsaken. Being cruddy was cool, snitching was accepted. It was like the game had gotten a lot weaker. While the streets became more dangerous, nothing was sacred. These kids would shoot anytime, anywhere at anyone: women, children, babies. Nobody was off limits. And everybody was calling themselves gangsters now. Even well-known suckers and rats.

I didn't really know when that had become so acceptable. But everybody was telling. So-called gangsters, hustlers and killers. Even some of the most popular rap artists and top TV characters were snitching. And dudes had the nerve to name themselves after them. It was sickening.

I stayed on top of Darrien and Ahmad and my nephews, Little Detauwn and Jordan; because I wanted them to know the truth about the game. It wasn't shit! There were no friends, no retirement plans and no future in it. In the end, all that was in it for your loyalty and honor was death, prison time and betrayal and I refused to let any of them go that route.

I pulled into the parking lot of the Maryland Department of Social Services and parked. Frank had told me about a 'second chance' program that helped people with criminal records, coming out of prison to start their own business. Which was cool because I was ready to put what I'd learned in Mr. Nuur's class to work. Like I said, it was hard for a convict, but I wasn't giving up.

"How may I help you, sir?" the fine ass, chocolate dime piece sitting behind the front desk of the *Social Services Building* inquired with a gorgeous smile.

"Well, ummmm," I stuttered, lost in her beauty for moment. "I ummm—heard about the ground floor program," I finally managed as her eyebrow arched.

Smiling at the effect I'm sure she knew she was having on me, she said, "One moment please" and picked her desk phone. She spoke to someone named Nyesha for a moment. From the sound of things, it appeared as if I had my days mixed up. "Name please," she held her hand over the mouthpiece of the telephone.

"Dakaron Truesdale," I revealed.

"What?" One of her freshly arched eye-brows went up in surprise. "Boy, oh my gawd!" she exclaimed, smiling from ear to ear. "Crystal, I am calling you back. Huh? Oh nah, girl, I got him. Don't worry about it. I'll get him signed up for Thursday session."

I watched as she hung the phone up, got up out of her chair, walked around the desk and threw her arms around me.

I was still trying to figure out what the hell was going on. I'm not going to lie though. I hugged her thick, chocolate ass back. *Damn!* I thought about stepping back. She was lovely and her hair, clothes, perfume and nails complemented her beauty.

"You letting me hug all on you and you didn't even know who I am." She placed her hand on her hip and twisted up her lips as I slowly took her in and sized her up.

She was right up my alley. Five-six, five-seven, thick, chocolate, confident and bad. Then she had the nerve to have on open-toe heels. "I know you're my type," I admitted, slowly licking my lips. Being in prison had taught me to appreciate every little detail of a woman.

"I see you still think you're a player though." She laughed, shaking her head. We locked eyes again and I tried to figure out exactly who she was.

To be honest, I thought that she had mistaken me for someone she knew. After all, I'd just done damn near twenty years in prison.

"I really can't believe you don't recognize me. That's crazy!" she said. "It's Margaret, boy!" she exclaimed.

"Margaret?" I repeated as she smiled. "Margaret Blevins?" I used her full name to be sure. "Hell no!" I fired when she nodded.

I hugged her again. "Wow!" I mumbled, letting her go. Margaret was still bad with a capital B. "How the fuck I miss that?"

"You're falling off," Margaret joked.

"Shiiid! Damn, what's up though?" I hugged Margaret again. She looked so fucking good. Time had really been cruel to a lot of women I used to know. But Margaret wasn't one of them.

I stood at Margaret's desk for every bit of an hour, talking about all kinds of stuff. Reminiscing about the good ol' days. She brought me up to date on her little brother. Shorty had got ten years for manslaughter and was looking to see the streets soon.

Margaret also gave me a guilty grin when I questioned her about the true info surrounding Jamaine's death. *"Real gangsters never talk!"* she declared and I left it at that.

"How you end up dealing with that nigga anyway? He's not even your type. You know you like that chocolate for real," I teased.

"It melts in your mouth, not in your hand, right?" Margaret played along.

"That's what I hear," I smiled as my mind went straight to the gutter. Margaret would probably shoot me too if she knew what I was thinking.

"Dakaron, I am not messing with you," Margaret blushed as if she knew what I was thinking. "How Chanae doing? I knew you're still chasing her."

I thought about Margaret's statement. I had honestly wanted to give Chanae a chance because that's where my heart was at. But, it was so hard to forget all the let downs, lies, and betrayal. I remembered the long, dark, lonely nights like they were yesterday. I'd never forget how she had continued on without me. Then there were the photos that never arrived. The money that never showed up and the letters that were never written.

"She's still around. But, I'm definitely not chasing her," I admitted, surprising even myself. The only people I usually talked to about Chanae were Saprina and my cousin Missy. And that was because I trusted them with my secrets and valued their opinions. They'd both kept it all the way gangster while I was inside.

"Nevertheless, she's still around though."

I knew that Margaret would never understand–women never did. Chanae was in my core, and a part of me felt responsible for a lot of the suffering she'd had to endure while I was gone. I blamed myself for a lot of her pain. I'd left her to fend for herself. Which was probably the main reason why I had allowed her to get away with so much. Things that we both knew that I would've never stood for, if I was on the streets. "What they say nowadays? It's complicated." I smiled.

"It ain't that complicated," Margaret assured.

"I'm telling you, the Chanae I once loved and adored— the one I wanted to spend the rest of my life with—is gone. Replaced by a shell."

I didn't want to go into how I really didn't recognize Chanae anymore and it wasn't because she'd put on a little weight. Because if I did then, I'd have to go into how some years had gone by where Chanae didn't write, visit or nothing.

"Life will do that to you, boy. Life and good-for-nothing ass niggas!" Margaret spat as if she knew from experience. "Every time you give yourself to one of these lames, you lose a piece of yourself."

"True," I agreed wholeheartedly. There was no such thing as a no-good woman. All no-good women were made no-good by no-good men. "But this is different. It's like she let the world suck the life out of her. I mean, the joy in her laugh is gone. Things that used to make her smile now make her angry." I tried to explain. But how do you explain that somebody's drive for life seems to be gone.

"Chanae used to love challenges. Now she dreads them. The light in her eyes has even faded. And I'm just being real. So, I don't know how to fix that. I don't know how to get us back to where we used to be."

"Y'all probably won't ever have that again," Margaret confirmed what I already knew in my heart. "What do you do for fun? You're probably going to need counseling."

"Imagine that!" I challenged. There was no way in the world that I'd go see a head-shrink. "I do hang out though, I be fucking around at the gym."

"I bet you do." Margaret laughed.

"Nah, not like that," I retorted, knowing exactly what she meant. There were a bunch of women at the gym trying to get at me though, but I wasn't into that. Especially all the stupid, wild, big, fake butts and stuff. "I really be up there working out. But dudes aren't ready. You know, you work out for different reasons in prison. It's not simply just about health and looking good. You're burning through pain, fighting for survival, preparing for the moment you get to pay everybody back for counting you out. That was what kept me going."

"Damn, boy, you need a hug," Margaret suggested after I finished venting.

"I know," I admitted with a smile. "That's why I want to take you out."

"Oh, I am not down with the free love thing," Margaret countered.

"What the hell is the free love thing?" I asked curiously.

'It's what I call 'relationships with no commitment', because it only requires the man or woman to be there during times of happiness. And it makes them free to bounce and leave the other uncared for in his or her sorrow," Margaret rationalized.

I continued to try my hand, but Margaret kept batting me down. She agreed to go out with me on a date, if I ever got my mind right and figured out exactly what I wanted to do.

After that, I filled out all the necessary paperwork for the ground floor program, sized Margaret up one more time and got out of there.

Man, if I ever get the chance, were my last thoughts as I walked out of the building.

***

The next morning, my daughters and I were coming out of Walmart when a couple kids pulled up in a brand new LS460 with an Ashanti Luxury grille package and a AFC 401 2 tone '4' lip rear, 2.5 front, killing it.

"What it do, A'myiah?" the driver spoke, disregarding me and Delmonte's presence.

"What's up, Vee?" A'myiah replied.

"Dakaron, right?" The kid extended his hand out the window.

"Yeah," I shook his hand. "And you are?"

"Venique, Venus and Monique's son," he revealed. "They say you're the one who spanked my father."

"They lied," I replied with the quickness, slightly pushing Delmonte and A'myiah behind me.

"I heard that," he smiled devilishly.

"Oh, that's ol' boy you were talking about, huh?" I heard one of Venique's little partners say from the backseat.

"Yeah, I think so," another one spoke up.

"Mann, yo stiff as shit," the same voice exclaimed and all the little kids laughed.

"You calling my mother a liar?" he challenged.

Never being one to back down, I had to catch myself. Plus, I had my daughters with me. "Nah, I'm just saying she got her facts mixed up," I replied, trying not to tell him off.

"Yeah, well, now that you're home and all, I'ma look into it myself," he alerted me.

"You do that," I encouraged, knowing that my secret was safe. The only dudes who truly know the story behind Monique's death were loyal to me.

"Oh, I will," Venique assured before pulling off.

I watched the car exit the parking lot. Back in the day, I'd been outside of shorty's house before the night ended. But, I was a different man now. I was taught to never be the aggressor in words, actions or deeds. Still, I wasn't stupid. I knew when a nigga was making a gentle threat.

"I didn't even know you knew Venique's father," A'myiah spoke up, surprised.

"Yeah, we used to run together back in the day. He's the one that put me in prison," I professed, refusing to lie to my children. "He lied on me and Frank like a coward."

"Are you the one that killed him?" Delmonte inquired. Which really surprised me. She was usually reserved, soft spoken and quiet.

"Of course not," I lied. Come on now, I was still a gangster at heart. So, you know I wasn't about to confess to the body I'd gotten away with. Even to my own children.

"A'myiah, me and you need to talk though. Because I need to know everything you know about these kids." I knew that I needed as much information as I could gather on Monique's son and his little crew just in case he was crazy enough to do something stupid. Like I said, I wasn't that far out of touch. I still knew how things went in the streets.

I made a mental note to get with my niece Latonya too because I knew that South Baltimore was her stomping grounds. So, if Venique was as live as my daughter had made him out to be, Latonya would not only know him. She would know where to find him.

Chapter Twenty-Seven

Reformed Gangster

"What's up, Cuz?" I greeted Frank, climbing into the car. "Ain't too much, trying to take it one day at a time," he replied as I closed the door. It had taken us almost a week to hook up due to scheduling. I'd told Frank all about Monique's son and how he'd pulled up on me outside of the Walmart. *"It's a different world, Dak, let them kids have it,"* Frank had cautioned after finding the situation real funny.

"How is the job thing going?" I inquired. My job search was going nowhere and starting my own business was proving harder than I'd initially thought, even with the assistance of Margaret and the 'Ground Floor' Program. I was starting to feel like there was a bigger plot to push me back into these streets, so I could fuck up and end up back in prison.

"Good for the most part. It's still strange working for the man," Frank admitted." What about you?"

"I done had a few part-time gigs, but nothing stable. I met this badass Washington D.C. sister's named Ladonna Harrison that manages the Giants across from the temp-agency. Cuz, let me tell you—" I gave Frank a quick rundown on Ladonna.

Shaking his head and smiling after I finished, Frank simply said, "You're something else, you know that, cuz?"

"You know I can't help myself when I see a fine, dark chocolate piece," I defended.

"You better get some discipline, Cuz!" Frank barked. "Anyway, what's on your mind though?"

"Honestly, I'm still thinking about Monique's son," I confessed.

"Come on, Cuz, you still stuck on that?" Frank questioned as if he couldn't believe it. "I told you the little kid probably just smelling himself. These kids nowadays do dumb shit for a different reason. They be out here chasing likes and clout on social media. Most of them aren't even cut like that. These little niggas aren't built for no bodies, Cuz. You get to dropping these kids, they're going straight to the police or social media."

"It's not just him, Cuz, shorty started making me think about other niggas who I'd gotten into it with back in the day!" I explained. "You know those type of niggas to never let a score go unsettled."

"Man, fuck them niggas, Cuz, you got to live your life. You got more important things to worry about. Delmonte drawing, A'myiah designing clothes. You got your niece Jamaine in college. Lor'De playing football. Come on, Cuz!"

"You right, Cuz, but Latonya told me this little kid was sneaky. Plus, she said he's getting a few dollars."

"Mannnn, Cuz, what they call money today is chump change for real," Frank assured. "These kids don't even know what getting money is. All they want to do is wear the latest gear, keep a few dollars in their pocket, drive new cars and pop pills all day. That's what they call getting to the bag!" Frank exclaimed. "I be trappin' off my nephews."

"That's the same thing Redburn said when I talked to him the other day."

"Old Redburn," Frank said with smile as if a fond memory had popped into his head. "What's up with that nigga anyway?"

"Nothing, still fighting. He said one of his rap-buddies just found a serious misconduct issue involving the police department."

"That's what's up. Where is he at now? Still out of state?"

"Nah, he's back down Jessup, Brockbridge. He said your man, Blade Runner down there with him."

"Hell no, stop lying, Cuz." Frank laughed.

Blade Runner was an old, institutionalized cat who liked to hide his fan and tier blades, whenever he went to court, so that his cell-buddies couldn't use them.

"That's my word, Cuz, that nigga still running around. Playing the same games too."

"Cuz, I thought he was home by now."

"Yeah or died," I added.

"Cuz, remember that time him and his cell buddy got to fighting, and the cell buddy came out all fucked up in the morning and the C.O. asked him what happened? What did yo say?"

"I caught monkey pox," Frank and I declared in unison, laughing.

"Blade Runner was like, nah, nigga. You caught these monkey paws," Frank continued.

I burst out laughing because I remembered the incident like it was yesterday. I'd slept right next the door to Blade-Runner at this time. "I need that, Cuz," I admitted wholeheartedly, still laughing. "I haven't laughed like that in a minute."

"The police was, like, *I see knots but I don't see no blood,* and forced them niggas back into the cell together." Frank had me thinking about all the crazy stuff that went on behind prison walls. "What else is on your mind though?"

"Shiid, what's not? Chanae, Delmonte and everything else," I revealed.

"What's up with Delmonte?"

"First of all, she's dealing with this little, skinny jeans wearing clown who don't know what to say out of his mouth. Cuz, I'm telling you if it was back in the day, boy—I'd do something with this little kid!" I exclaimed. "But I can't say nothing about him. It's almost like she's trying to pay me back for being locked up all her life."

"You got to give her some time to warm up to the idea of you being around, Cuz, my nieces and nephews the same way."

"We were cool when I was still in prison. She'd talk to me about anything."

"That was because she knew that you could not leave her. She could allow you into her world. Fear is a little girl's best friend."

"It's crazy you said that, because I heard something similar at the mosque last week."

"Are you still listening to the nonsense?" Frank teased as always.

"Don't do that, Cuz!" I warned but seriously I knew there was no ill intent. Me and Frank just always joked about each other's religious way of life, although we respected each other's beliefs. "I don't say nothing about you running around, following the loony-community on your Arab stuff," I joked, thinking about how the doctrines espoused by orthodox Sunni Islam and Christianity compelled you to accept principles and exhibit behaviors that were unnatural to who we were because they contradicted our true culture. The main two being that we are 'black and great'.

"Nah, seriously though, we all need something to believe in," I continued.

"Be it the truth or not," Frank retorted, "you got Chanae to go with you yet?"

"Shiiid, you'll probably have a better chance of getting her there than I will," I admitted.

"Why do you say that?"

"Because a lot of people can't handle the discipline of the Nation. And you and I both know that dudes done made a fad out of the Sunni community. I saw some pictures of Jamaine over Chanae's house the other day. Him and bunch of Muslim brothers with Holy Qurans in one hand and drinks in the other. These jokers had prayer-rugs and everything over their shoulders. And that's why everybody joined up. Just like in the joint. That shit a joke!" I fired.

"That's not why everybody join up, Cuz!" Frank challenged me and I could tell that he was offended.

"You know what I mean," I corrected, ready to let it go. Frank knew that I was right. When you didn't teach a person right, you automatically taught them wrong. That's why most of the guys in prison became Sunni Muslim now. They knew that they could continue to do all the same things they'd been doing and be protected while doing it. It wasn't much different from a gang. A bunch of wannabes using the strength of men and numbers to shield their cowardice.

The only real difference between a gang and the community in my eyes was the fact that in the joint, there was no one to hold you accountable when you were in the community.

'What is it that Redburn used to always say?" Frank questioned.

"I don't know. Redburn used to say a lot of things."

"About separation from people you knew."

"Oh." I paused for a second and thought because I wanted to quote Redburn correctly. "He said that, when you separate from a person for ninety days or better, you have to get to re-know them because people change like the seasons."

"Right," Frank agreed with a nod. "So, you got to get to re-know Chanae."

"That's what I been trying to do," I declared.

"Try harder!" Frank fired, making me smile.

Chapter Twenty-Eight

A Family Gangster

It was one of those rare occasions that brought everybody together at my grandmother's house. I was sitting at the kitchen table, watching the women in my family throw down, listening to the chitter-chatter. I really admired the women in my family. They were all black diamonds in their own right. As for the backbone of our family, she had never folded despite all the things she had endured including racism. Which was why her death was so hard.

I was holding up for the most part, trying to be strong like the rest of the family. After, all it was natural for a grandmother to go before her grandchildren, yet, losing Momma was like losing a leg, like taking a bullet straight to the heart. It was hard to let go. That was why I couldn't embrace the celebration-of-life concept.

I didn't care that Momma had died peacefully in her sleep. I didn't care that she'd lived to be almost eighty-five years old. I didn't care that she'd left behind a host of family and friends. To be honest, I didn't even care that she'd created a legacy and laid the foundation for our family to stand on. I felt cheated.

Everybody else had gotten to enjoy Momma's company for the last twenty years while I was rotting away behind enemy lines. So, I knew I had every right to hurt, to feel sad and to be angry.

"Uncle Dakaron," my nephew, Lor'De, came flying into the kitchen like the star defensive tackle he was.

'What's up, nephew?" I snapped out of my daze.

"Please come in here and represent!" Lor'De pleaded. "Jordan talking 'bout he can beat you on *Call of Duty*."

"Give me a minute," I requested, holding up my finger. I needed a moment to gather my thoughts because I knew that once I went into the living room with my nephews to play the game, it was over.

I took a deep breath, slowly got up and headed towards the living room. I needed something to take my mind off Momma for a moment anyway.

***

I had been sitting in the living room, watching my daughter busting my nephews' asses in *Call of Duty* for a good while, when One Love came strolling in, followed by Chanae. Jordan had already tightened me up. Now A'myiah was getting revenge.

"Hey, baby!" Chanae climbed into my lap and tried to give me a kiss.

"Watch out!" I snapped, rejecting the kiss, barely acknowledging her.

"Oh yeah," Chanae mumbled. "Sorry I'm late," she apologized, grinding her ass in my lap, making me mad that I instantly began to get hard. "I'll make it up to you," she teased and tried to kiss me again.

"Stop!" I ordered, jerking my head out of the way. I wasn't in a kissing mood, especially since she'd just showed up.

"Forget you then," Chanae pushed my head.

"Yeah, whatever," I declared nonchalantly. The effect she still had on me always amazes me.

'Hey, ma, when you go in the kitchen can you make me a plate?"

"I'll fix it, Ms. Linda," Chanae volunteered.

"Nah, I'm good. My mother going to make—"

"What you got an attitude for?" She rolled her eyes as if I'd done something wrong.

I tried to ignore Chanae and explained to my mother exactly what I wanted to eat. But she just kept mumbling little shit under her breath.

"Don't blame that on me," I fired when she complained about me leaving her. "I told you we're supposed to be here by twelve o'clock. Didn't nobody tell you to go out last night."

"Dakaron, please!" Chanae retorted. "I probably wasn't even five minutes late."

"It's doesn't matter if you were one minute later. You know how I'm about keeping my word!" I defended.

"So, you still should have waited a few minutes. You didn't have to leave me!" Chanae argued. "You see, Ms. Linda, if he stops living with you and just moves in with me, then we won't have to worry about time management. We can leave the house together and arrive on time."

"I know that's right." One Love smiled.

"Please don't encourage her, Ma!" I begged.

I knew that my mother loved Chanae like a daughter. I mean besides Detauwn's children's mother—Sarina—Ms. Spriggs and Samone, no other woman had ever gotten closer. However, One Love knew how much I enjoy living with her. Shiiid, all I ever talked about was staying with my mother for at least one year after I came home. I wanted to just enjoy her company. Plus, I knew that she was the only woman who wouldn't pressure or hound me about every little thing. She'd actually give me the time and space that I needed to slowly get readjusted back into society.

"I'm not encouraging nothing," One Love said with a grin. "I love having you in the house, son."

"As I love being there. Besides, Chanae has too many people coming out her house, Ma. I told her that before!" I fired, instantly regretting my words.

"Dakaron, I'm not paying you no mind," Chanae countered with a slight attitude. "Those are my friends. I don't say nothing about all your little X brothers and sisters."

"That's 'cause you got a lot more than I do," I fired to be smart, thinking about all the women and sometimes dudes Chanae hung out with.

"Yeah, well, you been gone a long time," Chanae shot back.

'Yeah, you too!" I retorted.

"What's that supposed to mean?" Chanae stared at me curiously.

"Nothing," I shook my head, ready to let it go.

"Nah, say what's on your mind," Chanae challenged. "You always talking that speak-the-truth-regardless-of-the-circumstances crap. The floor is yours."

I looked around the room. Everybody was watching, waiting. Even my cousins, Missy and them were standing in the kitchen doorway, wondering if I was going to finally speak my peace.

The truth was that I love Chanae dearly. Always had, always would. The problem was that, I wasn't sure if I was still in love with her. One minute, I knew that she was all that I ever wanted or needed. The next minute I didn't want anything to do with her. Don't get me wrong. The sex was even better than it was before I'd even gone to prison and we could still talk for hours. But, I just think that somewhere during my bid, between all the lost years, too much time had lapsed away and we began to grow apart.

The special unique bond we once shared was gone. The trust was destroyed. And I wasn't sure if I had the patience to build it again. The only thing that I did know for sure was the fact that, if Chanae and I ever wanted to make it, we'd have to rebuild our foundation from the ground up again. Because what we previously had was gone.

"If I had something to say, I'd have said it already," I assured, biting my tongue out of the guilt I always felt, when it was time to speak my truth.

I didn't want to hurt Chanae and I knew that if I ever really spoke my mind, that would be exactly what I'd ended up doing—causing a lot more damage than good. Besides, nobody really wanted to hear the truth nowadays. It hurt too much. That's why they were all content with being fake. Fake friends, fake photos, fake drugs, fake bodies. Fake everything! Everybody was caught up in the modern-day illusion.

I smiled inside because I was honestly at peace. That's what finding Allah and the Nation of Islam had given me. Knowledge of self, which in my mind equaled peace. And even though I knew that there was as strong a chance that Chanae and I may never be together again, I was cool with that because Allah knows best. Going to the Mosque and discovering how women could and honestly should conduct themselves changed how I viewed women hanging out all night in the streets and clubs. But really and truly, I found something to believe in that would never let me down as long as I never turned my back on it—Islam! And I couldn't say that about no woman I'd ever been with or any of the relationships I'd ever been in.

"Grandma!" Lor'De broke the silence. "Why are your shoes so old?" he asked, making Jordan and them laugh, killing the major tension in the room.

"Shut up, ugly face, and leave grandma alone," my niece Ta'nyah perked up, always ready to go off about her family.

"Don't tell him nothing," her sister—De'bre'anna—warned.

"Old?" One Love repeated, looking down at her own shoes. "See, son, one day you'll learn the value of a dollar. I can buy Nikes and Timber-whatchamacallit too. Got some upstairs your father bought me for Mother's Day. But guess what? Life is about more than clothes, shoes and cars!" One

Love schooled. "It's about family. It's about God. It's about working hard to lay the foundation for your future and the future of your children!" One Love continued. "If I spend all my hard earned money on nothing, I would have nothing."

"He wouldn't have nothing either, Ma!" I added my two cent knowing that my young nieces and nephews couldn't fathom the things their grandmother had to overcome.

"Don't let your eyes fool you, son. And that goes for all of you. People only show you what they want you to see. So, you have to look closer. Most of those people you see on the internet, driving around in fancy cars, living in big houses, do not own nothing! Then you got—"

I sat there and listened to One Love take the family to school until Antauwn walked into the living room and took over.

Antauwn broke down all the things that our family had been through and overcome. The loss of fortune, fame, family and friends. He talked about our father, Momma, Aunt Barbara and Journey–the daughter he and Samone had lost. Before he finished, everybody was in tears.

I can't even sit there and lie. I thought I knew all there was to know about our family, but, Antauwn put me up on something that I didn't even know. Something that impressed me enough to make me want to do some more family history research.

Chapter Twenty-Nine

Gangster Class

"You sharp, you conscious, you gangster, prove it!" I snapped, checking the rearview mirror. I was having a heated discussion with Darrien and Ahmad on my way back to Chanae's house. Apparently, some little South Baltimore punk had given Darrien a pack of synthetic weed to sell at school. "Don't ever let nobody use you," I continued. The truth was, I wanted to go put my foot in the little kid's ass. especially when I laid eyes on him. I knew the type of pure, untested, gangsters who'd fold under pressure. I wanted to roll up on him gangster style. But, I knew that I couldn't. Not nowadays. It was kill-these-kids-or-stay-out of-their-way.

"You hear me talking to you, Darrien?" I took a quick glance over my shoulder and saw him with his face buried in his phone.

"Yeah," he mumbled nonchalantly, barely even looking up.

"It's impossible to hear everything I'm saying and be on the phone at the same time, Darrien."

"I said, I'm listening!" he snapped and I almost reached back and pulled him into the front sit.

I didn't understand. I was trying to save his life. Trying to keep him from going down the same path I'd gone down because I knew exactly what the road led to: prison or death. I placed my eyes back on the road, took a deep breath and continued. "Real gangsters don't sell drugs, Darrien. They don't poison and destroy their own community. Real gangsters work hard to protect the community; real gangsters are altruistic. Do you know the difference between Little Italy and Jew Town and our community?" I questioned, knowing the answer.

"No," Darrien admitted.

"I know you don't." I was really starting to consider Frank's youth group ideas, because like he said, the school system wasn't teaching our children nothing. Real education was what you brought out, not put in. "But you're running around wearing a *Black Lives Matter* shirt." I shook my head in disgust. I really wanted to go upside his head. "I should've gone upside the little kids head."

"I'm glad you didn't do that. He's not no sucker!" Darrien declared.

"Darrien, that little kid is a pussy if I ever saw one," I assured. "I could've slapped the shit out of him. All he would've done was run and got twenty of his little buddies. But alone, by himself, one on one, he's a coward. He would be in the joint getting treated believe that. I know real gangsters when I encounter them. And your little friend is definitely not one. Shorty's a wannabe."

Ahmad laughed.

"Don't laugh, Ahmad, it's not funny. I'm serious! I don't want y'all to go through the same things I had to go through. I almost lost my life out here and for what? Nothing! A name, some clothes, a couple dollars? That shit doesn't mean nothing when your ass locked in a box for the rest of your natural life producing nothing! I have been in prison and seen guys who couldn't even get on the phone, couldn't go to the commissary. Guys who don't know where their next bar of soap or tube of toothpaste was coming from. That's why I'm so hard on y'all. Especially you, Darrien." I checked the rearview mirror again. I didn't know if I was being paranoid or if someone was tailing me. "Ahmad looks up to you and A'myiah the same way I used to look up to Detauwn and Antauwn. That's why you gotta lead by example. You got to change the legacy. I know so many penitentiary legends who are nobodies in the streets. Guys whose family won't even pay to bury them. But, if he hits any yard in the State of Maryland, they'll lay the red carpet out for him. Do you know the last time a man in our family went to college?"

"No," Darrien looked down at his phone again."

"Almost eighty years ago. In fact, before Jasmine went to Saint Mary's, nobody in our family had been to college since nineteen seventy-eight, seventy-nine when One Love had a full scholarship to Morgan State."

"I wasn't born yet," Ahmad interjected.

"Wasn't even thought of, baby boy!" I corrected, reaching over to the passenger's seat to rub the top of his head. "I don't want that for y'all," I explained because I knew that they already had to deal with some things that no child should have to deal with. "You understand what I'm saying?"

"Yes," Darrien nodded and I only prayed that I was getting through to him because I knew how I was when I was coming up. I wanted to be a gangster even if it killed me and there was nothing that nobody could've done or said to stop me.

"Who is that?" Ahmad pointed up at the photo hanging from the rearview mirror.

"A few good friends of mine I left behind when I came home," I explained honestly. "Real gangsters, not none of that stuff you see on TV or running around there. Men who—if you removed their status, wealth or power—would remain the same. Men who aren't made by materials things. But look, we'll talk about that later." I suddenly pulled the car over and threw it into *park*. "Darrien, you remember what I showed you about driving?" I questioned with my eyes locked on the wing-mirror.

"Yeah," Darrien replied excitedly.

"A'ight, look, when I get out of the car, I want you to climb up here and drive to your mother's house, a'ight?" I unbuckled my seatbelt. "Can you do that?"

"Yeah, I got it. But what's going on though?" Darrien looked around.

"Don't worry about that, let's go." I opened the driver's side door. "Tell your mother I had to make a run." I climbed out and stuck my head back into the car as Darrien climbed over the armrest and slid into the driver's seat. "And whatever you do, don't wait for me. As soon as I close this door, pull off."

I shut the door, tapped the roof of the car and waited for Darrien to drive off, then I walked towards the car that was following me.

I'd been gone a long time. But my senses were still intact. Some shit you just never loss. And being able to sense danger was one of them.

I noticed the cruddy tinted, driver-side window on the black J30 Infiniti crack as I approached and saw nothing, but a mouth full of gold slugs. *Monique's son's little homeboy*! I thought, instantly recognizing him as one of three kids who had been inside the car with Venique when he pulled up on me and my daughters in the Walmart parking lot.

"What's up, O.G.?" the husky kid behind the wheel nodded. Despite his size and numerous tattoos, I could tell that he wasn't no more than maybe nineteen or twenty.

"You following me, shorty?" I eyed him threateningly.

"What if I'm?" he questioned, rolling the window completely down to reveal the silver, rubber-grip, extended clip handgun lying across his lap.

I winced probably more out of shock than fear, and for a moment I didn't know how to take it. Was it a strong or subtle threat?

I didn't know if this kid was about to try and finish me or not. But, at that moment, the backseat window came down to reveal Venique's smiling face as he held up his phone, recording. "You should've seen the look on your face, O.G." Venique and his little homies laughed. "You didn't know what to do. I'ma post that shit on the gram."

I eyed Venique and his little baby-faced homeboy. They were really playing a dangerous game fucking with me. A game that I knew that they weren't ready for. I smiled to myself and thought: *These little kids better let sleeping dogs lie.* "I don't think you want to play me like a clown soldier," I warned.

"Ease up, O.G., it's all good!" the little dark-skinned, baby-faced driver smiled, showing his gold slugs again.

"Yeah, Unc, niggas ain't on nothing," Venique said. "I just pulled up on you to let you know that I looked into the situation with you and my father down the Cut and I still haven't been able to figure out if you were responsible or not."

"Why are you following me, soldier?" I questioned. All I could think about was Darrien and Ahmad being in the car.

"I just wanted you to know that I'm still in your rearview." Venique smiled. "I don't want you to get comfortable until I get to the bottom of the stuff with you and my father," Venique warned.

"Do you really know who and what your father was?"

"My father was a fucking gangsta!" Venique declared, making me laugh.

"Shorty your father was—" I caught myself before I went too far. I was about to bust Venique's bubble and tell him exactly who his father was. A fucking rat, coward and snake! A disgrace to the fucking game on all levels. But I humbled myself and remembered that I wasn't that guy anymore.

"—a cool guy," I continued after a long pause.

"If you know something I don't know, tell me."

"Just let me be, shorty," I pleaded, praying he wouldn't continue to poke the bear. "And don't follow me and my family again. Don't try to get my attention, nothing!

"There goes the old gangster my mother used to talk about." Venique smiled. "She said you used to really be something back in the day. You and my father. Said you were like my father's son. So, I guess we're brothers, huh?"

Venique joked and his little buddies laughed, but I didn't find it funny.

"Your mother forgot to tell you one thing though," I said.

"Oh yeah, and what's that?"

"That I ain't to be fucked with!" I declared menacingly.

"We'll see." Venique tapped the back of the driver's seat and told his man to pull off.

I stood there in the middle of the street, watching the J30 Infiniti until it disappeared. *HRDRD1B,* I locked the tag number in and prayed that there didn't come to time when I had to get back into the mud I'd worked so hard to climb up out of.

When I got to the house, Chanae was all over me. I peeped at Darrien and Ahmad disappointedly until she started asking me a thousand questions about some dude named DelmontX she'd discovered on YouTube. She wanted to know if I'd known or recognized him because he was a part of the Nation of Islam and had been housed at the North Branch Correctional Institution before. "Look at him!" Chanae ordered flashing me his photo. "He was down M-C-I-J when you were down there too," she explained.

"A'ight, that doesn't mean I know him," I said, eyeing the funny looking brother with the clean shave and bow-tie. "What is he talking about though?" I inquired for the sake of conversation, happy that Darrien and Ahmad hadn't said nothing about us being followed, because Chanae would've flipped.

"The same stuff you been saying for real. No nation can rise higher than its woman. You can tell a lot about a nation by the way it treats its women. When you want to tear a nation down, you tear down the woman. You know, all that stuff you be saying."

"Yeah, that's the teachings." I nodded but my mind was honestly somewhere else. "Where A'myiah at?"

"I don't know," Chanae admitted. "I think her and Sha'nyiah went to visit Omar, why?"

"Nah, I just wanted to know where she was, that's all," I replied truthfully, pulling out my phone. This little kid Venique had me leery. "Text and check on her anyways," I instructed, scrolling through my call-log until I located Frank's number.

I hit the call button and exited the room because I knew that only Frank could stop me from doing what I was thinking.

Chapter Thirty

Gangstacation

Captain Glover or rather Tiphani, as I now called her, surprised me with a trip to Hawaii. Let me tell you—I had a fucking ball. From the moment we left her fine mother and pretty little sister outside of her Virginia house, standing at the curve waving goodbye, to the time we landed at the Honolulu International Airport.

Tiphani's mother and little sister were both off the chain though. Her mother kept calling me a cutie pie and her little sister begged her not to put a hurting on me. But Tiphani knew better. She knew the young boy had major moves and serious staying power. You could always tell a tree by the fruit it bears. That's why I knew that Tiphani's mother was a peach tree because one of her daughters tasted like peaches and they were both just as thick.

Of course, I'd flown before, but never as a free man and never across seas. So, you know I went nuts, ordering all kinds of shit. I ran them stewardess crazy. Plus, I entered the Mile High Club. I even convinced Tiphani to place a blanket over her lap and allow me to eat that pussy while most of the passengers were asleep. We almost got caught twice by the air marshal. I suspected he knew there were bombs going off between Tiphani's legs by the way she was crying out for God.

When we stepped off the plane and exited the terminal, we were instantly greeted by four of the most beautiful, exotic looking women I'd ever seen in my life. Their skin was so fine and I could clearly see that they weren't wearing any make-up. They placed colorful Lei flowers around our necks as welcoming signs before kissing us each on both cheeks.

"Welcome to Oahu Island," one of women said before directing our attention to a cab. The scenery was so beautiful and amazing that I could've stood at the airport all day. The sun appeared to be closer, the waters seemed to be bluer and there appeared to be love in the air. I pulled Tiphani into a hug and kissed and thanked her for the trip. Then, I promised to eat that pussy out of the frame before the night was over.

"Why are you so nasty?" Tiphani giggled like a school girl and I loved it.

"Because you love it." I kissed her again.

We climbed into a taxi cab and Tiphani gave the driver directions to a place called *Sua's,* located in Waipahu City. All I kept thinking about was *Hawaii Five-O*—the cop show I used to watch in the joint with all the big Samoans and pretty women.

When we pulled up outside of *Sua's*—a nice bed and breakfast spot that appears to be sitting on water—two young boys ran up to the taxi cab and requested to take our luggage as we climbed out of the taxi.

I allowed them to help me remove our bags as Tiphani covered the cab fare.

"Welcome to *Sua's*," a big Samoan with two long ponytails hanging from opposite sides of his almost bald head approached with a gorgeous, supermodel looking woman and extended his hand. "I am Eddie and this beautiful woman here is my lovely wife Jackie." He gestured toward the beautiful island girl on his arm. "This is our place."

"Nice to meet you, bruh." I shook his hand as Tiphani accepted his wife's hand. "Dakaron," I said.

The cab driver hit his horn and slowly pulled off. "My brother Ryan," Eddie revealed, waving goodbye. "Right this way," he instructed before leading us inside behind the two little boys.

I sized Eddie up. I couldn't help myself; it was one of the fucked up things prison had done to me. Every stranger was a potential threat and every new location was a potential hazard. Eddie had some tribal shit tattooed on his large arms and muscular back. He reminded me a lot of Dwayne Johnson–*The Rock.*

I heard Eddie's wife Jackie asking Tiphani how long we planned to stay. Then, I seized the chance to checked the scene out for escape routes and all. Like I said, prison had fucked me up, but it also made me cautious. Tiphani kept telling me we weren't back in the States. But shiiiid, I'd rather be safe than sorry, especially with all the crazy shit going on throughout the world.

Once all the sleeping details were worked out and we were given our room location, it was time. I got Tiphani behind those closed doors and tried to knock the lining out of that pussy. I mean, I didn't know if it was the atmosphere or the little performance that she put on. But man, for some reason, I couldn't get enough of Tiphani and I chased her ass around the heart-shaped water-bed all night. I even finally convinced her to give me some of that phat ol' ass.

***

There was nothing like waking up to breakfast in head–I mean, bed. Tiphani definitely knew how to get a king up in the morning. I opened my eyes to find Tiphani paying homage to the throne.

"Now, that's how I like to start the day," I moaned, slowly running my fingers through Tiphani's hair as my head fell back into the pillow. "Damn, you give some of the best head."

It was something about that silent, slow neck that older woman gave that just always did it for me. I mean, don't get it twisted, I had a thing for that sloppy top too. But, when a woman knew how to make love to me with her mouth, it was awesome. I laid there and watched Tiphani go to work. It's almost as if it was just her and my dick. I'm talking about she never looked up. She just switched my dick from hand to hand, licking up one side and down the other, almost as if worshiping it and continued her silent but deadly attack.

After I nutted down Tiphani's throat, I was happy as hell. A good nut always gave me good vibes. On top of that, Eddie wasn't lying when he said that his wife could cook. Breakfast was very good. One thing that threw me off though, was the fact that the *Sua's* served everything with mayonnaise.

After jumping into the shower, Tiphani and I decided to hit the city and go sight-seeing.

Tiphani had me running around in an outfit reminiscent of Fred Flintstone. Hawaii was truly even more beautiful than any magazine or book could ever capture. The island was big too. We got to witness our first real volcano eruption. We went down to a white-sand beach and swam in water so blue that you could literally see the fish. Tiphani took all kinds of photos and posted them on Instagram and Facebook.

"I haven't seen an unattractive island girl yet!" Tiphani exclaimed out of the blue as we watched two belly-dancers moving seductively to the sound of drums.

"What made you say that?" I eyed Tiphani curiously. I mean, she knew that I wasn't tripping. She'd confessed to being a switch hitter and I was more than cool with that. Shiiid, I had a daughter, sister and a few of my nieces who went both ways. More importantly though, I love girls. All shapes, shades and sizes.

"Just thinking out loud," Tiphani confessed and I thought that was the end of it. But when we got back to our room at *Sua's*, the older of the two belly dancers was lying across the bed in nothing but waist-chains

"Go get her ready for me," Tiphani instructed, locking the bedroom door.

I started moving towards the bed, taking my clothes off without hesitation. *Man, I must be dreaming!* I thought as I stood over top of the belly dancer. Shorty looked like she'd fallen off the page of a *State Versus Us Magazine*. Like she could easily compete for America's Next Top Model.

"Oh, so that's what American beef looks like?" She gleaned up at me as my shorts hit the floor. "Please be gentle—I've never been with a black man before," she disclosed, carefully taking my dick into her hand.

"Don't worry, I got you, baby," I smiled, feeling like a king. Back in the States I was average.

I placed one of my feet up on the bed to give the belly dancer full access to my dick. I wanted some head from her pretty ass in the worst way. "Go ahead, suck that mother fucker," I encouraged.

She gently kissed the head of my dick and blushed. Then, she spat in the palm of her hand and began to long-stroke my dick with her soft hands. I looked over my shoulder and saw Tiphani getting undressed. Sex was always a game to her. A way to prolong her pleasure.

"If you call me Captain Glover, I'll make her deep-throat it." Tiphani walked up behind me and whispered into my ear before nibbling on my ear. "Welcome to Hershey Park, sexy," she added, snaking her arms around my waist until she could grab a hold of my dick. "That's it, sexy, be a good girl and take it a little deeper," she encouraged over my shoulder, holding the base of my dick with one hand while playing with my nuts with the other.

I was in heaven with a pretty ass, Hawaiian model between my legs, and a sexy ass, nasty dime over my back, kissing and rubbing all on my shoulders. I felt like I was in a *Blacked.com* video.

The belly dancer tried to take me down her throat deeper and started choking. She looked up at me before putting her head down in defeat and I swear to you, I almost nutted right then and there.

"Move over!" Tiphani directed, coming from behind my back to sit on the bed beside her. "I'ma show you how to drive the island boys crazy."

Tiphani's words made me want to wife her. There's was nothing in the world sexier than a pretty, intelligent, confident, nasty woman. Nothing!

"First, you gotta get it good and wet," Tiphani explained before giving her a live demonstration. My toes curled when Tiphani slowly inhaled me to the root.

'See how wet it is now?" Tiphani asked, coming up for the air, slowly stroking my dick. "Now you try," she encouraged before taking a moment to lick the pre-cum off the head. "I love the taste of his cum so much," she blushed, looking so fucking sexy.

The belly dancer innocently looked from Tiphani to me. "Go ahead, you aren't too good to eat after me, bitch." Tiphani's words appeared to spark a flame in the belly dancer because she started eating me up like she was hungry, trying to deep-throat.

"Take your time, sexy." Tiphani watched as the belly dancer tried to mimic her and ended up gagging a few times. "It's not going nowhere, is it, Daddy?"

"Nah, Captain Glover," I said, making Tiphani smile.

I stood there having the time of my life as Tiphani walked the belly-dancer through deep-throating. She never really quite got it to a T, but it felt good listening to Tiphani coach her about relaxing her throat.

"Breathe through your nose slowly. That's it, sexy. Now swallow." Tiphani had the belly dancer's long hair wrapped around her fist.

After I bust the first nut and watched the belly dancer give Tiphani a mouthful of cum, I was ready to fuck. I got Tiphani and shorty on the bed and went to work.

After a while, Tiphani and I began tag-teaming the belly dancer. I'm not even going to lie. We tore shorty's little pussy up. I loved watching Tiphani eat her pussy more than anything else though. It was such a turn-on. And Tiphani could eat some pussy too. She had shorty cumming like a river.

By the time we let the belly dancer go she was turned out, begging to spend the night. But Tiphani, I mean, Captain Glover wasn't having it. She wanted me all to herself.

"Stop by and see me tomorrow night and maybe I'll let you eat this pussy," Tiphani teased, slapping the Hawaiian beauty on her ass cheeks as she exited the room.

"Yes, mommy!" the belly-dancer agreed before disappearing.

"Now," Tiphani turned her attention back to me. I was laid back across the bed, propped up on some pillows, slowly jerking off. "I want you to fuck me good and deep."

Tiphani went in her luggage and began setting up the camera, and that was all I needed to see. As soon as she finished, I tossed her ass across the bed on her stomach, placed a large pillow underneath her hips, yanked her ass high up in the air, mashing her face into the bed and tried to murder that pussy up in there.

After handling her like a rag doll for a minute, I flipped Captain Glover over on her back, pinned her legs completely back until her toes were touching the mattress, then I went drilling for oil.

I fucked her good too. I knocked that pussy loose. Captain Tiphani Glover still had some of the tightest pussy I'd ever had.

I beat that pussy up! I thought to myself, smiling. *But man, she fucked the hell out of me*, was my last thought before my head touched the pillow and I went straight to sleep.

***

"Do you ever stop recording?" I inquired, honestly interested as Tiphani and I laid out on the beach.

"Hmm!" Tiphani continued to snap photographs of the beautiful skyline.

"Can you please put the phone down for a second and enjoy yourself?" I reached for Tiphani's iPhone. She'd been on that motherfucker, posting pics and comments since we'd arrived at the beach.

"I'm enjoying myself," Tiphani assured, pulling the iPhone out of my reach. "That's why I'm taking pictures and recording everything."

I just shook my head. There was no way in the world that she was enjoying herself with her face in the phone all day. It was crazy how nobody wanted to live in the moment anymore. Nobody wanted to take in the beauty. Everybody just wanted to post every minute of their lives. Don't misunderstand me. I knew that we lived in a world of technology. I personally used my phone to stay organized, informed and connected. But damn, some people spent their whole lives online, posting and commenting. Then they wondered why they couldn't find a good relationship. *Because your ass stays on social media all day!* I thought about all the women I knew who couldn't keep a man.

After sitting and watching Tiphani play on her iPhone for a while, I got an idea. "You say you can find anything on that thing?" I questioned.

"Yep," Tiphani replied without even looking up.

"What about people?" I asked, peeping over at the screen.

"Anything, anybody!" Tiphani declared, holding the iPhone screen up against her breast. "Stop being nosey. I'm telling my sister about you."

I instantly began to wonder if that was how Monique's son had kept rolling up on me. I mean, A'myiah and Darrien were always on them damn smartphones, playing on the internet too.

"Show me how to look somebody up," I requested, suddenly getting Tiphani's undivided attention.

"Well, it depends on what you want to know. I mean, there's Google for like federal information. Then, you have *Facebook, Instagram, Twitter* and *LinkedIn*. Some are more like personal stuff. You get to know who a person's dating and stuff," Tiphani explained, holding her phone up.

Sitting there listening to Tiphani made me realize that she could easily be a social media influencer. It also explained how phones had become so smart and people had become so dumb.

"Who are you trying to find anyway?" Tiphani gave me a curious look.

"My man, Big Al. I want to like *Instagram* and follow him on *Twitter*."

Laughing at me, Tiphani said. "You follow people on *Twitter* and like them on *Facebook*."

"You know what I mean."

"You are so stuck in time boy. But, I love it 'cause it's so sexy," Tiphani admitted. "What's your friend's real name?"

"Mmmm," I had to think back for a second. Dudes in the game didn't just throw names around. "Allen Griffin," I remembered the newspaper article.

Tiphani showed me everything there was to know about social media. We looked up everything Big Al had done in his life. She even showed me how to log into case-search and Maryland locator to find out how many cases a motherfucker had. By the time Tiphani finished giving me a step-by-step walk through the internet, I could've found D.B. Cooper, the infamous hijacker who'd jumped out of a commercial airline with a satchel full of cash, never to be seen again.

***

"As-salaam-alaikum, playboy! Welcome home." Frank was there to pick me up from BWI Airport as planned. "I hope you enjoyed yourself."

"Walaikum-assalam and you know I did," I replied, giving Frank some love. "Don't I look well rested?" I stepped back so that he could see the relaxed look on my face.

"You do," Frank admitted with a nod. "Where your girl Captain Glover at though?" Frank inquired, looking around for Tiphani.

"You know Glover shy and low-key around you."

"I don't know why," Frank said, taking the bag out of my hand.

"Cause she know you from over the jail."

"What? She think I'ma give her up or something?"

"Man, just come on, let's bounce."

I followed Frank to the ride and climbed into the passenger's seat as he tossed my bag in the trunk. "What's up though? I know Chanae been burning your phone up," I said, reaching for the MP3 Player when Frank got in the car. I'd stayed a few days longer than expected. But, I couldn't help it. Not after Tiphani brought another Hawaiian beauty in and we spent the next three days having threesomes.

"Yeah. But not for the reason you think." Frank looked over at me seriously. "We have a problem."

"What's up?" I just knew in my heart that Chanae had found out about Tiphani. *Fucking social media,* I thought.

"Monique's son found out the truth." Frank kept his eyes on me as I digested what he said.

"How?" was my next question.

"I don't know. I guess loyalty isn't only a thing of the past in the streets," Frank replied.

"Fuck!" I snapped, praying I wasn't about to have to kill this little kid Venique. "Why did Chanae call you though?"

"Look, don't pass out," Frank cautioned. "But a couple of Monique's son's little friends jumped on Darrien."

"He's fourteen, Cuz!" I spat, ready to strap up.

"He handled his business though. He definitely held his own." Frank smiled.

"How the hell you know that?" I look at Frank curiously.

"Chanae sent me the video that one of the little kids put online."

"Take me down there, Cuz," I demanded calmly, pulling my seatbelt across my chest.

"Come on, Cuz, you know I can't do that. Not while you're like this!" Frank replied and I just stared at him.

For a moment we sat there in total silence. Eyeing each other with different thoughts running through our minds. My mind was on murder and I'm sure Frank's was on staying out of prison.

"Cuz, we just got from beneath a life sentence. We know there are no winners in the street life." Frank broke the silence.

"I'm not trying to hear that shit, Cuz!" I retorted. "I got to protect my family."

"Protecting your family isn't always about taking a life, Cuz. Sometimes it's about giving yours."

Although I knew what Frank said was true, it was hard to agree. I mean, this was my son we were talking about. I'd walk through hell and hot water for Darrien. But if I murdered Monique's son, what about all the people who'd been there for me? *Shit!* I thought. I had to do something. I couldn't just let these kids attack my family and get away.

Still, Frank was right. If I was going to do something, I couldn't do it now. Not while my mind was in overdrive because I was only seeing red.

"You're right, Cuz, take me to Chanae's house so that I can find out exactly what's going on."

Chapter Thirty-One

Being Gangster's a Religion Too

After convincing Frank of the imminent threat Monique's son posed and getting him to understand my position, the first thing I did was look up my old gun connect—white boy Donny Hann from down South Baltimore up on social media. Once I realized that he'd either fell off the map or stopped posting on social media, I reached out behind the federal prison walls to my brother Antauwn's old partner—my man Anthony 'Buckey' Fields and lined some things up.

"I'm still trying to figure out who the hell white boy Donny is," Frank confessed suddenly as we sat on a park bench in Southeast DC, scrolling through photos on my phone, waiting for Buckey Fields' folks to show up.

"You still stuck on that, Cuz?" I questioned, while tripping off of Frank staring at Donny's Facebook profile.

"Man, I've been racking my brain trying to remember who yo is," Frank admitted. "I remembered Miss Sarah's daughter Doorean though. The little bad white girl you were on. I just don't remember yo." Frank continued to stare at Donny's photo.

"Hold, cuz," Frank reached for my wrist. "Who's that?" he inquired.

"You don't know who this is, Cuz?" I watched Frank shake his head.

"That's crazy." I really couldn't believe that Frank didn't recognize Venus.

"Show me another picture," Frank requested and I instantly swiped a few more photos by. "Oh, she Muslim too?"

"Yeah, but fuck all that. Who is it?" I asked again. "Who you used to want to fuck back in the day?"

"I don't know, Cuz." Frank gave up.

"Venus, Cuz! That's Venus!" I revealed.

"Hell no!" Frank snatched the phone out of my hand to get a better look. "Fuck no, Cuz, she done got badder." Frank looked at me as if I didn't know. "I mean she has always been right, but damn. Where these flicks come from?

"Instagram," I replied. "Tiphani showed me how to look people up."

"Damn," Frank drooled over Venus' picture. "I don't remember Venus being this phat. What? She got them butt shots?"

"Man, Venus has always been phat as a motherfucker," I smiled. "But fuck her," I took my phone back. "Check out Donny." I swiped back to Donny's picture. "You got to remember him. Especially after he was the one selling us all the guns when the stuff was going on with BulletEye-Ty and them. Yo was letting them burners go for dirt cheap."

I tried to think of something else, anything that may trigger Frank's memory of Donny. "What about white boy Sunny that used to sell all the weed out of Smitty's on the Boulevard? I know your big head ass remember slick ass Sunny?"

"Ain't no question," Frank smiled. "Slickest white boy. I ever met. Had the best trees in Pigtown too. That's the only son I remember Miss Sarah's having. Remember his sister Angel?"

"Of course, shorty was built like a brick house long before all of these other white girls started getting stacked off them butt shots!" I spat thinking back to how well put together as Angel was.

"Ayo, what's that gangster white bitch name who used to be with Angel all the time?" Frank inquired.

I thought for a second. He couldn't be talking about Becky; she was too young. "You're not talking about the dude Pie's baby mother Carrie, are you?"

"I said *gangster*, Cuz."

"What she look like?" I was trying to figure out who Frank was referring to.

"Man, I don't know, like Sharon Stone or something. Pretty white girl, dirty blond hair. She used to always come though and fuck with us. They said she was robbing shit back in the day."

I smiled when it hit me. Frank was talking about my baby. The thoughtless white bitch I knew handed me down. "Oh, you're talking about Mary, Cuz!" I declared.

"Absolutely," Frank confirmed. "White girl Mary. I fucked with shorty. No matter what she had done, her 'g' was always intact."

"True, true," I nodded in agreement. White girl Mary was definitely a gangster. "How you remember everybody accept Donny though?"

"I don't know, Cuz, I just can't remember yo," Frank replied as something seemed to suddenly capture his attention.

I looked in the direction where Frank's eyes were locked and instantly froze, there were two guys approaching quickly with what appeared to be AR-16's in their hands. My mind kept saying *run*! But for some reason I never moved.

"Where are y'all from, moe?" the first DC gunman asked, holding the machine gun at the ready.

I looked around again and tried to find my words. There was literally nowhere to run but open field.

"B-More," Frank said. "We're from B-More."

Shit! I thought. I'd left the Maryland Terrapins hat in the car.

"We're Terps fans!" I exclaimed suddenly, praying to Allah that these were Buckey Fields' peoples.

"Mannn, slim!" the first DC dude exhaled, lowering his gun with a smile. "Y'all my cousin Buck peoples from Baltimore?"

"Yeah," I nodded, breathing a sigh of relief.

"What happened to the Maryland Terps hat?" The second DC gunman inquired.

"My bad, I was slipping. I left it in the car," I admitted feeling like an idiot.

"Y'all lucky, moe, we almost gave y'all the business." The second DC gunman finally lowered his machine gun. "I'm just glad we could tell that y'all were not from around here. Otherwise, niggas would've squeezed first and asked questions last."

"Al-hamdulillah!" Frank professed.

"I'm Dakaron and this is my right-hand man, Frank." I extended my hand to the first gunman.

"Ain't no need for names, slim." He accepted my hand and shook it.

"Let's just take care of the business and get y'all out of here because there's a lot going on around here."

Buckey Fields' cousin took us to a spot located near Berry Farms and laid out some major weaponry. "This on the strength of fam," Buckey Fields' cousin explained, offering me anything I wanted.

I can't lie—I was tempted to snatch up a few joints. You know, the old me wanted to show them young boys his teeth, but the new me prevailed. Besides, as Frank explained, I wasn't getting war ready. I was just being prepared.

"Are you sure that's all you want?" Buckey Fields' cousin asked when I picked up the twin .357 Bulldogs and stuffed them into my carrying bag. "Like I said, any friend of family is a friend of mine."

I eyed all the artillery lying across the table eagerly. I'm sure Buckey Fields' cousins could see the hunger in my eyes.

Especially when he said that whatever I got was on the house anyway.

"Fam already footed the bill," he revealed. "Them young boys aren't playing fair. They got some serious heat nowadays!" he added and I knew that he was right. Every day somebody was getting worn out in the city with something big.

Still, I didn't need nothing with sticks, legs and drums hanging from it. I was old-school. So, when the beef was on, I didn't do any shooting from up the block or pull no drive-bys. I walked my man down, got right up on him, up close and personal like a true gangster and closed his casket.

"Thanks, but I'm good with these," I assured, holding the bag up. I just need something to get the job done."

"A'ight, slim, I'll tell my cousin you stopped by," he said, moving towards the table.

"Hold up." Frank stepped forward before Buckey Fields' cousin could fling the blanket back over the table to cover the weapons. "I think I do want something just in case," Frank confessed, making me look at him. "I mean you never know."

"My sentiments exactly," Buckey Fields' cousin smiled.

"I know exactly what I want too," Frank grinned, reaching across the table.

After Frank picked out his weapon of choice, Buckey Fields' cousin escorted us back to the city lines and just as quickly as it had begun, it was over. Within twenty minutes, Frank and I were back on the highway heading home.

***

"A'ight, so let me make sure I got it right." I paused to look at my daughter. Frank and I had been sitting at the computer with her, 'trolling' social media as she called it, viewing photographs of the main Young Crudy Buddies kids.

"Dhakiy?" I pointed at the slim, light-skinned kid on the computer screen with the gangstas in his head and A'myiah nodded. "Baby Dana?" I continued pointing at the next kid.

"Okay." A'myiah smiled, impressed. "Keep going."

"We both know that's Lor'Chuck," Frank interjected, touching the screen. "Shorty looks just like his father."

"You gotta see his mother—Miss Tiffany. Everybody say she spit Lor'Chuck out."

"Nah, shorty a spitting image of his father, ain't he, Cuz?"

"Hold up," I held my finger up because I didn't want to get sidetracked. I locked on the big youngen who'd followed me in the J30. I couldn't recall his name though.

"Damn what's shorty's name?" I snapped.

"Chimel, Chi for short," A'myiah disclosed.

"Right," I nodded, disappointed in myself. "He's the one from Harford Road, right?"

"Yep," A'myiah confirmed.

"Yeah, he's one of the Witherspoons," I stared at the dark-skinned, baby-faced, big youngen. It was hard to believe that he was only a teenager. I mean, just looking at him on the screen, I could tell that he was every bit of six feet, two-hundred-twenty pounds solid. *He's definitely getting that bulldog if something jumps off,* I thought to myself. Not only had he acted like he really wanted some smoke, but I knew that he came from a long line of wig-splitters.

"Which one recorded the fight?" Frank inquired.

"I'm not sure," A'myiah admitted.

"Probably this little bastard right here," Frank singled Dhakiy out.

"It wasn't Dhakiy," A'myiah retorted. "He don't be with that dumb stuff."

"Shiiid, he was the main one cracking jokes when they all pulled up on me the last time," I explained.

"He was probably just playing," A'myiah rationalized. "It be Chi and Lor'Chuck always wanting some smoke."

"If you say so," I dropped the issue, but I knew a gangster when I encountered one.

"Please don't do nothing to Dhakiy," A'myiah pleaded. "Sha'nyiah will have a fit."

"Hopefully, he don't have to do nothing to none of them." Frank took the words right out of my mouth.

"Listen, baby, I'm for peace first," I declared sincerely. "But at the same time, I'm not going to allow nobody to put my family in harm's way."

"I just know this isn't going to end good." A'myiah shook her head.

"Everything is going to be alright, trust me," I assured. But to be honest, I wasn't sure if I believed that myself. Especially when it came to dealing with these little senseless kids. In truth, I just wanted to talk to Venique and bring order to this little situation before it really got out of hand and somebody got hurt.

"Still, for the time being y'all stay away from down South Baltimore for a while," I instructed. "At least until all this stuff with your brother blows over."

"So how do you want to play this?" Frank looked at me after A'myiah stormed out of the room with a little attitude.

I stared at Frank. I honestly didn't have a plan yet. The only thing I know for sure was that Darrien wanted to see all of Venique's little homeboys one on one. "First, we seek peace," I replied.

"And if peace can't be had?"

"Then we bring harm."

Chapter Thirty-Two

Gangsterfied

Frank and I decided to meet Venique and his squad at the Baltimore Arena for a few reasons. The main one being security. Being that there was a Meek Mills concert and I knew that members of the Nation of Islam were on his security detail. I knew that the chances of Venique and his team getting something past them FOI's were slim to none.

"We still got over an hour, Cuz, why are you rushing?" I questioned as Frank sped down Howard Street. "We're not hooking up until eight-thirty."

"Yeah, well, I want to get there by seven," Frank retorted. "That way we can watch them like niggas coming in to see if they're up to something."

Downtown was packed. There were people everywhere trying to get a glimpse of Meek Mills. Personally, I didn't fuck with him. Especially, not after I'd heard his Breakfast Club interviews with Angie Martinez and *Charlamagne tha God.*

"I can't believe the city is coming out to support this dude," I confessed.

"Who? Meek Mills?" Frank questioned like he was surprised.

"Yeah."

"Shiid, I don't know why not. Niggas love Meek Mills in the city. You know he be riding with Chino and them." Frank explained. "Plus, he was supposed to be working on a movie called '*Charm City Kings*'. The movie is based on a documentary titled *12 O'Clock Boys*."

"I don't care what the dude is working on, he shouldn't have ever said that sucker shit out of his mouth. The crazy part is, there's this crazy ass C.O. down MCIJ who looked just like that sucker. Dudes even call him *Meek Mills*."

"I ain't a fan either. But I fuck with anybody who's putting on for the city."

"I know them boys who been twelve o'clocking. Lil' Ache and them wrote a song about that shit called 'One Wheel In The Air'."

"You're not telling me nothing I don't know, Cuz," Frank argued. "You know I been about that bike life."

"Oh yeah, your cousins did used to ride them bikes," I spat, remembering who Frank used to always go out Westport to ride dirt bikes with—his cousins.

For the next fifteen minutes, Frank and I tripped about the good old days when shit was so simple.

We were still arguing about who was the true wheelie king–Lil Net or Chino—when I pulled into the Baltimore arena's underground parking garage off Lombard Street and parked.

***

One night I prayed to God / I asked could he please remove the enemies from my life / And before I know it, I started losing friends—

The lights died down for a moment and the crowd went nuts as Meek Mills took the stage. I couldn't even lie, in prison, before I'd stopped fucking with Meek Mills. 'Friends' was one of my favorite classics because it spoke directly to all the so-called friends who'd ever left me for dead, counted me out or crossed me.

When Venique and his little goons finally found their seats, we'd been watching them float around the arena mob deep for the good part of thirty minutes.

"Let's go get something to eat," Frank suggested before anybody got too comfortable. "This isn't the place to discuss business."

Venique didn't say anything; he just gestured with his hand and his whole team moved out. *Power*, I thought, realizing that Venique really had the juice. I sized Young Dhakiy, Baby Dana and Lor'Chuck up too. There was no sign of Chimel. Which made me think Venique maybe up to no good. Especially since I'd clocked Chimel when Venique and them first arrived.

"Be on point, Cuz, the little kid Chimel lurking," I whispered just loud enough for Frank to hear me as we made our way towards the concession area.

"I'm hip," Frank assured nonchalantly.

When we got to the concession stand of Frank's choice, I realized why he chose the concession stand. Standing behind the counter, looking finer than ever, was the one and only Meek that I was a fan of. "How may I help you gentlemen today?" Frank's sister asked, looking as if she didn't know us.

"Let me see," Frank paused over the handwritten menu, "Yeah, umm, let me get the 'Evon' Special," Frank requested.

"Your luck, sir, I think there's one left," Meek smiled.

"What you want, Cuz?" Frank turned to me.

I looked up at the handwritten menu to see if there was a 'Linda' special or something but saw nothing. "Just give me a bag of plain chips."

After receiving our orders, Frank and I stood off to the side and let Venique and his posse order their food and drinks. Then, we all walked over to the landing, near the stand-up tables to discuss the reason why we were all there.

"Let's get to it," Frank broke the silence.

"The first thing we need to discuss is my son. You was out of order for sending your little puppies after my son. That—"

"Nah," Venique cut me off. "The first thing we need to talk about is you killing my father after he wasn't nothing but a friend to you, nigga!"

Okay, I thought. *That's what you want, shorty? That's what you're going to get.* "Your father wasn't a friend to anybody but himself!" I snapped. It was time to take the gloves off and expose Monique for the bitch that he was. "That's why he became a rat!"

"What?" Venique stepped into my personal space.

"Yeah!" I stood my ground. "Your father, Sebastian Monique, was a bonafide rat! Ask your mother about that. Tell her to tell you about how that coward sent me to prison for life. Or about how he was an FBI informant, since you wanna keep running around acting like your father was this gangster. So yeah, I clipped your father's nuts because he didn't deserve them. He violated everything we stood for, everything that he ever taught me."

Venique seemed to be at loss for words. He glanced around at his crew. He knew that he couldn't call himself a gangster and ride about no rat. "I ain't never heard no shit like that!" Venique challenged.

"Call your mother," I directed "Get her on the phone, she knows what's up. Venus testified on my behalf at trial."

Venique kept his eyes on me and pulled out his phone. "Why the fuck would my mother help you, nigga? She can't stand your ass."

I thought about telling him about his mother and I, but I decided to keep that to myself. No kid wanted to know the true history of their mother.

I could tell when Venus answered because Venique immediately started firing off questions. He wanted to know about Monique's 'G' status. Then, he asked about her involvement in my case.

It was obvious from the look on Venique's face that Venus was confirming everything I said. A few of Venique's homeboys started mumbling about 'not riding for no rat. Venique ended the call and stared at me for a while.

I stood there holding my breath, hoping and praying that I'd not have to kill this kid like his rat ass father. It would just be another life that snitching had ruined.

"My bad, O.G.," Venique humbled himself and I exhaled. "I didn't know that my punk ass father was a rat. Had I known that I'd have never pulled up on you like that."

I couldn't do nothing but respect where Venique was coming from. It took a real man to admit his mistakes. But still, lines had been crossed and blood had been drawn and there wasn't no coming back from that. "Enough said, but what about your little homeboys jumping on my son? How are we going to handle that?"

"I don't know, you tell me." Venique paused to take the straw out of his soda and put it into his mouth. "One thing that's not happening though. Niggas not doing nothing to my homies, that's for sure!" he added before taking a sip of soda.

I eyed Venique. The man I was today respected his stance. Loyalty was rare nowadays. However, the old, curious part of me wanted to put him to the test. Wanted to see if he could go the distance. You see, I knew that war wasn't about who was the most dangerous or had the numbers. It was simply about who was willing to go the farthest. Nothing more, nothing less.

"What about if we go to the gym?" Frank spoke up, knowing my plan.

"What do you mean, go to the gym?" Venique inquired as both he and I turned to Frank.

"Meaning we all meet up at the Uptown Boxing Gym on Pennsylvania Avenue and let Darrien and them go for what they know," Frank explained.

"I like that," I agreed, nodding. "That way Darrien gets to see whoever he wants to head-up with the gloves on and nobody has to die."

"What do you think, homie? You feel like representing on that lor'nigga?" Venique referred to Baby Dana.

"You already fucking know!" Baby Dana retorted excitedly. "Shorty a fucking spade," he added. "I'll trash his lor ass."

"Then, it's settled, "I said. "The next time we meet up, it will be at the gym."

"Just let me know when and we're there," Venique assured with a smile.

I knew that Venique and them were probably thinking that Darrien was sweet. But, they were all in for a rude awakening. Because I'd been schooling Darrien, teaching him some old-school combinations that would surely put the average joker on his back pockets. "I will do."

Chapter Thirty-Three

Gangster Triumph

Over the next few months, things began to settle down. Of course, this was after Darrien got up in that boxing ring and shined brighter than Lil' Tank on an HBO special. I wasn't sure where Chanae and I would end up, but Tiphani had convinced me to take the ride. "I know Chanae hurt you, Dakaron. And despite how hard you try to convince yourself that it doesn't matter, I know that it does, so, that's something that you have to deal with," Tiphani had explained. "I care deeply for you, Dakaron, I really do. But your heart is with Chanae. And until you deal with that, you can't move on." Those were the last words Tiphani said to me.

Chanae and I still had not moved in together though. I just wasn't be ready to take that step yet.

The first thing I made Chanae do was hit the gym with me. For one, I wanted to punish her. I wanted to put her through the ringer and make her jump through hoops. Like I said, Chanae never really had to give up nothing while I was in prison. She didn't even have to pay for a phone call. To be honest, I didn't think there was a woman on the East Coast dealing with a guy in prison who'd had it easier than Chanae, not one.

The other reason why I ran Chanae through the gym was because she'd picked up some weight over the years, and not just in the areas I liked. Now don't get me wrong, I have no problem with big women. Y'all know that some of the baddest women I'd ever fucked with or went for were thick– Lakeria, Officer Turner, Paula Coleman, Angela Thompson, even Detective Stanback. But, the way I fell for you, was the way I wanted to you to stay.

Meaning, if you were thick when I got a hold of you, I didn't need you getting skinny all of sudden, looking like a crackhead. The same thing went for if you are small, you shouldn't get all big. I was attracted to you as a whole–mind, body and beauty. I didn't need you to taking away pieces after we got together. It's a package deal! Call it what you want, I don't care. The woman I fall for is the woman I want. What the hell do you think still made Sweet Pea so damn attractive? Trust me, it wasn't just our friendship.

I'd finally gotten my online business off the ground, thanks to Margaret and the connects I got from the ERW class. I also moved into my own place. My apartment was small, but it was mine. I let Delmonte and A'myiah help me decorate the palace. We each took our own room. By the time we finished, the apartment looked like a bowl of *Froot Loops* with all the different colors. But they liked it, so I pretended to love it.

One of the first things I had to do though, was stop my niece from bringing her fast ass little friends past my apartment dressed in damn near nothing. The clothes the young girls were wearing nowadays were enough to drive an old man insane. And them little girls were built too. Sometimes I couldn't tell the difference. I mean, twice I'd gotten my niece's little friends mixed up with their mothers. But, I had serious discipline. Especially after the last incident. So, as soon as I realized my mistake, I tightened straight up. Still, I knew the best defense was no defense. So I just stopped them from coming to my spot all together.

"As-salaam-alaikum," I hit the speaker button on my cellphone and tossed it on the bed so that I could continue to lace up my Rockports.

"Walaikum asalaam, Cuz, what's up?" Frank's voice echoed throughout the bedroom.

"Ain't too much, about to go across town to see my cousin Lil Phil," I continued tying my boots up as I spoke with Frank and thought about how my cousin Little Phil had just given his time back and come home.

"What? You ain't been watching the news, Cuz? They're saying that COVID Nineteen thing is real."

"Yeah, well, life in prison was real too. And I survived that," I joked.

"See, you joking and shit," Frank said seriously. "My sister got that shit!"

"Cuz, I'm in the Nation of Islam," I reminded him. "I already know how the government plays it. That shit man-made," I declared sincerely. I'd been reading about exactly what was now happening for years. "I don't trust anything they say."

"So, what about this shit people are talking about? You taking that?"

"Hell no!" I retorted. "If history had taught me anything, it's to not accept help from the motherfucker who caused the problem in the first place."

"The Nation of Islam got you brainwashed, Cuz!" Frank exclaimed.

"Yeah, whatever, don't take that shit, Cuz, I'm warning you!" I cautioned.

"I don't fear anything but Allah, Cuz!" Frank snapped.

"Yeah, me too, that's why I'm not taking nothing, no shot, no pills, nothing!" I assured. I'd learned a long time ago how to eat to live and I took pretty good care of myself. "All I need is water, vitamins, oranges and exercise. Allah placed all of that in the earth."

Me and Frank continued to go back and forth about the so-called pandemic and who was actually responsible for it. Frank quoted a few doctors and White House recommendations. And I countered with a few scientific facts.

In the end, we got nowhere. Frank called me crazy and I still went to see my cousin Lil' Phil.

***

The next morning, I felt like shit, my head was hurting and I felt drained. Chanae wanted me to stay in bed until she got there but that wasn't my style. When something attacked me, I attacked back. So a cold was no difference. Plus I was used to fending for myself anyway.

I rolled out of bed, got my ass up bundled up and went out for an early morning jog.

I pushed myself to the limit and beyond. I drank a bunch of orange juice and got my squat thrusts in. Then I went six rounds on the punching box I had hanging up in my back room. I beat the bag like it owed me something. I wasn't laying down. Never had, never would.

By the time Chanae arrived, I was already sitting at the kitchen table, sipping hot chocolate, feeling better.

"You might be running a fever," Chanae suggested, lightly touching my forehead. "You feel warm."

"Now you sound like Frank," I said, removing her hand from my head.

"I'm good. Every time I got sick in the joint, I went straight at it, got the workout in and knocked it out."

"Yeah, well, maybe if you had listened to Frank and not taken your ass over to your cousin's house, you wouldn't have gotten sick!" Chanae fired.

"Sure you're right," I joked. "Listen, *COVID Nineteen* can't stop a black man with knowledge of himself and his enemy. Believe that!" I stated confidently.

Chapter Thirty-Four

Gangster Pandemic

Over the next year things went from bad to worse with the COVID-19 pandemic. I mean, people were dying left and right and I don't think no family went untouched. Antauwn and his entire family got hit hard, my sister Sarina got it hard. I even ended up with it myself

Still, I refused to take the vaccination. I mean, to each their own. If you wanted to take it, that was your business and if I don't that should be mine but that wasn't the case. Motherfuckers were attacking people for not wearing masks and refusing to take the shots. The whole world seemed to be divided behind that shit.

Crime spiked like crazy too. Especially in Baltimore, it was like once the government started laying people off, they started doing all kinds of shit to put food on the table. One of the things that tripped me out the most and showed me just how steeped in gross darkness and dead our children were, was the fact that they allowed—encouraged—people to wear a mask and they were still running around committing crimes without covering their faces.

The pandemic set a lot of things I had planned back. For starters, I had to fold my on-line business and give up my apartment. So, I finally moved in with Chanae and it wasn't so bad after all, despite the fact that we basically had to stay in the house together all day, every day.

Before long, I fucked around and knocked Chanae up. Yeah, she caught me slipping. Y'all know I could never handle it when she climbed on top of the dick and rode me to sleep. But, I wasn't mad, Chanae was still my heart.

Of course, Detauwn and Sweet Pea wasn't feeling me. But I always believed that sometimes people looked at the exact same picture and saw something totally different. Either way, I wasn't paying either one of them any mind. Besides, Sweet Pea had disregarded my feelings and opinion and let some lame put a ring on her finger.

I was happy with Chanae, and One Love was happy for me; that was all that mattered. I started writing a book called 'From the Making of a Monster to the Arrival of a Man'. It was based on my life and transition. I want everybody to know the truth about the game and how fake it was. Schooling Darrien and Ahmad was no longer enough. I wanted and needed the entire streets to know that the game that they love so much was nothing more than an illusion.

A trick to draw you into a way of life that was designed to kill you and your own people in one sense or another. I opened the book up with some words from the honorable Minister Louis Farrakhan that said, "Don't bother with black people if you don't have it in your heart to lay down your life for their freedom" and from there I got busy. I knew I could do it. It was just a matter of staying focused.

Chapter Thirty-Five

Gangsterproof

"Ma, I never got to choose what I wanted to eat," I declared, pulling up in front of my mother's house. We were just returning from grocery shopping for our coming 115th Family Reunion. "You barely even let me pick out my own clothes, then you can't choose where you sleep, what you eat or the type of clothes you wear. It's not like that no more, Ma. These women out here today allow these children to be grown. Remember how we used to have to call everybody mister or misses, say yes sir, no ma'am?" I questioned and my mother nodded. "It's not like that no more."

"That's 'cause you got babies raising babies, Dakaron, and everybody is so concerned with trying to be their child's friend instead of their parents!" One Love fired, always ready to give her opinion. "What they need is a good butt whipping. I'll tear their behinds up!"

"Ma, you can't beat these kids today. They'll call the police. Nowadays discipline is looked at as child abuse."

"And that's exactly why the kids running around acting crazy, taking all kind of drugs, blasting that damn music with their pants hanging all off of their backsides.'"

I'd been venting about Chanae and the way she allowed the kids to do whatever they wanted all week. They did what they wanted, got out of bed when they felt like it. To be honest, I don't know what to do. I asked Chanae several times to step back and let me handle the kids my way. But, she wouldn't do it. She wanted to keep babying them and that was causing friction between the two of us.

"That's why I told you to send the kids over here with me," One Love said as I climbed out of the car to come around to her side to open the door. "I'll get them back in line and I ain't worried about no police; they got to be able to make it to the phone."

"What you used to say, Ma? 'Straighten up or ship out'," I joked, holding the passenger side door open for her.

"Yep, you want to be grown, you can do it on your own." My mother accepted my hand as I helped her out of the car. "Thank you, sugar."

I escorted my mother into the house and came back out to start gathering the bags. That was when I realized my mistake. I'd violated the first law of the streets. *Never sleep!*

When I'd first pulled up with One Love and saw the joker posted up across the street from One Love's house, masked up, in all black, I should've known something was off. But, I never second guessed it. Why would I? Everybody in the world was running around wearing masks and the whole city wore black joggers.

Still, the full-face mask should've registered, but it hadn't and now as the shooter closed the gap between us, I knew that I was about to pay for my mistake with my life.

When the shooter brought the pistol up, I just froze up, dropped the bag of groceries, closed my eyes and braced for impact. But nothing happened. No shot went off, nothing.

"Nah, O.G.," the shooter mumbled. "Open your eyes and take it like a man."

I heard the shooter taunt and slowly cracked my eyes to see the barrel of something with a long ass clip and a slightly hidden smile behind the mask.

"Yeah, there you go, nigga," the shooter encouraged. "Hold your head up high, so I can give you this welcome home present."

My life instantly flashed before my eyes. I thought about all the things I'd still never gotten to do—like take Hajj, all the things I'd never get to say—like *Will you marry me?*

I felt the shooter press the business end of the gun to my dome and I prayed to Allah not to suffer. I'd suffered for almost twenty years in prison and just wanted it to be over with quickly.

Then, the shooter made his first mistake. Instead of just pulling the trigger and putting one in my head, he told me to get on my knees. Said he wanted me to beg for my life like some coward. His next and final mistake was stepping closer to me than he had to as I slowly followed his instructions.

"As a matter of fact, lay your bitch ass on your stomach, nigga!" He barked and I felt him jog the gun to my head and knew that it was now or never.

The instant my second knee brushed the ground, I drew back and punched him in the nuts with so much power that I was surprised he held onto the gun.

"Ahhhhh!" He cried out in pain and doubled over.

At that moment, I took off running down the street. I got about fifteen feet when the first shot rang out and breezed by my head. The second shot rang out about two seconds later and then the shooter started letting that motherfucker go.

I dipped in between two cars, cut out into oncoming traffic and got hit. I flipped over the hood of a Nissan and rolled out into the other lane of oncoming traffic. Somehow, though, I managed to get up and keep running. It had to be my adrenaline because I'd never even let the shooter get up on me.

All I kept thinking as I turned the corner and fled the scene was my mother. I mean, I was praying that she wouldn't come back outside to check on me. Because if anything happened to my mother, I'm talking about if a bullet had even grazed her house, it was doomsday for everybody.

I ran into the first store I saw and begged the young, light-skinned kid behind the counter to let me use his phone because mine was still sitting on the charger in my car.

The first person I called was my mother. Of course, I told her that somebody tried to rob me and I ran. Then, I made sure she was okay and hung up to call Frank.

"Hello," Frank answered on the third ring. "Who is this?"

"It's me, Cuz. I need you to come and scoop me now!"

"Calm down and tell me what's going on, Cuz." Frank must've heard the panic in my voice.

"Somebody just tried to kill me!" I exploded.

"What? Where?"

"In front of One Love's house!" I replied.

"One Love good?" I could hear the concern in Frank's voice.

"Yeah, a little shaken, but she's straight. I just got off the phone with her."

"Where are you now?"

I looked around the store for a name. "I don't know, just know it's about a quarter mile away from One Love's crib!" I said, covering the phone with my hand. "What's the name of this spot?" I asked the kid behind the counter.

"Pumpkins!" he replied.

"Where y'all located at?"

"Tenth Street," he uttered.

"I'm on Tenth Street, Cuz, at a spot called Pumpkins!" I revealed.

"That's the little orange store across the street from Bristol Place Apartments," Frank declared confidently. "I know exactly where you are. Don't move! I'm on my way." Frank's line went dead.

＊＊

"Come on, Cuz, you're just being paranoid now. How the hell you know it was Venique and them?" Frank questioned as we drove around Brooklyn looking for any tell-tale signs that might reveal who'd just tried to ice me out. "That shit was over a year ago."

"I'm not stupid Cuz, I saw the little kid gold slugs through the mask!" I assured, knowing exactly what I saw. "It was that little motherfucker Chimel or whatever his name is. The big, young one who related to the Witherspoons. His little ass smiled at me, Cuz, and I spotted the 'fear no evil' tattoo on the left side of his neck when I hit him in his nuts and he folded up."

Frank didn't respond. He just continued to drive around South Baltimore checking out all the hangout spots he'd known about from traveling back and forth to his uncle's house back in the day. After we left Brooklyn, Frank rolled through Cherry Hill and Westport. "You're looking for a fucking ghost, Cuz," I explained because I knew that Venique and his little band of buddies were behind the botched hit. "I already know exactly who did it."

"All I'm saying is we need some proof, Cuz," Frank rationalized.

"Nah, Cuz, *you* need some proof," I corrected. "I got all the proof I need."

"I'ma double back just in case," Frank mumbled, but honestly, I wasn't paying him no attention. My mind was already made up and I was going to smash Chimel's young ass as soon as I caught up to him and I didn't care what Frank had to say about it.

I was done with all the Mister Nice Guy shit; it was over. There was no more trying to be a better man. No more trying to keep the peace. These little bastards had taken a shot at me and missed. So, I had to make them pay for that. If only for no other reason than trying that shit outside of my mother's door.

"The shooter's long gone, Cuz, trust me. These kids are smarter than we have been giving them credit for!" I admitted even to myself, looking over at Frank. "To wait a year before they strike, that's serious. I can't do nothin' but respect that. I'm still respond though."

"Cuz, I'm not trying to fuck around and end up back in prison messing with these little kids out here," Frank confessed.

"Man, I ain't trying to go back to prison for messing with these kids either, but they came for my head, Cuz. What the fuck you want me to do?" I exclaimed.

"Fuck!" Frank pounded the steering wheel staring into space. "Let's ride through Pigtown."

"Nah, ride through up top," I instructed. "Ride right to the Carroll Street playground where they be at."

"Cuz, you know them little kids be out on that playground strapped up?" Frank cautioned.

"We're not going around there to beef, Cuz," I assured. "I just want to see who's out there and who's not."

Frank took a deep breath and shook his head because he knew that I was about to pull him back into the mud.

When we got up top, on the same strip that Dana, BulletEye-Ty and them used to control, Venique was sitting on one of the swings with a pretty, little, young girl on his lap not too far from his Lexus.

"What's up, O.G." Venique tapped the young girl on her thigh, signaling for her to get up as I climbed out of Frank's car.

"To what do I owe the pleasure?" Venique questioned as I approached.

I stared at Venique for a moment as his little soldiers began to surround him like a boss. I smiled; he was just as arrogant his father. "I came to do you a solid, soldier." I smiled.

'Oh yeah, is that right?" Venique's response seemed to amuse his little homeboys. "And what would that be?"

"I wanted to let you know that one of your puppies got off the leash and tried to bite me," I explained.

"This something you think? Or do you have some kind of evidence?" Venique took a quick glance at his crew.

"Does it really matter?" I inquired, feeling the tension rise.

"Not really," Venique and I locked eyes.

"You know back in the day, when a puppy ventures out on his own, we'd allow them to fend for themselves."

"Yeah, well, this isn't back in the day, O.G., we play by a different set of rules!" Venique retorted. "You come for one of us, every last one of us are coming for you. You see, we don't have any bosses. We don't answer to nobody."

"Maybe that's the problem," I said.

"Maybe not," Venique countered.

"I guess you didn't learn nothing from this situation with me and your father, huh?"

"Are you threatening me, O.G?" Venique got to his feet as his little crew advanced.

"Of course not," I put my hands up in surrender. "I'm just offering you a cautionary tale. Trying to see that history doesn't repeat itself."

"Mannn, Vee, let me spank this old, washed up ass nigga right here?" one of Venique's little, itchy, trigger-finger homeboys requested with hunger in his eyes.

"Nah, Dummy, chill." Venique waved him off before glaring at me patiently. The way a spider patiently glares at an insect after it had been trapped in its web. "See, O.G. I did you a solid." Venique smiled.

"You know, there a proverb in the Bible that says 'the one who walked with the wise will become wise. But, the one who had dealings with the stupid will fare badly," I quoted from *Proverbs* thirteen.

"Yeah, there's also something in the Bible about a time for everything, right? Like a time to leave and a time to stay. A time to talk and a time to get in your car and drive away!" Venique taunted.

"I hear you, soldier." I nodded and began backing up towards the car. There was nothing else to be said. The next time I cross paths with Chimel or Venique's little bodyguard, I was putting their little dicks in the dirt.

"One more thing for the record, O.G.!" Venique yelled out as I opened the car door. "I don't surround myself with puppies, I surround myself with wolves," he continued as I slid back into the car.

"Driving through just wasn't enough, huh?" Frank snapped the instant I was back the car.

"I just wanted him to know that I knew that they'd tried and missed."

"Why? For what? When the hell we start doing that?" Frank questioned my action before starting the car and pulling off.

I honestly didn't have an answer. "Did you notice who wasn't there?" was the only thing I could think to say.

"Of course, Chimel," Frank replied.

"Exactly," I agreed. "That's proof enough for you now?"

"What if I said it wasn't?" Frank questioned. "I mean, I didn't see the little kid Dhakiy either."

"I'ma still kill him, Cuz. I know what I saw."

"Just make sure you get that shit right."

"Don't I always?" I joked, but for whatever reason Frank never laughed.

Chapter Thirty-Six

A Gangster's Word Is Gold

The first thing I did before laying my first wolf-trap, was set up the perfect, airtight alibi. In prison, watching *'First 48'* and *'Law &Order: Criminal Intent'* had really showed me how powerful the alibi defense was in the courtroom. A good alibi could beat the case before it even began.

Shiiid, I knew some guilty dudes who are now walking the streets as millionaires, because of a solid alibi to put them somewhere else when the crime occurred and got them paid.

I gave A'myiah my phone and told her to take Darrien and Ahmad out to the movies and get something to eat. I also told her to be sure to order food and buy an extra movie ticket to make it look good. That is my little partner in crime. Plus, I had her to text Delmonte like she was me.

Getting the drop on Venique's little homeboy Chimel wasn't as easy as I'd thought. The young boy wasn't sleep. He was both cautious and calculating. He moved like he had all the time in the world. Never really in a rush. That made him hard to walk down.

I studied him for weaknesses such as drug use, hoe-chasing and social media addiction. But I found none. Chimel was probably the most focused 'YCB' member in the entire crew.

I got tired of waiting to find a chink in Chimel's armor and decided to double back for him later. I was bloodthirsty and wanted to send Venique a message that would let him know without a doubt that I would still knock a kid's dick-string loose too.

Now, Venique wasn't hard to get. In fact, he was probably the easiest because he loved to be seen, wanted to be known and chased women like they were going out of style. Venique was the total opposite of Chimel.

The problem was, Venique stayed surrounded by young wolves. I mean, everywhere this kid went, he kept at least two or three Young Crudy Buddy members with him. I'm talking about even going to the restroom. It was like if Venique shitted, one of his homies was there to wipe his ass. That's how I knew that they were really into some cruddy shit.

The first young Crudy Buddy member I picked off was the one who'd begged Venique to take my life. I caught shorty with his head in his lap like a true veteran and put him to sleep for good. Then, I picked another one of them little motherfuckers off after the funeral for the hell of it. A young, wild shooter my daughter identified as C-Bone.

It was so easy, like taking candy from a baby. I mean, these little kids put all of their business on social media. So, I just created fake Instagram and Facebook accounts, laid back and waited for them to post all their business. Mr. Nuur's class was paying off after all.

Once I knew where they were going to be and when they were going to be there, I just set the wolf-trap and went to work.

It took me a little longer than expected, but I finally discovered Chimel's weakness. He loves the gym. Now I knew why his young ass was so fucking big for his age.

I got a membership at the gym he attended and always waited for him to bounce before going inside. Then, I would just ask simple questions like, '*Who was just on this pull-up bar? Did somebody just squat this whole three-fifty?*' *etc.* I was all over Chimel ass.

After a while, I learned exactly when Chimel came into the gym and when he departed. Then, I concluded that the gym was the best place to get Chimel. It was quiet and low-key. Plus, Chimel would never see it coming. On top of that, his workout sessions were Monday through Friday in the evening hours, after school. Which made it even more ideal because most people work out during the day when they had more energy and more time.

The thing was that I knew that I had to really be extremely careful this time. Especially if I didn't want to end up back in prison. I mean, it wasn't like hitting the other two 'YCB' kids. I couldn't just throw on all black, slip on a pair of track shoes and walk Chimel down with a Kool-Aid smile. I couldn't just lay and wait outside of Chimel's house. Shorty was too alert. For this lick, I had to be strategic and cunning. My plan had to be well thought out because one slip-up would surely land me back in a box.

I didn't think that Chimel was armed inside the gym. He probably kept something tucked off in the car, but he definitely wasn't carrying nothing inside that gym. Still, I knew that if I wanted to really pull this shit off, I would need some help and the only person I truly trusted with my life and freedom was the only person who'd proved to be worthy, Frank.

Frank had fought me tooth and nail when I first brought up the idea, *"Fuck no, Cuz!"* Frank had snapped. *"Just roll up on his young ass at the light or something and knock his shit loose!"* he'd added before I had to remind him that this wasn't back in the days. There were cameras everywhere. And if the cameras didn't get you, people on their cell phones would, because everybody wants to be a reporter now. Everybody was trying to record something that went viral.

In the end, I used the fact that Chimel had tried to kill me outside of my mother's house to my advantage. Frank was just as crazy about One Love as I was. So, disrespect to One Love was disrespect to Aunt Evon.

***

Frank and I arrived at the gym separately. Not only that, but Frank was the first one to enter. Sitting back, watching my man strut across the parking lot towards the gym dressed like a woman had me laughing my ass off. It reminded me of the time we'd dressed up like hookers to knock a major East Baltimore player out the game for Monique back in the day. I could still remember the look on the dude's face when he realized that he'd taken the bait.

After Frank disappeared through the gym door, without incident, I sat in silence and patiently waited for Chimel's J30 to roll up. I couldn't believe that I was back in the killing field, hunting game. I'd vowed to never pick up the gun or bring harm to another human being again. But desperate times called for desperate measures. Besides, he'd tried to kill me and I had the right to defend myself.

That was even in my teachings. *Never be the aggressor in words, actions or deeds, but in the event that you are attacked then....* In so many words I had the right to flush a motherfucker down the toilet.

Still, Chimel was just a kid. A dangerous kid, but a kid nonetheless. He don't know the evils of the game the way I did and he was too young to understand the true consequences of his actions. The consequences nobody talked about. The family suffering, the sacrifices, the betrayal. All he knew or cared about was the rep he would gain after laying an O.G. down. And at his age, that was all that mattered. I knew this because I'd been Chimel years ago once. But, had it been up to me, I'd have stopped him from making the same mistake I made when I gave my life to the game.

I wished that we could've sat down and had an honest conversation, so that I could've told him about the 'hidden hand' and the strategically placed pitfalls. Because he couldn't fathom the power, wickedness and influence of the enemy though music, movies, books and the system that had been set into place. It was truly so much bigger than black and white.

Now, he would never understand the price that had to be paid for playing a game that nobody wins. Because he'd made a mistake that was about to cost him more than he could stand to lose. Chimel had gambled with his life and lost the day he took a shot at me and didn't finish the job.

I was sitting there fighting with myself about letting it go when Chimel pulled into a parking lot and climbed out of his J30 like he didn't have a care in the word. I followed Chimel with my eyes as he grabbed his gym bag and disappeared into the gym.

I watched the clock on the dashboard for forty-five minutes before I double checked my fake dreads and beard, grabbed my gym bag and climbed out of the stolen car.

I knew by now that Chimel should be heading for the locker room, preparing to take a quick shower.

I entered the gym, winked at the rainbow-shirt-wearing homosexual behind the counter as always and headed on for the locker room. As always, he waved back and stood there blushing from ear to ear. I guess he had a thing for muscular guys with dreads.

Frank was already posted up outside of the ladies' bathroom, down the hall from the men's locker room. He gave me the nod to let me know that Chimel was inside. "Any unwanted company?" I questioned.

"I didn't see anybody go in, but double check because I never went inside," Frank coached.

Moving quickly, I dipped into the locker room to see if anybody else was present. The locker room wasn't so big. But there were enough aisles for a motherfucker to go unnoticed.

The coast appeared to be clear. On top of that, Chimel had already hopped in the shower. So, that was a plus. I dipped back over to the entrance and signaled to Frank.

Then I sat the gym bag down and began to remove my gloves and the large ass butcher's knife I had hidden inside.

"Now what, Cuz?" Frank inquired, standing over top of me once he noticed that Chimel was already in the shower.

"We improvise," I looked up at Frank real quick.

The plan had been for Frank to slip up behind Chimel and put his big, young ass to sleep with his famous choke hold, so that I could cut his throat. But, now with Chimel already in the shower, that is out of the question.

With no time to waste, Frank and I quickly came up with another way to do the deed. To make a long story short, Frank would keep lookout while I went into the shower and stabbed Chimel to death.

I nodded to Frank and crept over on the steam-filled doorway of the shower and paused. Then, I slipped through the hole in the wall and saw Chimel standing under the shower-head, rinsing off with his eyes closed. He appeared to be enjoying the feel of the hot water.

Chimel seemed to instantly know that something was off. Maybe he felt my presence and noticed the way that I was dressed. Maybe the light, reflected off the murder weapon in my hand. Whatever the case, Chimel cracked the same confident Kool-Aid smile he'd had when he tried to walk me down.

"I knew you would come eventually," Chimel admitted, throwing up his hands to prepare for battle.

Before I could say or do anything, Chimel rushed me into a wall as I slammed the butcher's knife into his stomach and drew it upwards to open his belly up like a hog.

I instantly felt Chimel's blood and guts spill out all over my hands and arms as he rammed me into a wall like a long-backer and knocked the wind out of me,

The wound didn't stop Chimel. I don't even think he felt it because he began to pound my head into the wall like it was a hammer. Then, he wrapped his hands around my throat and lifted me up off of my feet.

This young motherfucker is strong! I tried to pry Chimel's fingers from around my neck. I don't know if it was the steam from the hot water or the lack of oxygen and dizziness, but my vision was getting blurry.

I brought the knife up and hit Chimel in his neck before he could crush my face in. Chimel definitely wasn't Monique. Not only did he have heart. But he was strong as a fucking ox. However, just when I didn't know how things would play out. Frank stepped into the shower area and cracked Chimel across the back of his head with a wooden scrub-brush or something.

"What the fuck took you so long, Cuz?" I went down to one knee, gasping for air. "He almost killed me."

"I thought you had him, Cuz," Frank went to peep out of the shower real quick. "We got to move!"

"Hold up." I took a few breaths, walked over to where Chimel's body had fallen, kneeled down by his head and cut his throat wide open.

"Help me drag him underneath the water, Cuz," I pleaded.

"Man, I'm not touching that nigga, Cuz!" Frank fired.

"A'ight, leave your DNA on him then." I hunched my shoulders as if I didn't care and Frank started dragging Chimel's body underneath the water himself.

Once we got Chimel's body underneath the shower water, we were both soaking wet. So, Frank and I decided to just put our heads down and walked out of the gym. I mean, our disguise looked like bad Halloween costumes. The water had basically destroyed them and I was hoping that we could skate through.

Frank now looked like a drag-queen who'd gotten caught in the rain and I looked like a penitentiary Jamaican boy who'd just fought his way out of an attempted shower gang-rape. To top it off, Chimel had knocked half of my dreads off.

"A'ight let's do this," I encouraged as me and Frank approached the corner where I knew we'd be under surveillance. "Whatever you do, stay up against the wall and don't look up."

Suddenly, we heard a loud call for help. I knew that there was no way that Chimel was still alive. *I cut that nigga's neck wide open,* I thought.

Always the one to think quick on his feet, Frank rushed over to the wall and broke the security glass out on the fire-extinguisher and used it to start spraying the sprinkler.

"What the fuck are you doing, Cuz?" I questioned as another scream echoed through the wall. We could also now hear footsteps quickly approaching.

"Shit!" Frank snapped, ignoring me to look around real quick. "Back up!" he ordered before flipping the fire-extinguisher upside down and smashing the bottom of it into a sprinkler until water began shooting out, which seemed to set off a chain reaction.

"What the fuck!" I held my hand up to shield my eyes as all the other sprinklers burst.

"Now let's move!" Frank commanded just as the sound of an alarm drowned out the distant scream.

"Head for the front door, everybody!" The desk client came speeding around the corner, shielding his eyes from the pouring water.

Frank and I exited the building in a hurry with everybody else, climbed into the car soaking wet and drove off. The amazing thing was that nobody paid us any attention, because everybody was trying to keep from having their clothes, cell phones, laptops and whatever else from being destroyed by water. So, nobody was the wiser.

Chapter Thirty-Seven

Gangster Secrets

After putting Chimel to sleep for good, I honestly couldn't stop thinking about him. My emotions were a tangled mess of guilt, empathy and confusion. It kind of reminded me of when I'd literally put the dirt over my childhood friend Tybo. Only difference was that back then, I was young, ignorant, easily influenced and only cared out of the love I had for him. Now, I actually knew better.

One minute I felt justified and the next I felt sick. Sick because I'd promised myself years ago, while in prison, that I'd never again help destroy my own community, I'd never again put myself in a position to leave my children. Yet, here I was again, having murdered three children whom could've just as easy been mine.

Take plenty! were the words that kept ringing in my head. *Take plenty!* Damn near every Nation of Islam brother I'd ever met would say, *Take plenty because the very same people you'll be out there trying to save, will be the main ones to give you hell.*

I struggled to calm my nerves. If the truth surrounding Chimel's murder ever came to light and hit the prison system, I'd be forced to cut ties with someone very close to me. *Why the hell did I have to go and kill this kid?* I questioned myself. I mean, I knew better. I knew what it was like growing up in the streets without an aim and a purpose. Without real guidance. Without real love for myself and kind, and without knowledge of self.

Chimel was just doing the only thing that he knew how to do. It was the same shit I did—gave my life to what I thought was a worthy cause. It took going to prison, being left for dead and waking up to realize that it wasn't. However, Chimel wouldn't ever have that chance.

I heard one of my favorite old classics pop up on my playlist and began hashing and rehashing the past as my thoughts spiraled out of control. I don't even realize that my eyes had filled with tears until I felt them slowly rolling down my cheeks.

I sat there and soaked in the haunting ballad giving voice to my own deepest pain. The song expressed not just only the anguish I felt, but also the profound need for change and healing if I ever wanted to help save kids like the ones I'd just brought harm to.

When I saw the shadow at the bottom of the door and head the light tap, I dried my eyes and quickly gathered myself. "Yeah, what's up?" I called out, wiping my face.

"You okay?" Chanae's inquiry made me twist my face up because I could never really tell when it was genuine or not. One thing living with Chanae had taught me was that love isn't always sincere. Sometimes it could be self-serving and manipulative

"Yeah, I'm straight," I replied.

"Oh, that was your jam right there back in the day," Chanae declared, opening the door. I could tell that she was fishing, trying to be nosey and figure out where my head was at and what I had going on. She always complained about my not being more open and holding things in.

Chanae hated when I sat in the back room alone, listening to my music. But, that was just another thing that prison had done to me. It made me play my card extremely close to my chest. Even with the people I love the most.

I mean, I was still compassionate and very giving. My love wasn't a fear-driven need for control or nothing. But still, when it came to other people's concern for me, I always viewed it as a means to an end. Simply put, I just thought it was the give before the take, the decoy before the hidden agenda.

"A'myiah still here?" I had no idea.

"Yeah, she's in her room waiting for Shaun to get here and pick her up. She's supposed to be going with Nydeer to that little boy's funeral tomorrow."

"I thought they aren't having no funeral due to the COVID stuff?" I questioned. "At least I think that's what the news said," I lied thinking about what I'd read on Chimel's Facebook page.

"Well, not a funeral. It's like a vigil," Chanae explained.

"Oh," I mumbled. "Tell A'myiah to come here real quick for me please."

"You sure you're okay?" Chanae eyed me curiously. I knew she was trying to read me. But like I said, prison had made me a master at concealing my feelings. It was a survival tactic.

"Yeah," I assured with a slightly forced laugh. "Thanks for asking though."

"You know you can talk to me about anything, right?"

"Of course," I lied with a smile for her benefit, another thing I'd picked up in prisons: *Always tell a woman what they wanted and sometimes needed to hear.*

"Now can you please tell my daughter to come here?"

"Yes, sir!" Chanae joked and pulled the door closed on her way out as I reached for my cell phone to call Frank.

Chapter Thirty-Eight

When Gangsters Collide

Frank begged me not to attend Chimel's memorial. He felt like it was too dangerous, stupid even. But I told him that I had to. For one, I don't trust my daughter being there alone and secondly, I knew that it would be one of the rare opportunities for me to pull up on Venique and to broker peace. It would be in a public setting so I don't suspect nothing too crazy to take place. Lord knows, I couldn't have fathomed the way things had played out.

The first thing I noticed when we arrived was that a lot of people love Chimel. They were wearing t-shirts and waving posters with his name and face on them. One pretty chick was passing out candles and balloons.

I was walking around, listening to people talk about how much of a good person Chimel was, when I ran into this mother—a very beautiful sister holding a baby picture of Chimel. I knew it had to be his mother because one of my childhood friends from up Park Heights was trying to console her.

I nodded and kept it moving. Seeing Chimel's mother like that made me feel ashamed. Knowing that I'd been the one who caused her pain broke my heart. I had to locate Venique and bring some order to this madness before more family members had to grieve.

It wasn't until the vigil actually started that I laid eyes on Venique and his crew. He spotted me across the crowd and he instantly began whispering to the kid Dhakiy. I saw

Dhakiy whisper to another kid who instantly disappeared into the crowd.

Then, I noticed Venique tugging at Lor'Chuck's arm sleeve before mumbling something into his ear also. A moment later I realized that Baby Dana and the other little kid were behind me.

I told my daughter and them that I'd be back and walked through the crowd until I was next to Venique.

"You got a lot of heart, O.G. Especially after you left my man like that without a fair chance to fight back," Venique mumbled under his breath. "You're going to answer for that though. You and everybody you love."

"I come in peace, shorty, but please don't threaten my family," I warned, ready to kill him where he stood about my family.

"Nigga, fuck you and your family!" Venique fired and it took everything in me not draw the .357 and knock his wig loose right then and there.

"Listen, shorty, I'm not trying to go down this road about no rat," I declared sincerely because at the end of the day, his father was a certified snitch.

"Oh, this ain't about my father no more, O.G.," Venique said. "This about you trashing my homies."

"Did you sanction that hit on me?" I was curious.

"Fuck outta here," Dhakiy finally spoke up. "Don't answer that dummy, this old, stiff ass nigga might be wired up."

"Did you send Chimel after me?" I questioned again but Venique remained silent. "It doesn't matter, shorty. You and I both know that once he took a shot at me and missed, he was fair game."

"And what about my other homies?" Venique turned to me. "What about T-Bone and Tigga?"

"I don't know anything about that," I lied. "My static was with Chimel."

"Come on now, O.G., I'm not stupid," Venique said.

"I'm telling you, I don't know anything about that. I don't play the collateral damage game," I reasoned with a straight face.

"So, what are you asking me, O.G.? You asking me to just let you walk away from this untouched? You know I can't do that. The wolf pack wants blood," Venique explained. "So, it's either yours or mines."

"A'ight, let's keep it in the streets then," I requested. "Between me and your crew. May the best man win."

Venique laughed at my suggestion. "Y'all old nigga really need to get with the times." Venique smiled. "I keep telling you this not back in the day O.G. When we start spinning niggas' bends, we're giving it to whoever we catch. Nobody's off limits."

"You know that can go both ways, right?" I stared at Venique to be sure he understood what I was saying. Because if anybody came for my family, all bets were off. I'd wipe out entire generation of family members all the way down to the pets.

"There you go with the ideal threats again." Venique stepped into my personal space.

"I don't make ideal threats," I declared, unfazed.

"Venique! Boy, if you don't sit your silly ass down!" A voice I instantly recognized from anywhere barked out of the crowds a second before a well-manicured hand went upside his head. "This is your friend's vigil and you're out here acting a fool. You too, Dhakiy, wait until I call your mother, boy!" Venus said before turning to me.

When we locked eyes, she immediately knew that it was me. Yet, her words wouldn't come out. I stared at her in silence, thinking back to all that shit she's caused. "How you doing?" I broke the silence. "It's been a long time."

I didn't really know what else to say. My mind was blank. I hadn't expected to see Venus.

Venus stared at me curiously before looking at her son. I think she was trying to read the situation. "Dakaron, please, he's my son," she pleaded the moment I believe it hit her because she knew better than Venique the type of hell I'd rain down on his little ass if he backed me into a corner.

"Ma, fuck that bitch ass nigga!" Venique exploded, trying to push past her. "His old ass is nobody."

"What I tell you about your mouth, Venique?" Venus popped him again. "Bye! Go make sure Chimel's mother is okay."

"But Ma—" Venique appealed.

"I'm not going to say it again, Venique!" Venus warned. "Go check on Ms. Melody."

Venique mean-mugged me for a moment and then slowly began backing up into the crowd.

"You too, Dhakiy!" Venus added.

"See you around, O.G." Dhakiy gave me an evil grin.

"No, you won't!" Venus interjected confidently. "Whatever this is, it's over, trust me."

Venus turned back to me with that old look in her eyes. She knew that something was going on and begged me not to hurt her child. I tried to convince her that she was tripping, but Venus wasn't green. She came out of the same mud as me. So without going into too much detail, I explained to her that the son was playing with fire.

"You're the one that started that shit!" I argued. "Why would you tell that kid that I killed Monique?"

"Because you did!" Venus retorted.

"I wasn't never even charged for that shit!" I reminded her.

"There's a lot of things you haven't been charged for." Venus looked at me knowingly. "But you and I know what's really good."

"Why would you tell the kid half the truth? You had him thinking Monique was this honorable dude and you know yo was a fucking snake!" I was starting to get angry. I was starting to remember how Monique and Venus crossed me.

"Did you tell your son I used to fuck your brains out? I bet you didn't tell his little ass that."

"Nobody thought you were ever coming home," Venus defended, looking around cautiously, hoping that nobody heard the truth. "Let's step over here."

"Oh, you're embarrassed now, huh?" I got louder. "You don't want your son to know the truth."

"Dakaron, don't fucking stand here and act like your shit don't stink too, nigga!" Venus rolled her eyes. "You were fucking your homeboy girl, Mister Honorable. Mister Righteous, you aren't shit either."

"Yeah, whatever." I brushed Venus' statement off. "Fuck all that though." I had to focus on the reason why I was there. "I came here to save your son's life. Before shorty get in over his head."

"If something happens to my son, Dakaron, somebody's going to jail," Venus threatened.

"Ain't nobody tell your stupid ass to pump all that dumb shit into shorty's head!"

"Like I said, everybody thought you were dying in prison." Venus' word hurt because I knew that they were true. So many motherfuckers had written me off.

"Well, I'm here now and I'm telling you, Venus, get your son before shorty fuck around and get himself killed." I looked at her seriously so that she would know that I wasn't bullshitting.

"Who the people my son got an issue with? Is it you?" Venus inquired.

Thinking quickly, I said. "Hell no! I'm just the go-between. I'm the one trying to keep the peace."

"Give me your phone." Venus held her hand out.

"Give you my phone for what?" I looked at her curiously.

"Dakaron, just give me the phone, damn boy. You act like I asked you for blood." Venus shook her head as I reluctantly handed her my cell phone.

I stood there and watched her hold our phones together while hitting a few buttons on the touch-screen before handing it back.

"You tell whoever you're being the go-between for that they don't have to worry about my son. I got him!" she guaranteed. "If they have any problems out of him, just have them call me."

"I don't have your number," I declared, twisting my face up.

"I just put it in your phone. I got yours too." Venus must've seen the look on my face because she continued before I could say anything. "Don't get all scared, nigga, I know you back fucking with Chanae dirty ass. She's my friend on Facebook. So, I put the number under your jail contacts. Just look for the number with no name attached."

"I'm telling you, Venus, keep your son on a leash. Because if he does something crazy with these dudes, they're going to come after him with everything that they got!" I warned one more time to make sure she got the point.

"Okay, Mister Go-Between, I know you're out here trying to keep the peace." Venus joked but she knew that I wasn't playing.

I left Venus standing there and made my way back over to my daughter and them. I was ready to go. "You ready?" I walked up on A'myiah. "Where did Sha'nyiah and them go?"

"In the store," A'myiah disclosed.

"A'ight, go get tell them to come on so we can go," I instructed, knowing that I had to drop them off.

I wasn't feeling right. Something seemed off. I knew that Venus had promised me that she could and would control Venique and I could see her standing across the street talking to him. But still, I couldn't locate Baby Dana, Dhakiy or that other little kid in the crowd and that just wasn't sitting right with me. Especially not when I saw Venique clocking me, playing on his phone.

Once A'myiah rounded the girls up and I got them to the car. I felt better, of course, they wanted to hang out, but I wasn't having it. I'd promised Shaun that I'd bring Nydeer straight home from the vigil.

I had just come to a stop at the top of the block when a minivan came out of nowhere and cut us off. *What the fuck!* I thought just before the side door slid opened, revealing Baby Dana and Lor'Chuck strategically sitting on the floor. Aiming guns.

"Get down!" I yelled, reaching over to push my daughter's head beneath the dashboard just as the sound of an automatic weapon began to rip through the night.

I heard the girls screaming as the gunfire got close. But it took me a second to realize that the car wasn't being stuck.

When I heard the unmistakable sound of screeching tires, I peered up over the dashboard and saw the now, bullet-rattled minivan burning rubber down the block.

I looked over to my left and saw a masked gunman I instantly knew was Frank, holding a Draco. The same burgundy Draco with the gold spray-painted clip Buckey Fields' cousin had given to him. But, I didn't say anything. Neither did Frank; we just locked eyes knowingly before he ran to jump into the car behind us.

"Everybody, stay down!" I shouted, stepping on the gas as I pulled off in the opposite direction.

I drove about two blocks before I allowed the girls to look up.

"Oh my God!" Nydeer fired first "Did y'all see that? They were shooting at us."

"No, they weren't," Sha'nyiah instantly corrected. "They're shooting at some guy in a black car behind us. He's probably the one who killed Chimel," Sha'nyiah rationalized.

Then, A'myiah added her two cents. I let them go back and forth for a minute to see what they knew, suspected and or had witnessed.

Once I figured out that they don't know much, I spun the narrative to make sure Chanae and them didn't know just how close we'd come to losing our lives.

TO BE CONTINUED...

The Birth of a Gangster 4
Coming Soon

Lock Down Publications and Ca$h Presents
Assisted Publishing Packages

BASIC PACKAGE $499 Editing Cover Design Formatting	**UPGRADED PACKAGE** $800 Typing Editing Cover Design Formatting
ADVANCE PACKAGE $1,200 Typing Editing Cover Design Formatting Copyright registration Proofreading Upload book to Amazon	**LDP SUPREME PACKAGE** $1,500 Typing Editing Cover Design Formatting Copyright registration Proofreading Set up Amazon account Upload book to Amazon Advertise on LDP, Amazon and Facebook Page

***Other services available upon request.
Additional charges may apply

Lock Down Publications
P.O. Box 944
Stockbridge, GA 30281-9998
Phone: 470 303-9761

Submission Guideline

Submit the first three chapters of your completed manuscript to ldpsubmissions@gmail.com. In the subject line add **Your Book's Title**. The manuscript must be in a Word Doc file and sent as an attachment. Document should be in Times New Roman, double spaced, and in size 12 font. Also, provide your synopsis and full contact information. If sending multiple submissions, they must each be in a separate email.

Have a story but no way to send it electronically? You can still submit to LDP/Ca$h Presents. Send in the first three chapters, written or typed, of your completed manuscript to:

LDP: Submissions Dept
P.O. Box 944
Stockbridge, GA 30281-9998

DO NOT send original manuscript. Must be a duplicate. Provide your synopsis and a cover letter containing your full contact information.

Thanks for considering LDP and Ca$h Presents.

NEW RELEASES

SANCTIFIED AND HORNY
by XTASY

THE PLUG OF LIL MEXICO 2
by CHRIS GREEN

THE BLACK DIAMOND CARTEL
by SAYNOMORE

THE BIRTH OF A GANGSTER 3
by DELMONT PLAYER

Coming Soon from Lock Down Publications/Ca$h Presents

BLOOD OF A BOSS VI
SHADOWS OF THE GAME II
TRAP BASTARD II
By **Askari**

LOYAL TO THE GAME IV
By **T.J. & Jelissa**

TRUE SAVAGE VIII
MIDNIGHT CARTEL IV
DOPE BOY MAGIC IV
CITY OF KINGZ III
NIGHTMARE ON SILENT AVE II
THE PLUG OF LIL MEXICO II
CLASSIC CITY II
By **Chris Green**

BLAST FOR ME III
A SAVAGE DOPEBOY III
CUTTHROAT MAFIA III
DUFFLE BAG CARTEL VII
HEARTLESS GOON VI
By **Ghost**

A HUSTLER'S DECEIT III
KILL ZONE II
BAE BELONGS TO ME III
TIL DEATH II
By **Aryanna**

KING OF THE TRAP III
By **T.J. Edwards**

GORILLAZ IN THE BAY V
3X KRAZY III
STRAIGHT BEAST MODE III
By **De'Kari**

KINGPIN KILLAZ IV
STREET KINGS III
PAID IN BLOOD III
CARTEL KILLAZ IV
DOPE GODS III
By **Hood Rich**

SINS OF A HUSTLA II
By **ASAD**

YAYO V
BRED IN THE GAME 2
By **S. Allen**

THE STREETS WILL TALK II
By **Yolanda Moore**

SON OF A DOPE FIEND III
HEAVEN GOT A GHETTO III
SKI MASK MONEY III
By **Renta**

LOYALTY AIN'T PROMISED III
By **Keith Williams**

I'M NOTHING WITHOUT HIS LOVE II
SINS OF A THUG II
TO THE THUG I LOVED BEFORE II
IN A HUSTLER I TRUST II
By **Monet Dragun**

QUIET MONEY IV
EXTENDED CLIP III
THUG LIFE IV
By **Trai'Quan**

THE STREETS MADE ME IV
By **Larry D. Wright**

IF YOU CROSS ME ONCE III
ANGEL V
By **Anthony Fields**

THE STREETS WILL NEVER CLOSE IV
By **K'ajji**

HARD AND RUTHLESS III
KILLA KOUNTY IV
By **Khufu**

MONEY GAME III
By **Smoove Dolla**

MURDA WAS THE CASE III
Elijah R. Freeman

AN UNFORESEEN LOVE IV
BABY, I'M WINTERTIME COLD III
By **Meesha**

QUEEN OF THE ZOO III
By **Black Migo**

CONFESSIONS OF A JACKBOY III
By **Nicholas Lock**

JACK BOYS VS DOPE BOYS IV
A GANGSTA'S QUR'AN V
COKE GIRLZ II
COKE BOYS II
LIFE OF A SAVAGE V
CHI'RAQ GANGSTAS V
SOSA GANG III
BRONX SAVAGES II
BODYMORE KINGPINS II
By **Romell Tukes**

KING KILLA II
By **Vincent "Vitto" Holloway**

BETRAYAL OF A THUG III
By **Fre$h**

THE MURDER QUEENS III
By **Michael Gallon**

THE BIRTH OF A GANGSTER III
By **Delmont Player**

TREAL LOVE II
By **Le'Monica Jackson**

FOR THE LOVE OF BLOOD III
By **Jamel Mitchell**

RAN OFF ON DA PLUG II
By **Paper Boi Rari**

HOOD CONSIGLIERE III
By **Keese**

PRETTY GIRLS DO NASTY THINGS II
By **Nicole Goosby**

PROTÉGÉ OF A LEGEND III
LOVE IN THE TRENCHES II
By **Corey Robinson**

IT'S JUST ME AND YOU II
By **Ah'Million**

FOREVER GANGSTA III
By **Adrian Dulan**

GORILLAZ IN THE TRENCHES II
By **SayNoMore**

THE COCAINE PRINCESS VIII
By **King Rio**

CRIME BOSS II
By **Playa Ray**

LOYALTY IS EVERYTHING III
By **Molotti**

HERE TODAY GONE TOMORROW II
By **Fly Rock**

REAL G'S MOVE IN SILENCE II
By **Von Diesel**

GRIMEY WAYS IV
By **Ray Vinci**

Available Now

RESTRAINING ORDER I & II
By **CA$H & Coffee**

LOVE KNOWS NO BOUNDARIES I II & III
By **Coffee**

RAISED AS A GOON I, II, III & IV
BRED BY THE SLUMS I, II, III
BLAST FOR ME I & II
ROTTEN TO THE CORE I II III
A BRONX TALE I, II, III
DUFFLE BAG CARTEL I II III IV V VI
HEARTLESS GOON I II III IV V
A SAVAGE DOPEBOY I II
DRUG LORDS I II III
CUTTHROAT MAFIA I II
KING OF THE TRENCHES
By **Ghost**

LAY IT DOWN I & II
LAST OF A DYING BREED I II
BLOOD STAINS OF A SHOTTA I & II III
By **Jamaica**

LOYAL TO THE GAME I II III
LIFE OF SIN I, II III
By **TJ & Jelissa**

IF LOVING HIM IS WRONG…I & II
LOVE ME EVEN WHEN IT HURTS I II III
By **Jelissa**

BLOODY COMMAS I & II
SKI MASK CARTEL I, II & III
KING OF NEW YORK I II, III IV V
RISE TO POWER I II III
COKE KINGS I II III IV V
BORN HEARTLESS I II III IV
KING OF THE TRAP I II
By **T.J. Edwards**

WHEN THE STREETS CLAP BACK I & II III
THE HEART OF A SAVAGE I II III IV
MONEY MAFIA I II
LOYAL TO THE SOIL I II III
By **Jibril Williams**

A DISTINGUISHED THUG STOLE MY HEART I II & III
LOVE SHOULDN'T HURT I II III IV
RENEGADE BOYS I II III IV
PAID IN KARMA I II III
SAVAGE STORMS I II III
AN UNFORESEEN LOVE I II III
BABY, I'M WINTERTIME COLD I II
By **Meesha**

A GANGSTER'S CODE I &, II III
A GANGSTER'S SYN I II III
THE SAVAGE LIFE I II III
CHAINED TO THE STREETS I II III
BLOOD ON THE MONEY I II III
A GANGSTA'S PAIN I II III
By **J-Blunt**

PUSH IT TO THE LIMIT
By **Bre' Hayes**

BLOOD OF A BOSS I, II, III, IV, V
SHADOWS OF THE GAME
TRAP BASTARD
By **Askari**

THE STREETS BLEED MURDER I, II & III
THE HEART OF A GANGSTA I II& III
By **Jerry Jackson**

CUM FOR ME I II III IV V VI VII VIII
An **LDP Erotica Collaboration**

BRIDE OF A HUSTLA I II & II
THE FETTI GIRLS I, II& III
CORRUPTED BY A GANGSTA I, II III, IV
BLINDED BY HIS LOVE
THE PRICE YOU PAY FOR LOVE I, II ,III
DOPE GIRL MAGIC I II III
By **Destiny Skai**

WHEN A GOOD GIRL GOES BAD
By **Adrienne**

A GANGSTER'S REVENGE I II III & IV
THE BOSS MAN'S DAUGHTERS I II III IV V
A SAVAGE LOVE I & II
BAE BELONGS TO ME I II
A HUSTLER'S DECEIT I, II, III
WHAT BAD BITCHES DO I, II, III
SOUL OF A MONSTER I II III
KILL ZONE
A DOPE BOY'S QUEEN I II III
TIL DEATH
By **Aryanna**

THE COST OF LOYALTY I II III
By Kweli

A KINGPIN'S AMBITION
A KINGPIN'S AMBITION **II**
I MURDER FOR THE DOUGH
By **Ambitious**

TRUE SAVAGE I II III IV V VI VII
DOPE BOY MAGIC I, II, III
MIDNIGHT CARTEL I II III
CITY OF KINGZ I II
NIGHTMARE ON SILENT AVE
THE PLUG OF LIL MEXICO II
CLASSIC CITY
By **Chris Green**

A DOPEBOY'S PRAYER
By **Eddie "Wolf" Lee**

THE KING CARTEL I, II & III
By **Frank Gresham**

THESE NIGGAS AIN'T LOYAL I, II & III
By **Nikki Tee**

GANGSTA SHYT I II &III
By **CATO**

THE ULTIMATE BETRAYAL
By **Phoenix**

BOSS'N UP I, II & III
By **Royal Nicole**

I LOVE YOU TO DEATH
By **Destiny J**

I RIDE FOR MY HITTA
I STILL RIDE FOR MY HITTA
By **Misty Holt**

LOVE & CHASIN' PAPER
By **Qay Crockett**

TO DIE IN VAIN
SINS OF A HUSTLA
By **ASAD**

BROOKLYN HUSTLAZ
By **Boogsy Morina**

BROOKLYN ON LOCK I & II
By **Sonovia**

GANGSTA CITY
By **Teddy Duke**

A DRUG KING AND HIS DIAMOND I & II III
A DOPEMAN'S RICHES
HER MAN, MINE'S TOO I, II
CASH MONEY HO'S
THE WIFEY I USED TO BE I II
PRETTY GIRLS DO NASTY THINGS
By Nicole Goosby

LIPSTICK KILLAH I, II, III
CRIME OF PASSION I II & III
FRIEND OR FOE I II III
By **Mimi**

TRAPHOUSE KING I II & III
KINGPIN KILLAZ I II III
STREET KINGS I II
PAID IN BLOOD I II
CARTEL KILLAZ I II III
DOPE GODS I II
By **Hood Rich**

STEADY MOBBN' I, II, III
THE STREETS STAINED MY SOUL I II III
By **Marcellus Allen**

WHO SHOT YA I, II, III
SON OF A DOPE FIEND I II
HEAVEN GOT A GHETTO I II
SKI MASK MONEY I II
By **Renta**

GORILLAZ IN THE BAY I II III IV
TEARS OF A GANGSTA I II
3X KRAZY I II
STRAIGHT BEAST MODE I II
By **DE'KARI**

TRIGGADALE I II III
MURDA WAS THE CASE I II
By **Elijah R. Freeman**

THE STREETS ARE CALLING
By **Duquie Wilson**

SLAUGHTER GANG I II III
RUTHLESS HEART I II III
By **Willie Slaughter**

GOD BLESS THE TRAPPERS I, II, III
THESE SCANDALOUS STREETS I, II, III
FEAR MY GANGSTA I, II, III IV, V
THESE STREETS DON'T LOVE NOBODY I, II
BURY ME A G I, II, III, IV, V
A GANGSTA'S EMPIRE I, II, III, IV
THE DOPEMAN'S BODYGAURD I II
THE REALEST KILLAZ I II III
THE LAST OF THE OGS I II III
By **Tranay Adams**

MARRIED TO A BOSS I II III
By **Destiny Skai & Chris Green**

KINGZ OF THE GAME I II III IV V VI VII
CRIME BOSS
By **Playa Ray**

FUK SHYT
By **Blakk Diamond**

DON'T F#CK WITH MY HEART I II
By **Linnea**

ADDICTED TO THE DRAMA I II III
IN THE ARM OF HIS BOSS II
By **Jamila**

YAYO I II III IV
A SHOOTER'S AMBITION I II
BRED IN THE GAME
By **S. Allen**

LOYALTY AIN'T PROMISED I II
By **Keith Williams**

TRAP GOD I II III
RICH $AVAGE I II III
MONEY IN THE GRAVE I II III
By **Martell Troublesome Bolden**

FOREVER GANGSTA I II
GLOCKS ON SATIN SHEETS I II
By **Adrian Dulan**

TOE TAGZ I II III IV
LEVELS TO THIS SHYT I II
IT'S JUST ME AND YOU
By **Ah'Million**

KINGPIN DREAMS I II III
RAN OFF ON DA PLUG
By **Paper Boi Rari**

CONFESSIONS OF A GANGSTA I II III IV
CONFESSIONS OF A JACKBOY I II
By **Nicholas Lock**

I'M NOTHING WITHOUT HIS LOVE
SINS OF A THUG
TO THE THUG I LOVED BEFORE
A GANGSTA SAVED XMAS
IN A HUSTLER I TRUST
By **Monet Dragun**

CAUGHT UP IN THE LIFE I II III
THE STREETS NEVER LET GO I II III
By **Robert Baptiste**

NEW TO THE GAME I II III
MONEY, MURDER & MEMORIES I II III
By **Malik D. Rice**

CREAM I II III
THE STREETS WILL TALK
By **Yolanda Moore**

LIFE OF A SAVAGE I II III IV
A GANGSTA'S QUR'AN I II III IV
MURDA SEASON I II III
GANGLAND CARTEL I II III
CHI'RAQ GANGSTAS I II III IV
KILLERS ON ELM STREET I II III
JACK BOYZ N DA BRONX I II III
A DOPEBOY'S DREAM I II III
JACK BOYS VS DOPE BOYS I II III
COKE GIRLZ
COKE BOYS
SOSA GANG I II
BRONX SAVAGES
BODYMORE KINGPINS
By **Romell Tukes**

QUIET MONEY I II III
THUG LIFE I II III
EXTENDED CLIP I II
A GANGSTA'S PARADISE
By **Trai'Quan**

THE STREETS MADE ME I II III
By **Larry D. Wright**

THE ULTIMATE SACRIFICE I, II, III, IV, V, VI
KHADIFI
IF YOU CROSS ME ONCE I II
ANGEL I II III IV
IN THE BLINK OF AN EYE
By **Anthony Fields**

THE LIFE OF A HOOD STAR
By **Ca$h & Rashia Wilson**

THE STREETS WILL NEVER CLOSE I II III
By **K'ajji**

NIGHTMARES OF A HUSTLA I II III
By **King Dream**

CONCRETE KILLA I II III
VICIOUS LOYALTY I II III
By **Kingpen**

HARD AND RUTHLESS I II
MOB TOWN 251
THE BILLIONAIRE BENTLEYS I II III
REAL G'S MOVE IN SILENCE
By **Von Diesel**

GHOST MOB
By **Stilloan Robinson**

MOB TIES I II III IV V VI
SOUL OF A HUSTLER, HEART OF A KILLER I II
GORILLAZ IN THE TRENCHES
By **SayNoMore**

BODYMORE MURDERLAND I II III
THE BIRTH OF A GANGSTER I II
By **Delmont Player**

FOR THE LOVE OF A BOSS
By **C. D. Blue**

KILLA KOUNTY I II III IV
By **Khufu**

MOBBED UP I II III IV
THE BRICK MAN I II III IV V
THE COCAINE PRINCESS I II III IV V VI VII
By **King Rio**

MONEY GAME I II
By **Smoove Dolla**

A GANGSTA'S KARMA I II III
By **FLAME**

KING OF THE TRENCHES I II III
By **GHOST & TRANAY ADAMS**

QUEEN OF THE ZOO I II
By **Black Migo**

GRIMEY WAYS I II III
By **Ray Vinci**

XMAS WITH AN ATL SHOOTER
By **Ca$h & Destiny Skai**

KING KILLA
By **Vincent "Vitto" Holloway**

BETRAYAL OF A THUG I II
By **Fre$h**

THE MURDER QUEENS I II
By **Michael Gallon**

TREAL LOVE
By **Le'Monica Jackson**

FOR THE LOVE OF BLOOD I II
By **Jamel Mitchell**

HOOD CONSIGLIERE I II
By **Keese**

PROTÉGÉ OF A LEGEND I II
LOVE IN THE TRENCHES
By **Corey Robinson**

BORN IN THE GRAVE I II III
By **Self Made Tay**

MOAN IN MY MOUTH
By **XTASY**

TORN BETWEEN A GANGSTER AND A
GENTLEMAN
By **J-BLUNT & Miss Kim**

LOYALTY IS EVERYTHING I II
By **Molotti**

HERE TODAY GONE TOMORROW
By **Fly Rock**

PILLOW PRINCESS
By **S. Hawkins**

BOOKS BY LDP'S CEO, CA$H

TRUST IN NO MAN
TRUST IN NO MAN 2
TRUST IN NO MAN 3
BONDED BY BLOOD
SHORTY GOT A THUG
THUGS CRY
THUGS CRY 2
THUGS CRY 3
TRUST NO BITCH
TRUST NO BITCH 2
TRUST NO BITCH 3
TIL MY CASKET DROPS
RESTRAINING ORDER
RESTRAINING ORDER 2
IN LOVE WITH A CONVICT
LIFE OF A HOOD STAR
XMAS WITH AN ATL SHOOTER